SPELL HOUND

A WITCH IN WOLF WOOD, BOOK 2

LINDSAY BUROKER

1

Morgen Keller, recent inheritress of a turn-of-the-century —make that turn-of-the-*previous*-century—farmhouse, grimaced at the chainsaw roaring outside as she padded to the kitchen. It was 6:01 am.

Technically, she couldn't complain, because the chainsaw had started up at the agreed-upon hour, but with wan morning light barely filtering through the fog and her skull pulsing with a headache, she realized she should have argued harder for quiet hours to extend until 8:00. It was bad enough her werewolf roommate had been out in the woods howling in the middle of the night.

"And here I thought country life was supposed to be more peaceful than city life."

The floorboards of the old house creaked with her steps, which she expected, but when she walked into the kitchen, something *unexpected* crunched under her bare foot. A *lot* of somethings.

Flustered, Morgen groped for the light switch and flipped it. The ceiling lamp flickered a couple of times before staying on and illuminating crunchy snack puffs scattered all over the floor. Her empty bag of PeaTos lay crinkled under the table. The day before, she'd left it on a shelf in the pantry, the top neatly folded over and secured by a clip.

"Lucky!" she yelled, certain her dog had been responsible.

But that didn't make sense. He slept like the proverbial log—as she well knew from the effort it took to shove him over when he flopped down in her bed—and he also wasn't known for raiding her stash of vegetarian snacks. If she'd left a bag of beef jerky within reach, that might have been a different story, but even before her vizsla charged into the kitchen, she'd decided he hadn't been responsible.

The fact that Lucky ignored the puffs strewn across the floor—aside from smashing a few more with his paws—and ran straight to the pantry door to sniff at the crack suggested he was on the trail of the true culprit.

Morgen grabbed the broom from the corner in case she needed to swat the destructive intruder to drive it out of the house. With her chosen weapon held aloft, she crept toward the pantry.

Lucky whined and snuffled, his tail wagging fiercely, as if he'd treed a squirrel.

"You don't have to kill whatever it is," Morgen said. "We like animals, remember? We'll just scare it out of the house so it can't further violate my snack foods."

The tail wagged even more fiercely.

Outside, the chainsaw had stopped. Morgen was about to grab the pantry knob when her roommate strode into the kitchen, more puffs crunching under his heavy boots.

At six-and-a-half-feet tall, Amar Guerrero, the forty-something werewolf who'd lived in Grandma's barn apartment for three years before she passed away, was an intimidating figure. As usual, he wore jeans and a leather vest that left his muscular chest and arms on display. Between the giant fang on a thong around his neck and his shaggy black hair, he looked like a caveman freshly thawed out of a glacier in the Alps. *He* would be a lot more likely to scare a mouse than Lucky.

"Are you all right?" Amar eyed the broom in her hands. "I heard you yell for your hound, as if invaders were charging the threshold of your home."

Morgen would have scoffed at such a notion, but in the three weeks since she'd come up to Bellrock, Washington, the property had been invaded by everyone from a real-estate agent who'd been murdered at her doorstep to a raven familiar intent on stealing a magical amulet to arsonist witches who'd set the barn on fire.

"They're charging the pantry, actually. I think I have a rat. Unless *you* had ravenous urges in the middle of the night and assailed my PeaTos." She pointed the broom toward the empty bag under the table.

"Assailed your what?" Amar asked in a deadpan voice, flicking a dismissive glance toward the scattered puffs.

"Snacks. They're made from pea and lentil flour."

His lip curled. "I'm surprised they're not assailed more often."

"Ha ha. They're good. Be ready in case a rat springs free, please."

"Ready for what?"

"To catch it and evict it."

"I'm a werewolf, not a house cat. No self-respecting apex predator would raise a paw to catch such anemic prey."

Lucky snuffled louder and clawed at the base of the pantry door.

"Lucky is interested," Morgen said.

"From what I've observed, *Lucky* is an apex couch-sleeper."

"That's not entirely untrue." Morgen, cheered by her fearsome company, however disdainful he was of PeaTos and rats, opened the pantry door with a flourish.

Lucky lunged in, inasmuch as he could with the low shelves

blocking him, and snuffled even more loudly as he nosed rat droppings on the warped linoleum floor. There was no sign of the intruder, but when Morgen knelt down beside Lucky, she could see more than one hole in the wall of the baseboard.

"Escape hatches," she grumbled with a sigh. "Should I get mouse traps? Or fumigate the house?"

She looked back at Amar, who now leaned against the doorjamb, his arms folded over his chest. It was possible he was checking out her butt, but she decided it was more likely he was simply amused and watching the show. Besides, as her ex-husband had pointed out more than once, her checkered flannel pajama bottoms weren't the most alluring sleepwear in the world.

"The house needs a lot of repairs," Amar said. "If it were in better shape, there wouldn't be access points for wildlife. In the past year, I remodeled one of the bathrooms for Gwen and replaced a lot of the wood and sanded and painted the porch, but home-building materials are expensive, so there was a limit to how much handiwork I could do."

"Yeah." Morgen remembered how much it had cost to have the kitchen and bathroom replaced in the house she'd shared with her husband. Since they'd both had good jobs and the Seattle housing market had appreciated a lot, it had been feasible, but now that she was single, unemployed, and living off her savings, she would have to think twice before even replacing the bag of PeaTos. "If I could figure out how one prepares the bioluminescent moss growing around the springs in Wolf Wood, maybe I could sell some of it to finance a few projects."

As she'd recently learned, the moss powder was a desirable—and rare and valuable—spell component in a performance-enhancing potion that witches could make. One of her grandmother's books had a recipe that used it, but she didn't know if one could simply dry and pulverize the moss to acquire the powder or if it had to be treated and prepared during some special ritual.

Until recently, Morgen hadn't believed in magic, witches, or werewolves. Learning that she had the blood of witches flowing through her veins had been a shock.

"I could use some lumber to finish rebuilding the barn," Amar said. "A month ago, I would have had enough money to cover it, but so many of my projects were destroyed or damaged in the fire that I'm starting from scratch and am behind on orders."

"Sorry about that," Morgen said, feeling guilty that she'd begrudged him his early-morning start time. It was her fault that the barn had been burned and he'd lost everything except what had been in his beat-up old truck. "I'll get you some wood."

Maybe she could ask Phoebe, the witch who ran the Crystal Parlor and who'd taught Morgen a couple of incantations, about how to prepare the moss. Assuming she could muster the courage to go into town to visit her. Since learning that Phoebe's sister Calista had been behind Grandma's murder, among other crimes, Morgen had been hesitant to visit. Just because Phoebe had helped out didn't mean Morgen could trust her.

Amar nodded. "After I finish the barn, I'll work on the house."

"Any chance you'd like to flip that?" Morgen turned the broom on the kitchen floor and started sweeping up the mess. "There's not any food in the barn for rats to assail."

He hesitated. "It is my workshop, and it was my home. I would prefer for it to be again—and to live there rather than in here."

"Because Lucky and I have cooties?"

Lucky was still sniffing at the holes in the baseboard, his tail in the air as his head repeatedly clunked the bottom shelf.

Amar hesitated again. "You are training to become a witch."

"So we can't be roommates?" Morgen smiled, but inside, she was stung. Sure, her relationship with Amar had begun when he sprang onto the hood of her car in wolf form and threatened to tear out her throat, but since then, they'd fought a witch and enemy werewolves together. He'd even admitted that his opinion of her had improved.

Why would he object now to sharing the big house? They weren't sleeping on the same floor or using the same bathroom. "My grandmother was a witch, and you got along fine with her, right?"

Morgen remembered Phoebe's suggestion that Grandma might have cast some kind of long-lasting control spell on Amar, and that was the reason he'd protected her and her property. Morgen hadn't run that by him. She didn't want to believe it was true—even if it was, it was possible Amar hadn't realized it—but everyone said witches and werewolves didn't get along.

"She was a private person, and I am a private person. And I lived in the barn, not her guest room. She did not disturb me."

"Am *I* disturbing you?" Morgen planted a hand on her chest. "I don't even go down the hall to your room."

"You are more disturbing than your grandmother was." He gazed at her, as if she should know exactly what he was talking about.

She didn't. "How can that be? My hobbies are reading and organizing the root cellar. *I'm* not the one running around with a chainsaw."

His eyes narrowed, and she regretted the comment. Carving furniture and artwork from slabs of wood was how he made a living.

"You simply are," he said tersely.

Though exasperated, Morgen didn't push him. She didn't like confrontation, not with enemies and not with friends—or strange furry roommates—either. She didn't even know why she was arguing. As an introvert, she liked her privacy and shouldn't want someone roaming around her house. More often than not, she'd preferred it when her husband hadn't been home. That was probably what had led to him calling her cold and aloof and filing for divorce.

"Fine," she said. "You work on the barn, and once I figure out how to turn moss into money, I'll hire some contractors to come de-rat the house. Are there many in town?"

"No."

"Are there *any* in town?" Morgen knew Bellrock was small, but it wasn't *that* small. After all, she'd met his pack mates and they'd been remodeling a house and installing landscaping at the time. "What about your, uhm, pack?"

His eyes flared with indignation. "They are not *my pack* anymore."

"Right. Sorry." She wanted to ask him what had happened, but he was so touchy that she didn't dare. "But would they be a good choice for this project?"

Morgen hadn't been drawn to the rough men when she'd met them, but she supposed she could tolerate more of their snide comments about witches and the insinuation that she was sleeping with Amar—or maybe controlling him with magic—if it resulted in the end of rat invaders.

"No," Amar said.

"Because they do bad work?"

"No."

"Because they wear wife-beater tank tops with pit stains?"

"No."

"Because... they kicked you out, and it's hard for you to be around them?"

His eyes flared again. "I left *them*."

He hadn't, she noticed, answered the second part of the question. She didn't want him to be uncomfortable around the contractors—especially since her experience with home-improvement projects was that they took forever—so maybe she would drop the idea.

"I'll try to find someone else," she said.

Amar shook his head. "Hire them. I don't care."

He strode out, floorboards creaking and boots clomping. The front door slammed shut.

Lucky must have decided he couldn't vacuum vermin out of the wall with the power of his sniffs, for he came and sat beside her, looking up expectantly with his is-it-time-for-breakfast expression.

"If you hadn't been sleeping so hard and had caught the rats, we wouldn't be in this situation."

He stood and leaned against her leg, tail wagging.

She sighed and patted him. She couldn't blame him. The house truly did need work. The laundry room—a converted porch—leaked when it rained, half of the windows didn't open, and a third of the outlets didn't work. When she'd opened the chimney flue, water and a bird's nest had tumbled down onto the grate.

Scratching noises came from a window. Morgen looked over in time to see a huge black raven spring away from the frame and fly out of sight.

"Is that Phoebe's kleptomaniac familiar again?" Broom in hand, Morgen headed for the front door. "Or is some *other* witch spying on me?"

Lucky whined pitifully, staying in the kitchen with his nose pointed toward the cupboard that held his dog food.

"I'll be back to feed you in a minute," she called, then stepped out onto the porch.

The raven hadn't gone far. It perched atop the partially rebuilt barn roof and gazed down at Amar with beady black eyes. He'd returned to a stump where a bear carving was in progress, but he hadn't missed its arrival. He stared balefully at it, his chainsaw in hand.

"Can you tell if that's the same one that was here before?" Morgen joined him, trying to remember if he'd been in the area when Phoebe's raven had spied on the house previously.

"It has been here before." Amar glanced toward the raised garden beds.

He'd mentioned seeing what might have been a fox familiar there once before. The witches of Bellrock were keeping an eye on the place.

"I guess I'll go see if Phoebe wants something." Morgen had wanted to ask about moss-powder preparation anyway.

"You should not go."

"She's the only witch in Bellrock who speaks to me without threatening me."

"That doesn't make her an ally. You thwarted her sister's plans."

"But I also installed a computer and inventory-management system for her."

"You think software counts for more than siblings?"

"In my family, it would."

The gaze he turned toward her suggested that was odd. He was probably right.

2

MORGEN MANEUVERED HER CAR DOWN THE MILE-LONG, POTHOLE-filled driveway with densely packed pines, firs, and cedars rising up to either side. It hadn't rained for a few days, so the potholes were less water—and duck—filled than usual.

To her surprise, Amar insisted on riding to town with her. In addition to hating witches and anything to do with them, he risked encountering the Loups Laflamme when he was out. Amar got along with the rival werewolf pack even more poorly than with his estranged Lobos Sanguientos.

"Do you know more about my standing with Phoebe than I do?" Morgen asked, wondering if he wanted to come along because he believed she was in danger.

"I know that witches hold grudges. And I've promised to protect you." He shifted, looking cramped and uncomfortable in the passenger seat of her compact electric car.

"You don't have to do that." Morgen almost said that she could take care of herself, but that wasn't true. She'd barely started learning about her witch heritage and the blood in her veins that allowed her to wield magical tools and cast incantations. Before her life had taken this unexpected turn, she'd been a database programmer for eighteen years. That hadn't exactly equipped her with the self-defense skills of a Navy SEAL.

"Gwen would have wished it."

"I hadn't visited since I was a kid. Grandma might not have remembered how much trouble I could get myself into."

"She knew about the coven here. She interacted with them, even if she was a loner and didn't work with them." Lone wolf that he was, Amar sounded like he approved of that.

A raven cawed and flew across the driveway, then flapped up toward the treetops. If Lucky had been riding in the back, he would have barked uproariously, but Morgen had left him in the house. Not all of Phoebe's customers appreciated having a friendly dog run up, stand on his hind legs, and put his paws on their shoulders. Oddly.

The raven banked and headed toward town.

"I guess Phoebe will know we're coming." Though Morgen didn't *think* the gray-haired witch had inimical things planned for her, she couldn't help but be nervous, and her palms were damp as she turned the wheel to guide them onto the paved road. Since it was only sixty-eight degrees out, she couldn't blame the summer heat for the sweat.

"The raven is herding you."

"Yes, I've heard they're the Australian shepherds of the bird world."

Amar gave her a sidelong look. "The witch will want something."

"If it's new inventory tagged and added to her database, I'm the girl for that."

"That was your previous employment?"

"Hm, sort of. I managed the supply-chain databases for a heavy-machinery manufacturer to help them make sure their products arrived on time."

"Sounds exhilarating."

"We can't all carve bears out of logs for a living."

That earned her another sidelong look. "Most people are smart enough not to mock werewolves."

"Does that include witches? Since you've got an ongoing feud with them, I assumed all kinds of insults were tossed back and forth."

"You do not want to become like them."

"No."

Morgen thought of the murdering Calista and the three witches who'd started the barn fire, one of whom had also branded Amar on the back of his neck and forced him to kill a real-estate agent. That brand was still there. What happened if that witch activated control over him again? She shuddered.

"I don't," she added and smiled over at him. "I apologize for teasing you. Thank you for coming along with me."

He grunted an acknowledgment.

Since it was a summer weekend in tourist-friendly Bellrock, the street parking was all taken, even in front of the Crystal Parlor. It was more likely the visitors had come to dine at the Timber Wolf across the street than buy hot-foot powder to keep ex-boyfriends away, but Phoebe didn't have dedicated spaces.

Amar eyed the log-walled restaurant, probably looking for signs of the Loup werewolf pack. Morgen hoped such signs did not present themselves.

She parked in an alley, and Amar accompanied her to the Crystal Parlor, his bare arms and wild-man attire drawing a few eyes. Before Morgen opened the door, he rested a hand on her arm.

"Be careful with her." Amar met her eyes, his expression grim. "If she's pretending to befriend you, it's because she wants something. *More* than computer help. She could have paid a teenager for that."

Morgen didn't point out that she had an advanced degree and was far more qualified to set up inventory-management systems than the average teenager. She almost mentioned that Phoebe had given her a similar warning about Amar, promising that werewolves didn't befriend, and certainly didn't voluntarily protect, witches. She didn't believe that, especially not after Amar had helped her infiltrate the Rainwater Estate to search for evidence related to her grandmother's murder.

She hoped Phoebe would also prove to be an ally and not an enemy, but she nodded and thanked him for the concern. She'd already been snarky enough with him that day. He didn't deserve that.

The raven cawed twice as it landed on the rooftop of the Timber Wolf, eyes locked on them. Amar lowered his hand and glared over at it, a faint growl emanating from his throat.

"Do apex predators catch ravens?" Morgen asked.

"It depends on how much the ravens irritate them." Amar leaned against the wall and nodded to indicate that he would remain outside.

Morgen was glad for the company, but she regretted taking him from his work. It sounded like he was far behind on completing orders.

"I won't take long," she promised.

A bell jangled as Morgen opened the door and stepped inside. A young, pale-skinned brunette in a sunflower dress and brown sandals glanced at her, then took a longer look.

Something about her was familiar, but Morgen couldn't place her. Maybe it was one of the handful of customers, mostly female, who came in to purchase hexing powders and the "Bitch Be Gone" herb blend.

The woman opened her mouth, then shook her head and rushed toward the back room. Morgen thought about saying something, since she knew that room was for storage and Phoebe didn't allow customers in there, but the back door slammed as the woman rushed out.

Morgen glanced over her shoulder, half-expecting to find that Amar had changed his mind and followed her in. It wasn't as if *Morgen* was frightening in any way. She hadn't even brought the kitchen broom along. But he remained outside, the side of his shoulder just visible through the large display window.

"Huh."

A chair creaked, and Phoebe stepped into view. She'd been reading in a corner hidden by the numerous racks and display cases that occupied most of the floor space and all of the walls. Her curly, graying brown hair made her look much older than the voluptuous Calista, who'd apparently had two recent lovers: the Loup werewolf she'd talked into working for her *and* the businessman whose house she'd taken over after murdering him.

"Hi." Morgen lifted a hand and pointed toward the back door. "Who was that?"

"A customer."

Between one eye blink and the next, Morgen remembered where she'd seen the young woman before, and she rocked back on her heels. Her property. That had been one of the three witches who'd lit the barn on fire and forced Amar to his knees, using magic to torture him.

If he'd come in with her, he might have roared in fury and sprinted after the woman to take his revenge. Or maybe not. He was wary of witches, understandably so. That young woman wasn't the one who'd pressed an amulet to the back of his neck to brand him, but if she traveled with the others, he would doubtless consider them all enemies.

And so would Morgen. They'd burned the barn to try to keep her from selling the property, which included the hundreds-of-acres Wolf Wood that surrounded the house. All they would have had to do was talk to her, and they could have found out that she hadn't intended to sell it. Maybe she had when she'd first driven up to Bellrock, but Grandma's letter had asked her not to. And now that she knew about the magical spring that gave life to bioluminescent mushrooms, mosses, and other plants that grew around it, she doubly wouldn't consider it. Those women—those witches—had chosen to make an enemy of her for no reason.

"A witch customer?" Morgen raised her eyebrows.

"Most of my customers are either witches or those who believe in our ways."

Morgen sensed that Phoebe was being deliberately evasive but didn't know how to get the answer she wanted out of her. Amar's promise that Phoebe wasn't a friend came to mind. His warning.

"But how many of them light fire to people's barns?"

"I heard about that," Phoebe said, "but those who did that aren't after you personally."

"Comforting."

"Now that you've taken Wolf Wood off the market, you shouldn't have to worry about them."

"Does *Amar* need to worry about them?"

Phoebe glanced toward the window, no doubt aware that he was there, even though she couldn't have seen him from her position. "He would be wise to avoid them. They've been hurt by werewolves, and he's very blatantly what he is."

What did *that* mean?

"Neither he nor they are what I wanted to talk to you about." Phoebe lifted a hand, waving for Morgen to follow, and headed toward the back room.

So, the raven *had* been sent to get her. Morgen was certain she'd given Phoebe her phone number, but the people of Bellrock didn't seem to be big into texting.

"How's the computer system working?" Morgen asked as she trailed Phoebe into the back, the storage room lined with shelves of colorful powders, mysterious liquids, and dried herbs. There were even a couple of small vials of the bioluminescent moss powder. They were locked in a display case, attesting to the value. "Do you need help with anything?"

"I'm getting the hang of it. Thank you." Phoebe opened a drawer and pulled out a cream-colored envelope with calligraphy on the front.

Under other circumstances, Morgen might have thought it an invitation for a wedding or equally festive occasion, but Phoebe's grim expression hinted more of funerals.

"My sister visited me last night for the first time in almost a year," Phoebe said.

As Morgen accepted the envelope, a tingle of energy flowed from the paper and up her arm. She almost dropped it. Maybe she should have. Things like ivory, bone, and stone could be turned into magical tools capable of delivering curses. Why not stationery?

"I would have been more pleased to see her if there wasn't an arrest warrant out for her," Phoebe added.

"I'm sorry about that," Morgen said, more because it seemed best not to ruffle feathers than because she truly was. *Calista* was the one who'd murdered her boyfriend, not Morgen.

"She brought it upon herself. As I feared she would."

"Oh?" Morgen might have relaxed an iota at hearing that Phoebe didn't approve of her sister's choices, but she still held the ominous envelope, so relief seemed premature.

"We've had differences of opinion for a long time."

"When you first spoke of your sister, I got the impression that she was dead."

Phoebe sighed and slumped against the desk. "Not dead, no, but we had a big fight before she left the Crystal Parlor, and we hadn't spoken since, so..." She twitched a shoulder.

"Was it about her plans to seduce a wealthy businessman and

try to get herself added to all of his bank accounts and credit cards?"

Phoebe's lips pinched together. Maybe Morgen shouldn't have been snarky. Just because there was a rift between Phoebe and Calista didn't mean Phoebe didn't continue to care for her sister. After all, Morgen and *her* sister didn't have the cuddliest of relationships, but they still looked out for each other.

"At the time, she didn't have plans to do that," Phoebe said. "Not as far as she told me. But she disparaged my store and berated me for having so few ambitions. She *also* wanted me to take it online. Take it online, expand, and start teaching about our products on the internet so we could gain more and more customers." Phoebe's tone turned dry as she added, "I'm such a natural with computers, so I'm sure that would have been easy."

Morgen would have offered to help her with such a project, but it didn't sound like Phoebe truly wanted to do it.

"She always cared more about gaining money and power in the traditional world than I did," Phoebe continued. "I don't understand it. It's not our way. Witches may defend themselves or help their loved ones with their magic, but they shouldn't strive to use it to gain power or subjugate others. Certainly not to *harm* others. That is not what our mentor taught us long ago. Perhaps it's good that she passed on before she could witness how Calista's... priorities changed." Phoebe shook her head. "I have not read the message, but I fear it won't be light-hearted and amicable."

"Nothing written in calligraphy on fancy paper ever is." Morgen eyed it, wondering if she should read it in front of Phoebe or take it out to the car. This wasn't what she'd come for. "Do you, by chance, know how the bioluminescent moss powder is prepared?" She pointed to the vials in the display case.

Phoebe arched her eyebrows. "Are you thinking of going into the production business?"

"I need to finance the rebuilding of my torched barn."

If Phoebe felt any guilt about being associated with the witches who'd done that, she didn't show it. "That's reasonable. The moss isn't the only valuable thing growing in Wolf Wood—it's unfortunate that you didn't come up and learn from your grandmother before she passed—but it's the rarest and sells for the most, to those handful of souls who know how to make use of it. If you need help finding customers, let me know. I can put you in touch with them."

"For a cut of the proceeds?"

"As I said, I'm not the raving capitalist that my sister is. I would offer my assistance in exchange for something less pecuniary."

"Computer help?"

"You spoke of the possibility of selling my goods online. The Crystal Parlor is currently without a website."

"You could get started on eBay."

"Do you think my eclectic clientele is there?"

"I think everyone is there." Morgen suspected witch paraphernalia of all sorts was on the auction site. "But I'm sure I can help you set up a website and a shopping cart. There are plenty of out-of-the-box solutions these days."

"Excellent. I can get you in touch with buyers. When it comes to the curing process, however... I don't know it. I'm a master of ancient lore and incantations, but as I told you previously, I'm not a crafter, nor do I know much about preparing components. Calista would." Phoebe's eyes grew wistful as she gazed toward the shelves of ingredients.

"I'll be sure to ask her for tips the next time she tries to coerce me into a one-man helicopter that she plans to crash."

"Perhaps you can find another resource. There are other crafters in the coven."

"Like the one that darted out the back door as I came in?"

Phoebe smiled faintly. "Wendy has some talents in that area, but she is young and not that interested in the world she was born into. I do not expect her to stay in Bellrock for long. She would prefer playing *video games* to learning witchcraft. If you could make amends with them, her older sisters might be more likely resources."

Make amends? *Morgen* hadn't been the one to pick a fight with them.

"Admittedly, it takes them a while to warm up to strangers," Phoebe continued. "That's true of most of the local coven."

"So I suppose this isn't an invitation to join?" Morgen held up the envelope.

"No. Calista couldn't give one, regardless. She was cast out. Her crimes are not acceptable to our people."

But magically coercing a werewolf to murder someone was? To Morgen, the idea of being welcomed by the local witches and learning more about her heritage was appealing... but not if they were criminals.

"Perhaps the knowledge you seek is among your grandmother's belongings," Phoebe suggested.

Since Morgen had already sorted and organized most of what was in the root cellar, she didn't think it was, but maybe she had missed something. She would have to peruse the various grimoires again. Maybe she would even make a searchable online database containing all the recipes in those old books. That sounded a lot more appealing than dealing with stranger-hating witches.

Morgen took a breath and broke the seal on the envelope. A single card was tucked inside, the writing using the same elegant handwriting and calligraphy pen.

You have destroyed my world and made an enemy. You and your scruffy werewolf had better watch your backs. I'll have my revenge on both of you and unfettered access to Wolf Wood as well.

3

"WELL, IT'S NOT A WEDDING INVITATION." MORGEN SHOWED THE letter to Phoebe.

She frowned as she read it and shook her head slowly. "I do not know what my sister is capable of these days or how real her threat is."

"Given that her former business partner was found buried under a cairn in his backyard, I'll take it as very real."

"I suppose that's wise."

"I'm not sure how to watch my back though. I have to sleep some time." Morgen hoped Phoebe would suggest some defenses that she could plant around the house and barn to keep out witches. Thus far, her searches of Grandma's grimoires had turned up enchantments that could curse someone or cause unseemly growths to sprout on an intruder's body, but it was unclear if said curses and growths could deter a visitor or were simply a punishment that would pop up days later. As much as Morgen wanted to cover Calista in warts, she would prefer it if fireballs burst out of the lilac bushes to blast the woman if she trespassed.

"You should get a familiar. Zeke warns me if someone is snooping around my store or home."

That wasn't the security Morgen had been thinking of, but she asked, "How does one get a familiar? And does magic make a familiar more intelligent than the average animal?"

"Somewhat. It's more that they have a link with you and understand your desires. As to how one gets one, there's a ritual." Phoebe walked to a bookshelf, selected a leather-bound tome, and opened it to a page in the middle. "You can borrow this if you want to try."

"Will I end up with a raven?"

"Perhaps. If one deigns to come to you when you do the ritual. Cats are also typical, though I don't know if there are any roaming around in Wolf Wood. The wolves infesting the place would eat them." Phoebe pursed her lips with disapproval.

"My dog Lucky would chase a cat anyway. For that matter, he's convinced that your raven would make a succulent morsel."

Given how obnoxious that raven had proven thus far, Morgen might not discourage that.

Phoebe's disapproval turned to disdain as she said, "Dogs are atypical companions for witches. Especially one as boisterous as yours. They're large and rambunctious, and they're poor at moving subtly around to observe nature and humanity on your behalf."

Or spying on newcomers to town...

"Well, I've had him for three years, and he's staying. Any familiar that wanders out of the forest and wants to work with me will have to get along with him." Which might be a lot to ask. After all, Lucky was a hunting breed. He hadn't been trained to be a hunter's companion, but his instincts told him to seek out and catch fowl, lizards, rats, squirrels, chipmunks, and other inimical forest creatures. "Actually, it would be easier if *he* could be my familiar. Though he's not typically up at night, keeping an eye on me." Or on the rats invading the kitchen... "Is that possible?"

"You do *not* want a dog for a familiar. Such a creature, if sent out to do your bidding, would be too dumb to avoid being picked up by the pound."

"He's not dumb."

"Dogs are all dumb."

"They have bigger brains than ravens, I'm sure."

"Size doesn't mean anything. Ravens are very clever. Listen to me. I have decades of experience. Dogs are fine for companions but not as familiars. It's unlikely the coven would even allow you into meetings with a *dog* familiar." Phoebe shuddered, as if she was imagining Lucky running around, knocking over cauldrons and trying to nosh on other witches' familiars.

"The coven isn't allowing me into meetings now," Morgen pointed out.

"They are aware of you and observing you."

How wonderful.

Phoebe handed the book to Morgen with the page marked. "Read about the ritual, gather the ingredients, memorize the matching incantation, then don your grandmother's amulet and go out in the woods in the evening. You'll build a fire, perform the ritual, and wait for an animal to visit you. Don't be in a rush. The first creature that comes might not be the one most appropriate for you. You'll know in your heart when it's right. You'll have a deep and meaningful spiritual connection with its eternal soul."

"Lucky and I had that last night when he was stealing my pillows."

"It won't be your dog," Phoebe snapped.

"Fine, fine." Morgen held up the book. "Thank you for this. I'll look for shopping-cart software that will work for the Crystal Parlor."

Unfortunately, it sounded like Morgen was on her own for

figuring out how to *cure* the moss. That was the word Phoebe had used. Well, she could handle it. And she would make enough to pay for rat-proofing the house.

"Excellent. I look forward to doing business with you." Phoebe hesitated. "Do you have a return message for Calista?"

"Do you know how to reach her?"

Another hesitation. "No. But she may come back and ask me. I don't know."

"No message. Though I don't know why she blames me for what she brought upon herself. She's the one who wanted to force me to sell my grandmother's land to her."

"Things might have been easier if you'd gone along with her. She didn't want to develop it, just have access to the resources."

"If she's the capitalist you say she is, she might have turned it into Disneyland for Witches, started charging admission, and figured out how to turn the whole forest into a profit center."

Phoebe opened her mouth, what looked like an objection on her lips, but closed it again and sighed. "I'm not positive you're wrong."

"Just try to get her to leave me alone, please. I don't want a fight with anyone. I just want to do my own thing, like Grandma did."

"I think… it's too late for that."

Great.

Shaking her head, Morgen walked toward the front door. A couple of girls in torn jeans were *oohing* and *aahing* over rose quartz obelisks that looked vaguely like sex toys. The label did promise rose quartz was the most romantic and compassionate crystal in existence.

Once outside, Morgen handed the note to Amar. "We've been threatened and we're to watch our backs."

Not surprisingly, he scowled as he read it.

"Will she seduce another werewolf to send after us?" Amar sneered, crumpled the paper, and threw it in a trash bin as he strode toward the side street that led to the alley where they'd parked.

Morgen was more worried about the werewolf-control spell than seduction, but she didn't bring it up. He got touchy about such things, and the note had already put him in a surly mood.

As she trailed him down the alley, the sound of glass shattering came from the main street. She paused and looked back. Had someone taken a baseball bat to a car window?

A teenage boy in overalls with tools stuffed into the oversized pockets ran into their alley. He was grinning fiercely, his black hair flopping in his eyes, but his expression changed when he spotted Amar.

Amar pointed Morgen toward the wall and stepped past her to face the oncoming boy.

"*Hola, tío, ¿como estas?*" the kid asked.

"Arturo!" Amar said sternly. "*¿Qué hiciste?*"

Morgen couldn't interpret much of the rapid-fire exchange, but she could guess Arturo had thrown a rock through a window by the way he kept running down the alley while glancing over his shoulder. Amar reached for him, but he ducked and sped away even faster. Morgen thought Amar, who was just as fast and much stronger, could have caught the boy and hoisted him over his shoulder, but he didn't.

As the kid disappeared around a corner, two pale-skinned men wearing Ray-Ban sunglasses and what Morgen could only categorize as luxury athleisure-wear ran off Main Street and into the alley. She recognized the Loup pack's taste for expensive clothing right away and remembered Deputy Franklin's implication that they had ties to important people like the mayor and that they owned part of the Timber Wolf and other establishments in town.

They'd clearly been chasing the kid, but they came up short when they spotted Amar. He puffed out his chest and stood in the middle of the alley, blocking their way. Arturo had disappeared around a corner, and Morgen thought they should do the same instead of picking a fight, especially when the boy might be a juvenile delinquent.

"It's the lone Lobo," one of the men said. One of the *werewolves* said.

Neither was one of the three Loups that Morgen and Amar had faced a couple of weeks earlier in the Timber Wolf parking lot, but they looked just as belligerent.

"Go to your car, Morgen," Amar said without letting his gaze stray from the werewolves.

She took a couple of steps in that direction, mostly so she wouldn't get in his way if a fight broke out, but she refused to leave him to battle alone against superior numbers. He probably only wanted to buy time for the kid to get away, but who knew what the fight would escalate into?

She gripped her amulet, thinking of the incantation she'd learned that could let her control a werewolf. Possibly. She had chanted it to Amar when he'd been under Calista's control, but whether it had worked or not was debatable. He'd been trying hard to resist Calista, and it might have ultimately been sheer willpower that had allowed him to free himself.

Still, Morgen would try to do *something* if this turned into a fight.

"You the one who thought it would be cute to break our window?" one Loup asked.

"Like a foolish *child* instead of a lone wolf without a pack to protect him?"

Their accents were faint, but it was clear they weren't from the area any more than the Lobos were. Someday, Morgen would dig up the story of how Mexican and Canadian werewolf packs had converged on Bellrock. Assuming they survived this encounter. It was too early in the day for any of them to shift—at least, according to what Amar had told her—but even as humans, werewolves were strong and dangerous.

"I don't break windows or play games." Amar crouched in a fighting stance as the two men prowled closer. "And I am not a child, Gabin."

"But you're alone."

Morgen resisted the urge to raise her finger and point out that Amar *wasn't* alone. She knew what they meant, and she also didn't want to draw their attention to her.

"Some say you killed Antoine," the one he'd called Gabin said. "The deputy found him dead in Rainwater Estate with his throat ripped out. Rumors say you were there."

Amar didn't reply. He only crouched, ready to fight. He'd battled three Loups before and held his own, but Morgen didn't know if he would have won that skirmish if she hadn't grabbed a blowtorch and helped. This time, they hadn't driven his truck to town, and she didn't have anything in her car that could be used as a weapon. Why had she stopped stuffing that staff with the antlers in there? It had only maimed her upholstery in a *few* spots.

As the men glared at each other, she rehearsed the werewolf-control incantation in her mind, but she realized she couldn't say it without possibly affecting *Amar*. What if her magic put him under a spell that left him defenseless while not affecting the two werewolves farther away? Damn it, she couldn't risk it.

One of the men drew a dagger, hatred in his eyes as he focused on Amar. The other lifted his fists, and they stepped forward, clearly intending to attack together.

Morgen looked around for an impromptu weapon and spotted a beer bottle on the cement. As the two Loups sprang at Amar, she lunged and plucked it up.

Amar dodged the man with the knife and threw a lightning-fast punch at the face of the other. The Loup jerked his head to the side, but Amar still clipped him. While he reeled, Amar shoved him into the knife-wielder. The man stumbled into his comrade, and Amar lifted a foot and kicked him in the chest. The Loup with the knife elbowed his buddy away as he tried to get around him to attack Amar.

For a second, Morgen had a clear target. She hurled the bottle at the knifeman, hoping to knock the blade out of his hand. Her aim was abysmal, but she got lucky, and the bottle flew high instead of wide. It thudded into the man's nose.

She hoped that would knock him out, or at least leave him stunned and weeping, but his eyes only widened with rage, and he focused on her for the first time. While his ally recovered enough to launch a flurry of punches at Amar, the Loup raised his knife and charged at her.

She cursed and backed up but smacked into the wall.

"Under the moon's magic, turn the snarling hound from angry foe to witch bound!" she blurted as she prepared to swing her purse at him. It was all she had.

He halted two feet away from her, the knife poised to plunge into her chest. Not trusting that her incantation had worked, especially since Amar and the other Loup were still fighting, Morgen ran several steps to the side.

The Loup didn't follow her. He didn't even look at her. Instead, he stared blankly at the wall.

Good. Amar could finish with the other one, then deal with this guy. Or Morgen and Amar could simply hurry to the car and leave the area.

With a roar, Amar hurled his opponent into a brick wall. The man cried out in pain, but he managed to land on his feet. He growled at Amar and rushed back at him.

The Loup that Morgen had ensorcelled blinked slowly a few times. Was the spell already wearing off? The knife remained in his grip, the wicked blade long enough to hack down a small tree.

Figuring she should disarm him, Morgen crept back in and

tugged it free. His fingers were slack, so she was able to, but he frowned and belatedly tightened them. He was definitely fighting the spell.

Maybe there was something else she could do to him before he recovered his faculties, something to put him out of the fight. With his knife in her hand, she risked creeping closer to him again. She bent down and slid the sharp blade under his bootlaces. It sliced through them like butter.

She meant to end her sartorial sabotage there but noticed how thin his designer belt was. Made from thin canvas, it featured a red snake undulating across its black length. She stepped around to the man's back, grabbed the belt, and slipped the knife under it.

He tried to step away, but the blade proved its sharpness once again and cut the belt in half. He growled and turned around, shaking his head. And shaking off the incantation?

Morgen scurried back, hoping he would trip over his bootlaces —and his pants—if he lunged after her.

But before the Loup could contemplate it, Amar appeared behind him, lifted him under the armpits, and threw him against a big blue trash bin. Too bad the lid was down, or the man and the remains of his designer clothing could have taken a bath in refuse. His pants did sag impressively as he crumpled to the ground.

His buddy was groaning on his knees nearby as he gripped his ribs and blood flowed from his nose. He clambered to his feet, shot a dark glare back at them, and staggered back toward Main Street. The other Loup gave them the middle finger before shambling off after his comrade. His pants drooped off his hips and butt. He cursed, grabbed the waistband, and hurried out of sight.

"Nicely done." Amar lowered his fists and smirked at her.

He didn't mention the incantation. Maybe he hadn't heard it over the din of his own fight.

"Thanks. Mind if we leave now?" Morgen worried the Loups would return with reinforcements.

"I encourage it."

Before they reached the car, Arturo popped out of an alcove, a hammer clenched in his hand. Morgen jumped, thinking he was a threat, but he lowered the tool when he saw them.

Amar and Arturo exchanged a quick conversation in Spanish. It sounded like the kid had realized Amar had started a fight on his behalf and had been coming back to help.

Amar finished by shrugging, thumping Arturo on the shoulder, and continuing toward Morgen's car.

She hesitated, realizing this might be an opportunity to ask if the Lobos were interested in working on her house. If Arturo could deliver a message to his elders, she wouldn't have to drive around town looking for the pack. Something that might be unwise with angry Loups in the area.

"Do you work on construction with the rest of your pack?" Morgen asked before the boy could trot off. "Or is that a tool for window destruction?"

Arturo lifted his chin. "I work *hard* with my uncles and cousins. I only threw a rock because those stupid *pendejos* said they were going to run us out of town and that Pedro is a runt."

"Well, if your pack is looking for work, I need some remodeling done." She almost added *and a barn repaired*, but Amar was glaring at her from the car. Even if she only wanted to lighten his load, he might be offended if she tried to hand the job he'd promised to do off to someone else.

"We're pretty busy, but I'll tell them." Arturo shrugged and took off.

Morgen had no idea if anyone would get in touch with her or if the teenager would even deliver the message. Well, there was no hurry—aside from saving her pantry from rats—and she still had to figure out how she would pay for labor and materials.

"I don't suppose you know how my grandmother prepared her

glowing moss?" Morgen asked as she joined Amar, hoping the question would distract him from his glowering.

"I do not. All I need is lumber, and I can continue the repairs on the barn and then work on the house. You do not need to hire anyone." He climbed into the car and shut the door.

She slid in beside him. "As soon as I figure out the moss thing, I can give you money for wood."

He looked out the windshield while radiating displeasure. Such a grumpy werewolf.

"Maybe if I can find an animal familiar, it'll have some ideas." Morgen smiled at him and held up the book Phoebe had lent her.

"Familiars obey commands, nothing else. If you want knowledge of how to process the moss, find one of the witches who sell it."

"You mean the witches who've been sneaking into Wolf Wood to steal it? Like Calista?"

"She would have the answers you seek."

"I think I'll just scour the internet and Grandma's books."

"I will hold my breath while waiting for funds for lumber."

"You're in a crabby mood today." Her own mood had been lifted by seeing a Loup hobbling away with his trousers sagging off his butt. Too bad that hadn't entertained Amar as vastly.

He looked over, his eye starting to grow puffy from a punch he must have taken. Maybe that was why he hadn't been entertained.

"Understandably so," she said. "That was nice of you to help the kid. You're a good man."

Amar grunted and looked forward again.

A surly, crabby man but a good man. Morgen drove off, hoping she could figure out how to make some money without going to her enemies for help.

What had happened to the good old days when her most hated enemy had been the anonymous evildoer who stole her Diet 7-Ups out of the fridge at work?

4

THE INSTRUCTIONS FROM A COOKING SHOW EMANATED FROM Morgen's phone as she measured ingredients for vegan mole poblano. She looked forward to tasting the *richness* and *depths of flavor* that the chef promised.

Maybe the scents that would soon waft out the kitchen window would send subliminal comfort to Amar that would soothe the disgruntled state he'd been in since she'd given her message to Arturo. Actually, he'd been disgruntled before that too. Essentially, since she met him. The aggressive hammering going on at the barn currently did not suggest his state would change soon, no matter what she cooked.

Morgen stepped over Lucky to retrieve tomatoes from the refrigerator, which prompted him to thwack his tail hopefully against the floor. He was sprawled on his side, tongue lolled out, as he recovered from an hour of hunting vigorously around the garden and barn.

"Just so you know, mole has chocolate in it, so you won't be getting any, but I've got some deli meat to put on your kibble. Special toppings."

That earned more tail whacks.

"I'm going to assume that chocolate isn't poisonous to werewolves. Just because dogs can't have it, and wolves are kind of like dogs, doesn't mean anything, right? Amar is human most of the time, and human digestive systems like chocolate just fine. There's only a little in there anyway. Less if I keep sampling." Morgen took another square of chocolate and popped it in her mouth. One had to make sure one's ingredients were suitably fresh for cooking, after all.

She was in the process of making corn tortillas—Grandma's kitchen had *everything,* including a cast-iron tortilla press old enough to have fed troops at the Alamo—when the hammering outside stopped. The sound of a vehicle rumbling up the driveway made Morgen put everything down and peer out the window.

A huge blue truck with tinted windows was driving up. It gleamed, especially in comparison to Amar's beat-up 1960s Ford parked out front.

Maybe these were the Lobos, already coming to talk about her project. That truck was newer and fancier than anything she'd seen at their job site, but since she hadn't invited anyone else to come to the house, she didn't know who else it could be.

She turned off the cooking show and hurried outside, wanting to speak with them before Amar strode up and said he could handle everything by himself.

When she stepped onto the porch, shutting the door so Lucky couldn't follow her out and jump on people, Amar was indeed standing outside and facing the vehicle. His back was rigid, and his face was frosty. Great.

Morgen jogged down the porch steps, intending to greet whichever of his kin had come, but Amar thrust a hand in her direction.

"Stay out of this," he barked.

"But isn't that..." She let the words trail off, realizing the lack of ladders and other tools that were typically visible in the bed probably meant this wasn't someone's construction truck. There also wasn't a logo or company sign on the side, as she would expect on a business vehicle.

In the house, Lucky put his paws on a windowsill and barked his disapproval of not being allowed out.

The driver and passenger doors opened at the same time, and two men in slacks and boots stepped out. Morgen's shoulders slumped. She didn't recognize the passenger, but the driver had been there for the fight at the Timber Wolf. It was the Loup she'd scared off by applying a blowtorch to what had been, at the time, his furry belly. He wouldn't have fond memories of her.

The two men focused on Amar as they strode toward him. He held his ground, his jaw clenched. A slight bend to his knees suggested he was ready to spring away—or spring at them—if they turned aggressive, but he waited for them to make the first move.

"Guy. Chace. What do you want?" Amar asked. "I'm positive the homeowner didn't invite you up to her property."

"The homeowner you're mooching off, loner?" the one he'd called Chace asked. He wore sunglasses even though it was a cloudy day. Maybe he was hungover.

"You killed Antoine," Guy stated, lifting a hand to his comrade to cut off more chitchat. Judging by the hair on that hand and running up under his sleeves, he was as furry in human form as he was in wolf form. "Did you think we wouldn't find out?"

"He tried to kill me first." Amar glanced at Morgen. "I was defending myself."

She grimaced. He'd been defending *her*. If she hadn't asked for his help, he wouldn't have been in that mansion where Calista's werewolf could attack him.

Probably. Amar had originally gone over there alone,

intending to kill Grandma's murderer. He and the Loup might have ended up butting heads no matter what.

"You defended yourself to his *death*. Lucien wants you dead."

"But he didn't come to face me himself," Amar said.

"Oh, he will. He sent us to issue a challenge." Guy pointed between Amar's eyes. "In three nights. The full moon. At the Deer Creek trail. You know the place."

"I know it."

"Be there. Bring your female as a witness if you want." Guy sneered disdainfully at Morgen. "Or that boy who likes to break windows. Someone to tell the rest of your pack that Lucien dueled you and killed you fair and square."

Morgen raised her eyebrows at being called someone's *female* but kept out of it.

"Because you're afraid there'll be repercussions from the pack if you kill me?" Amar growled.

"Not if it's fair. You know the rules of the wild."

"I know the rules."

"Three nights, Lobo. Be there."

They climbed into their truck and turned it around, leaving deep tire tracks in the grass as it roared off.

"I don't like them," Morgen said.

Amar joined her at the base of the steps. "I will try to finish the barn before the duel."

"Because it's going to rain and you don't want your shop towels to get wet? Or because you don't think you'll make it back alive?" Her gut churned at the idea.

He shook his head grimly.

Morgen hadn't encountered the leader of the Loups yet and didn't know how formidable he was. Or if their pack would play fair. What if they said it would be a one-on-one duel, but they planned to jump Amar with their whole pack and take revenge for the death of Antoine?

"Is there anything I can do to help?" Morgen thought of her werewolf-control incantation.

As if he knew what she was thinking, Amar frowned at her. "Witch magic is not an honorable weapon to bring to a battle."

"Magic? Hey, I was just thinking of giving you a plate full of *enchiladas de mole poblano* to give you strength before your battle."

He squinted at her. Funny that they'd known each other only for a few weeks, and he had no trouble telling when she was lying.

"Are you sure *they* intend to be honorable?" she asked.

"No."

"Then you should have a backup plan."

"Even if they are not honorable, I will not besmirch my own honor by using *magic*." His lips reared back from his teeth, as if he were in wolf form now.

"Shouldn't you at least figure out if they're planning a trap? It's too bad I don't have a familiar yet. If I had a raven, I could send it to spy on their lair. Assuming they have such a place. Do they? Do you know where it is?"

"In the hills above town, they have a log lodge with a pool, a tennis court, and a putting green."

"A tennis court and a putting green? These are not the amenities I associate with wolf lairs. Though I guess the logs are on point, or at least consistent with their restaurant."

Maybe Phoebe would lend her the use of Zeke. Could witches do that? Lend out their familiars? Admittedly, the raven wasn't that subtle. If Morgen performed the ritual and got a familiar of her own, that would be better. Maybe she could request something sneaky that few people would notice. A rat? A raccoon? A garter snake?

"You will not go there," Amar stated. "Or *send* any creatures there with witch magic."

"Are you sure? Spying would be a good idea. Then you can be prepared if they plan to betray you."

"You will not get involved." He faced her, gazing challengingly into her eyes. "This is my problem, not yours. You have enemies enough to worry about."

"Just the one, I think. Those other three witches shouldn't be out to get me anymore, now that I took the property off the market." She hoped.

"Just one that is far more experienced and formidable at witchcraft than you."

"Yeah, but I could write code around her in a programming competition. I bet she can't even run a simple search query."

"I'm not joking, Morgen. Leave the Loups for me. You should study your witch heritage and learn to place wards around your property so that strangers can't come up whenever they wish."

"I *have* been looking for information on how to do that. I'll try to learn." Morgen was tempted to ask him for an address or at least the street that the log *lodge* was on, but if she did, he would know that she intended to go against his wishes. Maybe she could figure out some other way to help him. "I've got a mole sauce to finish first. Will you join me for dinner?"

She smiled cheerfully, hoping he would believe that she'd agreed to heed his wisdom and that, even if she could convince a sneaky animal familiar to come work for her, she wouldn't send it off to spy on his enemies.

His eyes only narrowed further. "What will be *under* the mole sauce?"

"Enchiladas with a mushroom filling."

"*Mushroom*?" he mouthed.

"Cheese and onions too. It'll be delish. Bring your appetite."

5

As Morgen spread aluminum foil on a patch of grass at the edge of the trees, she decided she should have started making her fire pit earlier if she wanted to do her ritual this evening. She also decided she should have Googled *how to make a fire pit*.

She'd started out dragging rocks to this spot from around the property to create a ring, but the perky grass peering up from within it hadn't seemed right, so she was covering it with aluminum foil and planned to scrounge some dirt to pack atop it. *Then* she could build a fire. Something else she needed to Google how to do. All of her brothers had been Boy Scouts when they'd been kids, but Morgen and her sister had always preferred books to playing outdoors. She remembered *reading* about children who had adventures in the woods and learned to fend for themselves, but her own meanderings had rarely taken her out of the yard.

"Are you preserving that for later?" Amar asked from behind her.

Morgen kept from jumping but barely. For a big man, Amar tended to walk up quietly, more like a feline than a canine. "What?"

He pointed at the aluminum foil. "You're wrapping that grass like your leftover enchiladas."

"I'm making a bed of aluminum foil, not wrapping anything."

"A bed? To tuck the grass in for the night?" His blue eyes twinkled. He'd either gotten over his earlier grumpiness or he was so amused at how she made a fire pit that his mirth was forcefully overriding his dour tendencies. No doubt temporarily.

"I need to make a fire at the edge of the woods for the familiar-finding ritual." Morgen waved toward Phoebe's open book. She'd propped it against one of her gathered rocks. "I didn't want to do it *in* the woods, because I could envision branches overhead catching fire."

Her grandmother had wanted her to preserve Wolf Wood. Lighting it on fire wouldn't be in line with those desires.

"So I'm doing it here." Morgen finished with the aluminum foil and started placing rocks again for her ring.

"You know that's not going to keep the grass from dying, right?"

"I just didn't want it to get in the way. Do you want to help?"

"Make a fire or with your ritual?"

"A fire. I *know* how you feel about rituals."

"Rituals don't offend me if they're not used dishonorably against one's enemies." Amar moved a couple of the heavier rocks for her. "Or to cause warts to grow on one's tenant's toes."

"I trust my grandmother didn't do that to you. I've seen you naked a couple of times now. I don't remember warts."

"I didn't know your perusal had been that thorough."

"I thought about flinging an arm over my eyes and looking away, but we were engaged in battle at the time."

"Gwen threatened to put warts on my toes because I was pestering her, but she never did it." Amar pointed to the branches she'd gathered from beneath the trees. "Your wood isn't seasoned. It's going to be hard to burn."

"It might be seasoned by the time I finish this fire pit. How long does it take?"

"Six months to a year," he said dryly.

"Oh."

"I'll get some from the stack behind the house. Gwen occasionally put the hearth inside to use. I trust that indoor fires aren't sufficient for rituals."

"Probably not for rituals where you're trying to lure wildlife in from the forest, no." Not to mention the bird's nest that had fallen down from the chimney when she'd investigated the hearth earlier in the week.

"Luring wildlife from the mouse hole in the pantry won't do?" he called back over his shoulder.

"I'm going to resist throwing something at you, but only because I approve of this new development where you show off your sense of humor."

With Amar's help, Morgen finished the pit and got the fire started. Meanwhile, twilight descended on the yard and the woods grew thick with shadows.

Lucky came over to check out the fire, and she watched to make sure he wouldn't step in it or burn his snout. His only experience with flames came from the gas fireplace in her old house that turned on with a flick of a switch.

"I will go hunt while you ritualize," Amar said.

"You're not full from dinner?"

Morgen hadn't been sure if he would eat her food, but after a couple of hours spent putting together that meal, she'd been pleased that he'd wolfed down several enchiladas. She'd picked the recipe thinking he might appreciate something from his homeland, even if he never spoke of his background and might have left Mexico decades ago. Also, she was on a quest to make every savory dish containing chocolate that she could find. It shouldn't be relegated to sweets.

"Full?"

"Yes. Full is what most people get after eating six enchiladas."

"With only mushrooms inside?"

"They were filling mushrooms. And, again, *six*."

"It was a good appetizer. Also, as the full moon approaches, the call of the night—the call to *hunt*—grows harder to resist." His eyes seemed to glint as he gazed out into the trees, and he looked more like a predator than a man.

"Don't eat anything that's trying to come out of the woods to become my familiar, please."

"So, nothing small, obnoxious, and with a glazed look to its eyes?"

"I suppose that describes Zeke. Though ravens aren't that small."

"Compared to a wolf, they are." Amar lifted his nose in the air, took a deep inhalation that expanded his chest, and reached for his vest, as if he meant to remove his clothing and change right there. He paused and glanced over at her.

"Around the corner, if you wouldn't mind." She waved to the barn. "I'm too busy getting ready for my ritual to perform a wart inspection."

He held her gaze, that predator vibe still emanating from him, and she hoped she hadn't offended him with her suggestion. If he wanted to strip next to her fire and spring immediately into the woods, she wouldn't stop him. It wasn't as if she *could.*

"As you wish," he murmured, his eyelids drooping as he kept holding her gaze for a long moment before turning away. He strode to the barn, removing his vest as he went.

By the firelight, she could make out his powerful back muscles shifting under his bronze skin, and a silly part of her regretted asking him to step out of sight. It wasn't as if she wanted to drag him off to bed, but he was nice to admire, the shaggy hair notwithstanding.

As he rounded the corner, she decided that his hair fit him. Wild hair for a wild man.

A moment later, Amar appeared again, now a powerful gray-and-black wolf. He loped into the trees without glancing over at her. She hoped he wasn't irked with her. Probably not. When he was in his wolf form, he probably forgot all about humans and their silly notions of clothing and propriety.

Morgen gazed after him, even after he disappeared from view, until wood snapped in the fire pit and startled her. She shook her head and grabbed the book to reread the details about the ritual. Earlier, she'd skimmed through it to make sure she had everything she needed. The ingredients she was supposed to sprinkle into the fire included various powders and dried herbs, and then she would consume a vial of Crater Moon Spirits, which sounded alcoholic or hallucinogenic or both.

"You'd think it would be the animal that needed to get high or drunk to agree to this, not the witch." Morgen picked up the vial and eyed the purple contents by the light of the fire.

Whatever it was, it wasn't rare. She'd found eighteen vials of it in a rack in Grandma's cellar. Hopefully, it was still efficacious. Grandma had failed to label her potions and tinctures with *best by* dates. Should Morgen ever start making her own, she wouldn't be so lax. Even if potions weren't inspected by the FDA, it was proper to list ingredients, calorie content, serving size, and expiration dates.

She lined it up next to the small vials of powders and herbs in the grass beside her, then finished reading the entry. A sentence at the end made her pause. *As with other rituals, maximum effectiveness will be achieved by chanting the incantation while nude.*

"Uh. Phoebe didn't mention that when she shared the other two incantations with me."

Maybe because deducing enemies' weaknesses and

commanding werewolves weren't *rituals*. They also hadn't required a fire or powders.

"I wasn't planning on getting naked on the lawn," she admitted.

Lucky ambled up and flopped down beside the fire. Now that it was getting dark, his urge to hunt had ended. Dogs didn't have a lot in common with werewolves.

As she re-read the bit about nudity, hoping she'd misinterpreted the sentence, Lucky rolled onto his back, head bent sideways, and crooked his forelegs in the air. Dogs, of course, were always naked, so he wouldn't likely comment on the matter.

"You're more of a free spirit than I am," she said.

He wriggled around, scratching an itch.

Her second read confirmed that nudity was highly suggested for rituals. Morgen sighed and peered all around, half-expecting someone else to drive up to the property if she got naked. Given how out of the way this place was, and that the driveway was a mile long, unannounced visitors *should* have been rare. And yet...

"More likely, Amar will come back and wonder what the heck I'm doing."

Or maybe he wouldn't even notice. As far as Morgen could tell, he didn't have any interest in her, sexual or otherwise. It might not even register to him that she was dancing naked around the fire.

That was fine with her. She hadn't come up to Bellrock looking for a werewolf boyfriend. Still, she'd lost a little weight since switching to her vegetarian diet, and it would have been nice if *someone* admired her for it. Or at least noticed. But at forty, she supposed she was past the age of being admired for her body. Jun hadn't batted an eye over her improved health, and he'd called her diet a *crazy hippy phase*.

"Getting older sucks, Lucky."

He flopped over on his side and closed his eyes.

"I guess I don't have to worry about you attacking whatever familiar wanders out of the forest."

After listening to make sure she didn't hear anyone walking or driving up, Morgen removed her clothes, everything except her grandmother's amulet. She set them close by in case she needed to lunge for them quickly.

Next, she drank the substance in the vial—it tasted like fermented beet juice and burned going down her throat. Lastly, she sprinkled the powders and herbs over the flames and lifted the book to read the incantation. No, *chant* the incantation. while walking around the fire and trying not to trip over the rocks. That was a challenge since it had grown dark enough to make reading hard. She ended up using her phone's flashlight and imagined she made quite a picture, walking around the fire naked while holding a book open under her phone.

"More things Hollywood didn't get right about witchcraft," she murmured, then read the thankfully short passage. "Under the moon's magic, bring forth a minion, furred or scaled or fanged, to join the lady's dominion."

Morgen didn't feel any tingle of magic to suggest the words had done anything. Maybe the woodland creatures—furred, scaled, and fanged—hadn't thought much of the weak rhyme. She supposed there weren't many words that rhymed with minion. Or familiar, for that matter.

In case it helped, she repeated the incantation. She recalled that she also hadn't felt anything when she'd effectively cast the spell that showed enemies' weaknesses. Not until the illusions had formed before her eyes.

Hopeful, Morgen closed the book and peered into the forest as the fire burned lower, orange embers emitting heat that warmed her bare skin as the night deepened. Damp grass pricked at the soles of her feet.

An owl hooted in the trees. She raised her eyebrows.

"An owl familiar would be pretty cool," she whispered, wondering if they were on the coven-approved familiars list. "If a raven works, why not an owl?"

Would it matter if her familiar refused to be active during daylight hours?

The sound of wingbeats drifted to her ears. Maybe the owl *was* responding to her ritual.

It came into view, flying between the trees and toward her. Morgen resisted the urge to wave vigorously and say, "Over here, over here!" It *knew* where she was.

As the owl sailed closer, she wondered how she would communicate with it. Both Phoebe and the entry in the book had been fuzzy on that, mentioning only a spiritual connection.

For a moment, the owl looked like it might land right next to her—or on her—but it remained ten or twenty feet above the ground. Its wings flapped, and it kept going, flying past her without stopping.

Something moist splatted on Morgen's bare shoulder. The owl soared through one of the barn windows and disappeared inside. Morgen examined her shoulder.

"You're kidding me." Grimacing, she grabbed the water bottle she'd brought out for hydration, not to bathe bird poo off her naked body. Had she known that would be required, she would have brought a towel. Perhaps soap, sanitizer, and a loofah as well.

The squeal of something dying came from the barn, making her jump. Lucky sat up, his ears cocked. The owl flew out the window with a rat clutched in its talons, then flapped back into the woods.

"I don't think that was my new familiar, Lucky."

He sprang to his feet and ran into the trees after it. As if he was going to catch an owl flying twenty feet above the ground.

Morgen shook her head and finished cleaning her shoulder while debating on going into the house to get a towel. Would that officially end the ritual? Maybe she should stay out here a few more minutes to see if any less disrespectful creatures flew, crawled, or slithered out of the woods.

As she debated, the feeling of being watched came over Morgen. She listened hard, hoping nobody was coming up the driveway. She didn't hear any vehicles, only the occasional chirps of insects from the woods. She peered into the trees again, hoping to see a friendly future familiar stroll out, but her pessimistic side posited that her watcher was more likely some creepy stalker.

Lucky hadn't come back yet, and that also made her uneasy. How far had he followed that owl? She couldn't hear him snuffling and rummaging in the undergrowth.

Something glinted in the shadows. Two somethings. Eyes reflecting the orange of her fire. They were high enough off the ground that they had to belong to a dog or a wolf. Maybe a deer?

"Lucky?" Morgen called softly as she grabbed her clothes. "Is that you out there? Come on back."

She tugged her shirt on, not bothering with a bra, then grabbed her pants. The eyes disappeared. She didn't think they had belonged to Lucky.

Amar? Would his blue eyes have reflected the firelight like that? Eerily? Unblinking?

"Lucky," she called again, louder this time. He didn't usually go that far from her, and he should have returned by now.

Morgen shoved her feet in her shoes without tying the laces. She felt less vulnerable with her clothes on—and the eyes gone, or at least their reflection—but she couldn't shake the uneasy sensation that she wasn't alone. Once more, she called for the dog. Again, he didn't come. Where *had* he gone?

After turning on her phone's flashlight app again, Morgen headed for the trees. She wouldn't wander far into the woods, not now that full darkness had fallen, but that path that led to the spring was back behind the barn, and she figured she could follow it without getting lost.

In the campfire, a log shifted and fell. Morgen paused, worried about leaving it. The flames now burned low, and the grass around her makeshift pit was too damp to catch fire easily, but childhood imperatives by Smokey the Bear came to mind.

"Not going far," she muttered.

She would keep the fire in sight and call a few more times for Lucky. He'd probably caught the scent of something else and had his nose stuck under a bush. Eventually, he would come back.

Before she'd taken more than a few steps down the trail, she spotted a light up ahead in the trees. A small prick of light, like someone else's flashlight.

She paused, well aware that she didn't have a weapon. Even though this was Grandma's property, and there *shouldn't* be anyone roaming around out here at night, a wolf hadn't pulled out a flashlight. Someone was out here. Someone stealing some of the valuable bioluminescent moss? The light *had* come from the direction of that special spring.

Morgen ran back to the house. She was half-tempted to ignore the light and ask Amar about it in the morning, but what if someone stole all of the moss out there? It was her plan for paying for renovations, and maybe even the taxes on the property when they came due.

Besides, Lucky was out there somewhere. She had to go find him. The thought of him running up to unfriendly thieves with guns—or witch wands—scared her.

She used the amulet to let herself into the root cellar and grabbed a camp lantern and the largest weapon within reach, the staff with antlers at the end. Someday, she would figure out if it had magical powers that she could use to zap enemies. For now, she would be relegated to pronging nefarious foes.

"What could go wrong?"

6

As Morgen crept down the path through the woods that led to the spring, her staff gripped in both hands, she lamented that she hadn't taken the time to put on socks. Grit and pieces of grass competed with the clammy insides of her shoes to distract her as she advanced. The light appeared ahead again, and she dared not stop to fiddle with them.

It kept appearing and disappearing and moving. It definitely belonged to someone with a lantern or flashlight. She had no idea what she would say when she reached the person. Maybe nothing. She didn't want a confrontation, especially when her security werewolf was off hunting. And Lucky was… who knew where. She still hadn't seen or heard him.

The night air grew hazier as she followed the trail closer to the spring, the trickle of the stream audible off to the side. Fog? There hadn't been any back at the house, but it was on a hilltop, so maybe that made sense. Still, the way it grew thicker as she drew closer to the light made her uneasy. *Uneasier*.

Another light appeared, this one a ball of yellow. It floated between the trees, well above ground level. The fog deepened. Soon, the faint blue glow of the mushrooms around the spring and the green of the bioluminescent moss draping the trees grew noticeable. Reassured that it still hung from the branches, she almost turned around, but a barefoot woman in a flowing dress came into view.

Morgen snapped her flashlight app off and ducked behind a tree.

Her heart pounded as she breathed shallowly, not wanting to be heard. Several seconds passed before she risked peering out.

The woman was pacing back and forth and waving her arms in some kind of dance. A ritual? One that didn't require nudity? The woman gripped a stick in one hand. No, it was a wand. She waved it in the air, as if she were conducting an orchestra.

Two other women came into view, dancing along different routes. The lights Morgen had seen floated in the air above them, and water below glinted with their reflection. The spring.

The three women were familiar, and before Morgen glimpsed any of their faces, she was certain they were the witches who had lit the barn on fire.

The oldest, a brunette of about thirty, gripped a knife instead of a wand. She stepped close to a tree and sliced off strands of the glowing moss.

Damn it, they *were* here to collect it.

Morgen gripped her staff in both hands, wishing she dared charge out there and demand that they stop.

The knife-wielder dropped the moss into a bag that the youngest witch held. It was Wendy, the woman who had been in the Crystal Parlor that day.

Morgen clenched her jaw, wishing she'd pushed Phoebe harder for information on the trio of witches.

"Is it working?" the third woman asked. Her blonde hair hung in curtains to her waist, and she appeared to be in her mid-twenties.

The dancing paused, and all three women stopped where Morgen couldn't see them through the trees. She held her breath, hoping they wouldn't be able to use their magic to sense her out here.

"I think so," the eldest said. "If we can avoid any more dog interruptions, we should be good."

Morgen's blood chilled. Lucky had been here? What had they done to get rid of him?

Someone started chanting. Mist curled around Morgen's legs, growing thicker, almost palpable. The cold moist air caressed her skin like a presumptuous lover. It was hard not to fear the magic these three could wield. They'd brought the powerful Amar to his knees.

"Someone's watching!" one of the women said abruptly.

"It's *her*."

Shit.

Morgen debated between confronting them and sprinting back to the house. As she stepped out from behind the tree, one of the witches muttered something under her breath.

"Come forth!" the woman called to finish her incantation.

The urge to obey came over Morgen. Not *again*.

Frustrated, she strode toward them, her legs following the command against her wishes. Morgen longed to smack the witches over their heads with her staff instead of obeying magical compulsions. She hoped she could.

"What are you doing here?" Morgen asked as the women came into view.

As she'd suspected, they were the three who'd been on her property before. Two were scowling. Only Wendy appeared more uncertain than irritated.

"*Again*," Morgen added.

The oldest woman opened her mouth to speak, but foliage

rattled to the side of the spring. An animal glowing with a faint green light bounded through the ferns. Lucky?

He splashed into the water. The blonde witch pointed her wand at him.

"No!" Morgen raised her staff and charged her, but her arms wouldn't obey her desire to crack the weapon down on the woman's head. She couldn't swing it at her target at all.

Swearing, Morgen gripped her amulet and willed it to help her break the spell.

Lucky yelped and ran out of the water and toward her. Morgen couldn't tell what the witch had done to him, but fury rose up inside her like a volcano erupting. Once again, she lifted the staff, and this time, her arms obeyed her.

"Look out, Nora!" Wendy called, but the witch didn't react quickly enough.

Morgen smacked the staff down onto the arm holding the wand. The witch—Nora—cried out and released her weapon as she skittered back, almost tripping over the stone bench that overlooked the spring.

"Get her," the eldest ordered. "And get the moss."

"Don't do anything to her," Wendy said. "It's her property."

"She *clubbed* me."

Yeah, and Morgen would do it again.

A howl came from the woods. Amar? Another werewolf?

Morgen didn't care. These bitches had hurt her dog. She swung again at Nora—*she'd* been responsible—but even as Morgen connected, cracking her on the shoulder, the eldest witch lunged in and threw a powder at Morgen's face.

The gritty substance got in her eyes and coated her mouth. It tasted like rotten fungus, and Morgen had to pull back. She kept the staff up to defend herself, but her eyes watered, making it hard to see.

A snarl followed on the heels of the howl. Unlike Lucky, who'd crashed through the foliage, the wolf came in as silent as death. Gray-and-black furred, with the power of the apex predator he'd promised he was, Amar sprang at Nora. She tried to dodge out of the way, but he was too fast. He bore her to the ground under his weight.

The woman who'd thrown the powder grabbed another fist of the stuff as she chanted something else. Afraid the words would let the witch control Amar, Morgen lunged at her. This time, she stabbed with the antlers instead of using the staff like a club. They pronged the witch in the side, and her hand spasmed open, releasing the powder prematurely as her chant faltered.

"Sorry, wolf," Wendy said, pointing a wand of her own at Amar.

He yelped as some power knocked him away from Nora. As if a hurricane gale had blasted him, Amar rolled several feet and tumbled into the spring with a splash.

Morgen rushed at Wendy, swinging the staff toward her hand, hoping to knock her wand away too.

But Nora sat up, her arm bloody from Amar's fangs, and cried, "Stop, servant!"

Morgen froze.

Damn it, she thought she'd overridden that compulsion. She struggled to move her arms and legs as the three witches ran away, Nora gripping her injured arm and cursing all the way.

As they crashed through the foliage, moving farther from the spring, the power gripping Morgen lessened. She took a step and then another. Should she chase after them alone? That seemed dangerous.

Besides, she was more worried about Amar and Lucky than catching the witches. Splashes sounded behind her. She turned and found Amar back in his human form, wet and naked, rivulets of water running down his muscular arms to his clenched fists.

"I *hate* witches," he snarled, looking in the direction they'd run, as if he were contemplating chasing them down and killing them. If they hadn't had some magical power over him, Morgen was certain he would have.

The bag they'd been filling with moss lay slumped near the bench. At least they'd failed to complete their theft.

Amar looked over at Morgen, his face still savage with anger, then took several jerky steps toward her.

"Ah, I was just trying to help you." Morgen stepped back, afraid his condemnation of witches included her. Those three had fled, but she was still here. A suitable outlet for his temper?

"I know," he said, his voice still a growl.

She stepped back again and bumped into a tree. Though she still gripped the staff, Morgen couldn't imagine using it on him. The words of the incantation to control werewolves came to mind, but she couldn't imagine using that on him either, not again. Not unless she had no choice.

He stopped right in front of her, close enough that she could have reached out and touched him.

"I know," he repeated more softly, though his eyes were intense.

The witches' floating lights remained, shedding warm yellow illumination on his naked shoulders. On his entire naked body, Morgen was sure, but she made a point not to look down.

Amar lifted a hand to the side of her head, fingers pushing through her hair. Surprise jolted her, and she opened her mouth to ask what he was doing. But the words didn't come out before he leaned in and kissed her.

She stood slack for a long moment, confused since he'd given no indication that he was attracted to her. And a minute ago, they'd been fighting against enemies, enemies that might still be out there. This wasn't the time for... whatever this was.

His kiss seemed almost angry as his mouth pressed hard against hers, a growl deep in his throat. Maybe it should have scared her, but it wakened a part of her body she'd almost forgotten she had, a part that found this—*him*—appealing and urged her to step closer, to lean into him.

But Morgen always thought with her rational mind, not base instincts and urges. This wasn't her style.

She reached out, intending to push him away, or at least ask if he'd lost his mind—was it possible one of the witches had ordered him to do this for some weird reason?—but when her palms touched his hard chest, her fingers merely ran up it to curl around his shoulders.

Maybe it wasn't wise, but she let herself kiss him back. And enjoy it, even though she shouldn't have. Something about this seemed wrong, the tension in his body dangerous. He growled again and shifted closer, pressing her against the tree—and against him—and stroking her through her clothes. He slipped his hand under her shirt, callused hands caressing her bare skin.

She should have put a stop to it, but she didn't want to. It had been ages since she'd experienced anything like this. Had she ever? Her ex-husband hadn't been the growly savage sort, not by a long shot. She never would have guessed she could find something like this interesting, and yet...

Just as she was thinking it might be all right to see where this went, since it was off to an intriguing start, Amar pulled back. Abruptly. As if a spell had broken.

Had it?

Amar opened his mouth, on the verge of saying something. Instead, he released her and sprang away.

Before she could gather her wits to ask if he was all right, he disappeared into the woods without a sound. If not for her hammering heart and her aroused body, she might have believed he'd never been there.

A long moment passed before she recovered enough to straighten her clothes and remember that Lucky was out there somewhere. He'd been her primary reason for coming into the woods, but he'd disappeared again.

"Lucky?" She whistled, hoping he hadn't chased off after the witches.

Rustling came from the bushes alongside the trail. He bounded out, as if this had all been a fun game, and ran toward her.

He was still glowing green.

Morgen slumped against the tree. "Please tell me that'll come off with a bath."

Lucky wagged his tail cheerfully.

7

The next morning, Lucky was still glowing. By the light of day, the green nimbus wasn't as noticeable as it had been the night before, but it was very distinctly *there*.

Against his wishes, Morgen had plunked him down into the tub before bed, using soap, water, and a scrub brush on his short copper fur. This had resulted in *her* being thoroughly doused—not to mention water droplets hitting the light fixtures, window, and bathroom mirror every time he'd shaken himself—but it had done nothing to diminish the glow.

Now, Morgen stood in the kitchen, gripping her chin and considering her tail-wagging dog. Other than his new nimbus, he seemed fine. Before breakfast, he'd gone out to run around the house and barn to check all of his favorite spots. After coming back in, he'd scarfed down his food and wagged hopefully for more.

"Does one call a witch for a problem like this?" Morgen mused. "Or a vet? Or a ghost hunter? You kind of look like an apparition now."

If Amar had been around, she would have asked him, but he

wasn't working on the barn or any of his projects this morning, and it didn't look like he'd spent the night in his room. She'd peeked in warily that morning, the puzzling kiss from the night before on her mind. Puzzling and... arousing. It had prompted the kinds of dreams that she'd thought she was well past the age of having.

She wondered if Amar was deliberately avoiding her now. If that kiss had been spurred by some spell, he might be angry or embarrassed.

Lucky leaned against her leg, reminding her that he should be the priority.

"Right. I'll call the Crystal Parlor." Morgen grabbed her phone, wishing Phoebe had shared her private number.

So far, Deputy Franklin was the only person in town whose number she knew. As far as she could tell, Amar didn't have a phone. She wondered how his clients ordered their furniture, decorative bears, and modern interpretations of totem poles.

The call went to voicemail. She left a message, requesting help with glow removal, then checked the internet to see if Bellrock had a vet. Normally, she wouldn't think such a person would have a clue when it came to glowing fur, but people in this town seemed aware of the local witches and werewolves, so maybe they knew ways of dealing with supernatural side effects.

"I wish I knew whether they'd thrown a powder at you, cast a spell at you, or if you'd rubbed yourself all over some biolumines-cent mushrooms," Morgen said.

Instead of enlightening her, Lucky ran into the living room and put his paws on the windowsill. Did that mean someone was coming? She hoped not. Nothing good ever came of guests visiting this place.

She found the number for the sole vet listed in Bellrock. Dr. Osvaldo Valderas. As she dialed the number, she walked to the kitchen window to peer outside. Thus far, no vehicles had come up the driveway, but Lucky whined from the other room. Maybe Amar had wandered out of the woods and was about to get to work.

"This is Dr. Valderas," a man with a cultured Spanish accent said.

Surprised he didn't have a receptionist, or at least screen his calls, Morgen gave a flustered, "Hi. I'm a new client, and I have a three-year-old vizsla who needs... a checkup."

"I do annual examinations on Thursdays, and I'm booked for the next few weeks. Does the eighth work for you? I have two morning appointments available."

"Would it be possible to get in earlier? He's also got an acute problem."

Outside, a beat-up black truck rumbled into view. It looked like she was also about to have an acute problem. Lucky started barking.

"He sounds healthy," Valderas said dryly.

"It's a skin issue. He had a run-in with some weird people in the woods, and now he's, uh, glowing." Maybe she shouldn't have admitted that, but she worried the vet would make her wait weeks if she couldn't convince him that Lucky needed to be seen sooner.

Though she could take him to another town for an appointment, or even drive back to Seattle to see her regular vet, she had a feeling the person most qualified to handle glowing dogs was here in Bellrock.

After a long pause, in which she worried he would accuse her of prank calling him, Valderas asked, "Is this Gwen Griffiths' granddaughter?"

"Uh. Yes."

How could he possibly know that? She was calling from her personal cell phone, not the land line at the house, so it wasn't as if he could have recognized the number. Had she become infamous in town? Her introvert sensibilities cringed at the thought of any kind of celebrity—or infamy.

"I can fit you in at two today. What's the dog's name?"

"Lucky."

"I've got you down. You know where my office is?"

"14 Euclid Ave?" she asked, reading the address off the website.

"Yes. Ring the bell before you come in, and leave your shoes on the porch."

She blinked at these strange instructions but didn't want to question him, not when he was agreeing to see Lucky on short notice. "Okay. Thanks."

He hung up without saying goodbye or wishing her a good day.

"Customer service in this town is decidedly lacking."

Two brawny men in jeans and tank tops slid out of the cab, and two younger men—teenagers—vaulted over stacks of lumber to drop down from the truck bed. Morgen recognized one of them. Arturo.

As she walked out to meet the men, she glanced around, hoping Amar lurked somewhere nearby. Just because he hadn't slept in the house didn't mean he wasn't within earshot. With most of the barn roof repaired, he could have moved back in there. The windows still needed replacing, to keep owls from swooping in to hunt, but he probably didn't care.

Unfortunately, she didn't see him. Even though he hadn't approved of her desire to hire his pack, Morgen would have been more comfortable negotiating with them if he was around. The Lobos she'd met at their last construction site hadn't appreciated her *witch blood*.

The thought brought to mind Amar's snarled *I hate witches* comment from the night before.

Surprisingly, a woman slid out of the cab after the men. She seemed familiar, though Morgen hadn't met her before.

A beauty with lush raven hair with a bluish sheen to it, she slipped her arm around the waist of the man who'd been driving. He wasn't well-dressed, but his jeans weren't torn, and his tank top lacked the pit stains common among some of his men. Also, he was as handsome as she was pretty, with a few days' worth of beard growth along a strong jaw. His muscles were more lanky than bulky, but he radiated raw power.

"I'm Pedro," he said. Amar's brother. "You're the witch who needs to be serviced?" His eyebrows twitched.

The woman swatted him on the chest and said something stern in Spanish. Pedro only looked more amused.

"I'm Morgen, and I need some remodeling done. I have an infestation problem."

Lucky barked, claws scrabbling at the windowsill.

"A rat infestation problem," she clarified, lest he think the property was overrun by vociferous dogs.

Given how subservient Lucky acted around Amar, Morgen suspected that barking would stop as soon as he caught a whiff of these guys and realized they were werewolves, but she would prefer not to let him out where he might pester them.

"We are not pest control," Pedro said.

"I know. My, uhm, roommate suggested that some repairs might improve the situation and make it less likely for vermin to get in."

"Roommate?" the woman asked. She hadn't given her name yet. Her nostrils flared as she sniffed the air. Was she another werewolf? "Is that all Amar is to you? You have his scent on you."

Morgen's cheeks heated as she remembered the kiss of the night before, but she'd showered since then. She shouldn't have anyone's *scent* on her. "I made him some enchiladas, so he was hanging out in my kitchen."

"Is that so?" The woman's eyes crinkled as she smiled.

She couldn't possibly have known about the night before, but

Morgen couldn't turn down the flames torching her cheeks. Not until she realized with a jolt why the woman was familiar. It was the smile and eye crinkle that clued her in. The expression was identical to the one she'd had in Amar's drawing, the one Morgen had glimpsed in his glove compartment.

Was this a woman that he'd loved? And that his brother had ultimately gotten? Was that why Amar had left the pack? Or been forced out?

"Show us the house and what you want done that my brother is unable to do," Pedro said, smirking past Morgen's shoulder.

Even without looking, Morgen was sure Amar had appeared.

"He's capable of doing many things," Morgen said, "but he's busy, and I don't want to take advantage of his kindness. I'd prefer to pay to have the work done quickly by a crew."

As soon as she figured out how to turn that moss into money. The night before, she'd brought the bag the witches had left back to the house and stretched some out on the kitchen counter, hoping that would be sufficient to cure it. She doubted she could afford to pay for the remodeling with her savings. Besides, she would prefer to make that money stretch until she figured out what her next job would be. Rare moss aside, she couldn't imagine that being a witch paid well.

"Busy, yes," Pedro said. "Doing his pretty art. What you need is a strong team who knows how to get a job done efficiently, quickly, and professionally. You do not need *el artista*."

"Artists are valued for what they bring to the world," Amar said coolly, coming to stand beside Morgen, though the sidelong look he gave her suggested he'd come to keep her out of trouble, not because he wanted to interact with the pack.

Would his kin attempt to swindle Morgen if she didn't pay attention?

"Yes, you're so valued that you're driving a truck that can barely get around without a horse team to pull it. *Señor* Ferguson has that same model out front with his collection of antique farm equipment, isn't that so, Maria?" Pedro winked at the woman.

"Would you prefer I run around like one of those Loups and flaunt my success?" Amar clenched his jaw.

Pedro spat on the ground, as did the rest of the male Lobos who'd gathered around to listen. "Death to the cowardly Loups."

"How are you doing, Amar?" the woman—Maria—asked quietly, the amusement in her eyes fading to concern as she looked him up and down.

Something in her expression made Morgen want to bristle, the hint that maybe once they'd been lovers. Morgen attempted to smooth her imaginary hackles. Even if that was true, it wasn't any business of hers. As soon as the Lobos left, she intended to ask Amar about the night before, because she was positive there had to be an explanation for that kiss. There was no way he'd abruptly been overcome by a deep desire for her and hadn't been able to resist the urge to act upon it.

"You've lost weight," Maria added when Amar only answered with a shrug. "Are the enchiladas not filling?"

That made Morgen's hackles go right back up. She'd spent a long time preparing that meal, and she *knew* it had been filling. And *good,* damn it.

"I don't always remember to eat," Amar said.

"Perhaps you should find someone who cares enough to remind you." Maria glanced dismissively at Morgen.

Morgen couldn't keep from scowling at her, though Maria had already looked away. Morgen had just met Amar a few weeks ago. It wasn't her job to feed him.

"Enough of this nonsense," Pedro said. "Let's get to business."

He was giving Maria a scowl of his own. Maybe he also didn't like the sympathy she was showing to Amar, the reminder that those two had been something once.

"I'll show you what needs to be renovated," Amar said and strode briskly toward the front porch.

Morgen blinked and lifted a finger. Wasn't *she* the homeowner here?

But the men strode past her without a glance.

"Don't be offended," Maria said. "That is their way. They are very take-charge."

She smiled after them, watching Pedro's ass with a smile curving her lips.

"Uh huh," Morgen said. "And you like that?"

"I am of the pack. I understand them."

"Are you the alpha female?"

Maybe Morgen should have called her sister to get more advice on wolf hierarchies and social structures before inviting the Lobos up. But Sian continued to be flummoxed by Morgen's insistence that she was dealing with werewolves instead of simple wolves. And Morgen wasn't positive their pack structures would be the same as those of the non-shape-shifting woodland creatures. Thus far, Amar hadn't explained much to her about how werewolves worked.

"I am," Maria said.

"Because you're the strongest female in the pack?" Morgen had only seen one other female in the presence of the men and wasn't positive she'd been a werewolf. "Or because the strongest male chose you?"

Maria's smile widened, growing a touch predatory. "He is the alpha of the pack because *I* chose *him*." She strode after the men, her long legs taking her up all three porch steps in one stride. "Come. Perhaps they will let you choose the paint color."

"Oh, lucky me."

Morgen intended to choose a lot more than that, especially considering she would be the one paying. After she put Lucky outside so that he wouldn't be in the way, she caught up to the group, but they'd started speaking rapidly in Spanish. Reluctantly, she let Amar take the lead.

Maybe that was for the best. He'd been doing repairs around the house for Grandma for the last couple of years, and he knew a lot more about what still needed to be done than Morgen. As long as the laundry room roof was repaired, the mouse holes sealed, and she got a modern update to the pale-blue icebox in the kitchen, she would be delighted.

Unfortunately, Pedro took a lot of digs at Amar, making at least one snide comment in every room. Morgen had no trouble understanding those. Pedro also went out of his way to slide his arm around Maria's back, especially when Amar was watching. Amar didn't seem to burn with envy or do much more than sigh and lift his eyes heavenward, but now and then, the insult hit close to home, and his back stiffened like a ramrod as he strode out of a room. Arturo and the other teenaged Lobo seemed confused by their leader's antics, but the other man only shook his head knowingly.

Morgen wished *she* was in the know. She would have liked to defend Amar from the barbs, but most of the time, she didn't know what they referred to. By the end of the tour, she regretted asking the Lobos up to look at the house and decided she wouldn't hire them, even if they were the only outfit in town. If she assisted Amar, maybe they could do the majority of the renovations themselves. He clearly had experience in that area.

Once the group returned to the porch, Morgen was about to say the pack needn't bother giving her a quote, but Pedro halted and planted a hand on Amar's chest.

"The Loup leader is after you, no?" His face was utterly serious, the snide smirk that had lingered throughout the tour gone.

"He sent one of his lieutenants up to challenge me to a duel on his behalf," Amar said. "Because I killed Antoine."

"You can beat that hairy bastard in a fair fight, but will he fight fair? Or will he sic his whole pack on you? They've ganged up on us Lobos before."

"I know."

"They've even willingly gotten into bed with witches." Pedro bared his teeth as he glanced at Morgen. "Not that you'd object to that, I guess."

"I'm not in anyone's bed," Amar growled without looking at Morgen.

She clenched *her* jaw. Again, she wished she hadn't invited the Lobos to the house.

"Good, *hermano*. Keep it that way. You know what you do still reflects on us."

"As what *you* do reflects on me."

"Once a Lobo, always a Lobo." Pedro smirked as Amar shook his head. "Where's the meeting spot and when?" Pedro went on. "We'll come and make *sure* they don't cheat."

Amar didn't answer. Why not? Morgen wished he *would* have his pack—his old pack—with him to make sure their enemies played fair.

"Tell us, Amar," Maria said. "You know we'll find out one way or another. We'll be there for you." She lowered her voice and met his eyes. "Always."

That tender look fired up Morgen's emotions again, making her want to push the woman away. It didn't help that Maria was a beauty and that Morgen felt frumpy and old in her hiking pants and hoodie. She experienced a rare urge she hadn't felt in years to go shopping and spruce up her wardrobe, and maybe update her no-makeup-and-hair-unstyled look.

She frowned at herself in disgust. That wasn't necessary. She and Amar weren't dating, nor was she interested in dating *anyone*. Even if she were, she wouldn't change her look just because some pretty alpha female was in the area.

"The Deer Creek trail," Amar said. "When the full moon comes up."

"We'll be there," Pedro said. "I'll even take your place and fight for you if you want."

"That's not necessary," Amar said.

"No? You know I kicked your ass last time we fought." Pedro smiled smugly at Maria.

"I know you think you did," Amar grumbled, glancing at Morgen.

Pedro laughed. "With my jaws around your throat, it was definitive, *hermano*."

"I can handle my own fights."

"Whatever you say. Witch," Pedro said, turning toward Morgen, whom he'd ignored for the entire house tour, other than briefly listening to her input on kitchen flooring and paint colors, "I'll do some math and have one of the boys bring you a quote." He handed her a business card with his number on it. "You can decide if you want us to do the job for you."

"I'll look forward to it." Morgen managed to keep her sarcasm out of her tone. Barely. And only because she wanted the Lobos to show up for Amar's duel and watch out for him.

"I'll bet you will." For the first time, Pedro gave her a long once over. Then he winked at Amar and strolled to his truck, making Morgen certain that had been a dig at his brother rather than a sign of interest in her. Some brother.

Given that he swatted Maria on the rump as they got into the truck, interest from Pedro would be a nightmare rather than an honor.

"I think I hate your pack," Morgen said as the truck drove away.

Amar, his face a mask, strode off without a word.

8

Morgen watched Amar disappear into the barn and debated whether to leave him be or go after him. Most of the time, she was inclined to give him his privacy and not pry, but she had too many questions. Actually, she just had one question. Whether that kiss had been by choice or if he'd been ensorcelled.

Though maybe that wasn't the most important thing to learn. What she *should* want to know was how to un-ensorcel him. The kiss didn't matter. What *did* matter was that one of those witches had forced him to change into wolf form to murder a real-estate agent and still had the ability to control him.

Morgen wished there was a way to bring that woman to justice, but at the least, she should be trying to figure out how to remove the brand from the back of Amar's neck. She wanted to free him from ever being controlled by a witch again. Was it possible to do that? Maybe she could make him a protective amulet or talisman that would do the job. There were entire grimoires on talismans in Grandma's collection. From what she'd seen, most were to deter bad luck or spiteful fairies, but there had to be some that served as protection from magic.

She headed toward the barn and peeked warily through the sliding door. There weren't any lights on inside—they'd been knocked out in the fire and not yet repaired—and the sky had clouded over, leaving only wan daylight filtering through the windows. It took a moment for Morgen's eyes to adjust and pick out Amar standing between a dresser and a table with a sander on it. They were two of a handful of pieces of furniture that he'd been able to salvage after the fire.

He wasn't working on either, merely staring broodingly at them. Morgen hesitated before walking in, sensing that he would prefer to be left alone, but she wanted to help him. Would he let her? And, if she *could* make a talisman, would he be willing to accept it? A gift from one of the witches he loathed?

She walked quietly inside and stopped a few feet away, not wanting to presume to put a hand on his shoulder or get too close, even if they'd been much closer the night before.

When she opened her mouth to ask him about that, he stopped her by speaking first.

"I let him win."

"Ah, pardon?"

"My brother. He's not a better fighter than I am. I let him win."

That wasn't even remotely what she'd intended to question him about, but curiosity prompted her to ask, "Why?"

"He challenged me because he wanted Maria, and he believed that if he bested me, she would go to him."

"And he did and she did?" Morgen asked, trying to follow the logic. Was fighting prowess the only reason a woman—a werewolf woman—would choose one man over another? That was hard to believe, but the Loups and Lobos seemed to be strongly influenced by their wolf sides.

"I believed that she wanted to be with him at that point. He... makes her laugh. He always did. I've never had that knack."

"You are a touch dour," she said.

Amar looked over his shoulder at her. Dourly.

It probably didn't hurt that Pedro was so handsome. Amar was appealing, in his untamed, wild-man kind of way, and he certainly had a nice body, but Pedro had those chiseled facial features that photographers coveted. Morgen thought he was an ass, but maybe personality didn't matter to some.

"Some women like dour and broody," she offered. "Maybe they aren't moved to guffaws in your presence, but you've got a dry wit." She'd been accused of having that herself. Alas, she couldn't remember Jun—or any man—guffawing as a result of it. "It could prompt a laugh here and there. You never know."

Amar looked away again. "Even though Maria traveled at my side, because I led the pack at the time, my brother was the reason she originally joined and became one of us. I think she was always drawn to him because of that."

"Became a werewolf? That's not hereditary?"

The next look he gave her was somewhere between pitying and incredulous, as if he couldn't believe she didn't know how werewolves worked.

"You do know I didn't believe in you—or witches—until a few weeks ago, right? You can't expect me to know everything about werewolves. Especially when you're far from chatty and revealing."

Amar turned to face her fully and touched the side of his neck. "The bite of a werewolf under a full moon turns a person into a werewolf forever."

"Oh. Yeah, I guess Hollywood tells us that, but Hollywood also taught us that the Enterprise could visit a new planet in a new star system every week simply by hopping around the galaxy at warp speed. It's not the most trustworthy resource when it comes to scientific accuracy."

He gazed at her without comment, his face harder to read now. She had no idea what expression was on her own face. Horror? Concern? It hadn't occurred to her that all these werewolves roaming around could bite people—people like her?—and change their lives forever. And was it also an enslavement of a sort? Did the magic of the bite bind a person to a pack? To the one who had chomped on him or her?

"I thought it might be hereditary," Morgen said, "because you call each other cousins and brothers."

"We're bound by the magic of the wolf pack, not blood ties. I watched my parents die, shot by criminals, and was an orphan before the pack found me and gave me another family."

"How old were you?" she whispered.

"Ten."

"I'm sorry. That must have been rough." An inadequate thing to say. Even if it had happened long ago, the horrible event must have shaped him forever.

"Yes."

"So, Maria left you after you and your brother fought and he won?"

"I knew they wanted each other, but I was... still attracted to her. It was difficult not to be resentful when I saw them together, especially since he was so smug about it, as if he'd won a trophy, not a person. Pedro and I squabbled often." Amar touched a scar on his shoulder, suggesting a werewolf's idea of a squabble involved fangs. "It was easier to leave the pack than to stay and make everyone uncomfortable."

"Even if it was lonely?"

"I like being alone," he said shortly.

It sounded like a lie. If it were true, would he have stayed here for three years after finding his way to Grandma's property?

"Do you still miss her? Maria?" Morgen wasn't sure why she asked, but she wanted the answer to be *no*, that he was long over her.

He shrugged. "It doesn't matter."

"Ah. I just ask because..." She cleared her throat, looking for a diffident way to ask about the night before. A part of her didn't want to bring it up at all. *He* hadn't. Maybe he wanted to pretend it hadn't happened. Hell, if it was because of some spell, maybe he didn't even remember that it had happened. "I was confused about last night," she said vaguely.

His brow didn't furrow in puzzlement, so that probably meant that he remembered it. But he didn't speak, merely gazed at her, his shaggy hair hanging to either side of his face, his blue eyes neither warm nor cold. She sensed that he didn't want to talk about it.

"Did the witches make you, uh, kiss me? So they could get away more easily or something? It's not that you're not nice and all, but I thought we'd agreed that you're not—that we're not... interested in each other." She felt like a liar saying that, since her body had been quite interested in that kiss the night before, but he wasn't her type, and he'd made it clear she wasn't his type either. If anything, it sounded like he was still pining over Maria.

"Olivia, the oldest sister and the one who placed this brand on me—" Amar pointed at the back of his neck, "—can use her magic to force me to obey her. We discussed this. I did not desire to kill the real-estate agent."

"I remember. I just wasn't sure why she would force you to..." Morgen waved at her lips, but maybe it would be better to drop this. It didn't sound like the kiss had been of his volition.

But did that mean it wouldn't happen again? What if that witch—Olivia—still resented Morgen for some reason and forced Amar to come to her bedroom in the middle of the night for *more* than kissing? She shivered at the thought of him being turned into a fearsome enemy to her rather than an ally, but that had almost happened in Calista's garage, so she already knew it was possible.

The fact that Morgen had memorized that werewolf-control incantation was some small comfort, but she still didn't know how well it truly worked. It had made the Loup in the alley pause, but did it have the power to override another witch's spell?

"You'd have to ask her," Amar said after a long pause.

"Can I? Do you know where those three witches live, by chance? You said they're sisters, right? Phoebe wouldn't tell me much about them."

"Don't trust her even if she does tell you. She could set you up to be trapped. She's known them—her own coven—far longer than she's known you."

"I know. I was thinking... Do you believe it's possible that I—or, if not me, a real witch that I could bribe—could make you a talisman that would keep anyone from controlling you?"

Amar's brows lifted. "It may be possible. Witches make many talismans. I've mostly heard of them cursing or hexing others, but they create things to protect themselves from the magic of enemies. And the power of magical creatures." He touched his own chest.

"Grandma left behind a lot of grimoires, and I've only scratched the surface of what's in them. I can spend some time reading and see what I can find."

He walked closer to her. "You would make such a talisman for me?"

"If I can learn how, sure. I mean, absolutely. I would rather not have witches making you do things to me. Or other innocent people either. Nobody deserves that, and I'm sure you don't want it on your conscience." She went from thinking of Christian's death to their conversation about bites turning people into werewolves, and she had to fight the urge to step back as he stopped in front of her, close enough that she could have put a hand on his chest.

What if Olivia had commanded him to bite her the night before instead of kissing her? For that matter, what if a werewolf lost control in the throes of passion and bit someone he was being intimate with? Did the intent behind the bite matter?

It hadn't been a full moon the night before, she reminded herself. She hadn't been in danger, at least not of being turned into a lycanthrope. Never mind that the full moon was coming up in a couple of days.

"*You* wouldn't be able to control me either," Amar said, watching her through narrowed eyes, "if I had such a talisman. That wouldn't bother you?"

"Uh, no. I don't want to control you." Morgen hesitated. They'd never discussed her attempt to do so in Calista's basement. She'd assumed that he understood that she'd only been trying to save her own life, but was it possible it had been more effective than she'd realized? And that Amar resented her for it? His avowal of how he hated witches once again came to mind. "You know when I said that incantation in Calista's garage that I was trying to keep you from killing me, and nothing more, right?"

"I know," he said softly, "but it bothered me that you learned it. You barely know anything of your blood or of witch ways, but you know that."

"Only because Phoebe gave the words to me. Given all the werewolves in this town, it seemed smart for me to learn to defend myself against them."

"She wanted you to use it on *me*."

Morgen shook her head, but wasn't he right? That *had* been the reason Phoebe had given the incantation to her. Because she believed Morgen was in danger from Amar.

"She only gave it to me so I could defend myself," Morgen reiterated. "I genuinely don't want any magical control over anyone."

"No? Some witches don't trust that werewolves won't attack them and always have a spell on hand when they're around us. Some find it stimulating to control a werewolf like a loyal pet." His lips reared back in a lupine snarl. "To have the power to order him or her to attack on one's behalf. To kill."

"I find it exasperating just to talk to one." Morgen took a step back, not appreciating the way he was looming and watching her as if she were a criminal about to pull a knife. "And you can be assured that I have zero interest in murdering people. I'll start researching and let you know if I can figure out how to make a talisman."

Morgen turned and strode for the door, also having zero interest in continuing the conversation. She didn't appreciate his insinuation that she might be anything like those power-hungry witches.

"Morgen," Amar said softly before she reached the door.

Warily, she looked back.

"I would appreciate that," he said.

She raised her eyebrows.

"If you could and did make me such a talisman, I would appreciate it. It angers me deeply to be under someone else's control."

"I'm sure it does." Morgen thought of their kiss again and wondered if he'd stalked off into the woods afterward to wipe his lips and wash his mouth out with water. It was stupid, but that thought bothered her as much as everything else.

9

Dr. Osvaldo Valderas's two-story blue Victorian house was located a block off Main Street and uphill. From the porch, Morgen had a view past the Roaming Elk Inn and putt-putt course to Rosario Strait. Through a drizzle that had dampened her cheeks and Lucky's fur on the walk from the car, a freighter was visible, taking shipping containers somewhere to the north.

Lucky, still beaming green like a glow stick at the roller-skating rinks of Morgen's youth, snuffled at the floorboards of the covered porch. It looked like a residence, not a vet's office, but a plaque on the wall by the door showed the doctor's name and hours. A smaller sign stuck to an ornamental metal mailbox offered a phone number to call in case of after-hours emergencies.

Morgen took a photograph of it before ringing the doorbell. "Just in case you ingest something you shouldn't or tangle with barbed wire on a hike."

Lucky cocked his head and gave her a puzzled look.

"Do I need to remind you of the raccoon that purposely led you into that downed fence? On a long holiday weekend, mind you." As she recalled, every injury that any of her dogs had ever experienced had taken place late at night or over a weekend and had required an expensive trip to an emergency vet. "I'm amazed you opted to start glowing on a weekday. Though I can't blame this on you. I should have put you in the house before I started dancing nude on the lawn."

"You may enter," said the same baritone voice that had spoken to her on the phone.

Morgen blushed. She hadn't noticed the intercom next to the mailbox. "Thanks."

"Shoes off, please," the man—Dr. Valderas—reminded her as she opened the door.

Given that the hundred-year-old Victorian was in impeccable shape, Morgen couldn't blame the vet for wanting to keep it nice, but it did seem a little strange, given his clientele.

"You better not have mud between your toes," she whispered to Lucky as they stepped into a foyer.

Just inside the door, a bench had cubbies under the seat for shoes, jacket hooks mounted to the wall above, and an umbrella holder to the side. Morgen stuck her shoes in one of the cubbies as a man stepped out of what would have been the living room—or *parlor*—had this been a regular house. It had been converted into an office and exam room, and what would have been the dining area held waiting-room furniture. A door beyond it kept her from seeing if the kitchen was an actual kitchen or if it had also been altered for the business. She imagined cabinets full of medicines instead of fine china and a fridge containing specimens waiting to be sent off to a lab.

Morgen lifted a hand to greet the approaching man. He wore pinstripe trousers with suspenders, a gray embroidered vest, and a creamy button-down shirt with the sleeves rolled up, revealing ropy forearm muscles. His short silver hair matched a tidy goatee and mustache, and he had striking forest-green eyes. His feet were adorned with less striking Birkenstocks and gray wool socks. The no-shoe policy either didn't apply to him, or those were his comfortable house shoes.

"I'm Dr. Valderas." He extended an olive-skinned hand not toward her but toward her dog. "And I presume this is Lucky."

"The incandescent Lucky, yes. I'm Morgen."

"So you informed me on the phone."

Lucky wagged tentatively at the vet, then lowered to his belly, much as he did with Amar. That made Morgen wonder if Valderas was also a werewolf and another member of the Lobos, though his accent was different from theirs, and his dress was a *lot* different. She wasn't the world traveler that her sister was but thought he might be from Spain rather than Mexico. Could he have been adopted into their pack after he came to America? And was it rude to ask if one's new vet was a werewolf?

"Yup, just thought I'd remove all doubt. Thanks for seeing us on short notice."

"Yes." Valderas waved for them to follow him into his office, and Lucky padded after him as if he understood perfectly. "Has he experienced any changes to his appetite or other behavioral peculiarities?"

"Just his usual behavioral peculiarities."

Valderas looked at her as if he would have preferred to have his discussion with the dog rather than the human. Since he seemed humorless, Morgen vowed to keep her attempts at levity to a minimum.

"When did this glow start?"

"Last night. He ran up on some, uhm, strange women in the woods doing a dance or ceremony, and they were throwing witch powders around."

"*Witch* powders? Or *which* powders?"

Uh oh. If he didn't have any familiarity with witches, this might have been a pointless visit.

"Powders made and carried by witches. You do know about the

witches and werewolves in town, don't you?" She raised her eyebrows, refraining from asking if *he* was a werewolf. If he was oblivious to the supernatural stuff around Bellrock, she might have missed her guess. It was only Lucky's reaction that had made her think he was a werewolf. He seemed fit and had a presence about him, but that didn't mean he was, as Amar put it, an apex predator.

"I'm aware of them." Valderas grabbed a thermometer and stethoscope, but he knelt and ran his hands over Lucky before putting them to use.

He looked at his fingers, as if he expected something to come off and make them glow. It didn't. And Morgen slumped. She had a feeling this guy wouldn't know anything about the substance. She should have stopped in at the Crystal Parlor, but a *Closed* sign had uncharacteristically been hanging from the door, so that might not have been an option.

As Valderas examined Lucky, Morgen gazed at titles in a bookcase near the desk. Most were the types of tomes on veterinary medicine and anatomy that one would expect, but she halted her perusal in surprise at an old book, the title on the binding written in silver: *A Treatise on Lycanthropy.*

"Do you treat many werewolves?" she asked.

Valderas followed her gaze to the shelves. "Let's just say that I had a reason to want to learn everything about them a few years back."

"Is that when the Lobos and Loups came to town?"

"It's when the Loups decided to expand the size of their pack," he said coolly. "Whether people were interested in joining or not."

She stared at him, wondering if she fully understood the implications of his words. "They forced people to become... werewolves?"

Valderas turned his head and spread his fingers toward the side of his neck. There were faint scars there. Bite marks?

Morgen's conversation with Amar tumbled to the forefront of her mind, especially the part about how some witches didn't trust werewolves and always had spells on hand to defend against them —or take control of them. If the werewolves could bite others and turn them involuntarily into one of their own kind, maybe that precaution was understandable. She didn't think Amar would turn on her—or *turn* her—as he seemed far too honorable for that, but what if someone forced him to? More than ever, she wanted to find a way to make a talisman to ensure that couldn't happen.

"I do not treat them," Valderas said. "I'm not like the weak-minded fools who like what they did to them and now meekly concede to their demands, even handing over control of their establishments. Hell, control of this town. The mayor runs with them at the full moons."

"The Loups or... all of the werewolves?" This new revelation made Morgen a lot more uneasy about having had the Lobos in her house. She hadn't agreed to have them work on the property, and she didn't plan to, no matter how reasonable a quote they gave her, but what if they were offended when she rejected them?

"The Loups are the ones who turned numerous of the townsfolk." Valderas went back to his exam of Lucky, who stood patiently for the temperature-taking, something he usually objected to with a lot of whining and an attempt to hide behind Morgen. "When they arrived, there were only a handful of them. Rumor has it their pack was devastated after battles with Canadian werewolves up north. Here, there were only the Lobos, who'd come a couple of years earlier, and the Loups thought they could build their ranks and drive them out. But the Loups weren't sufficiently able to control all of those they turned, so they ended up at a stalemate with the Lobos. For the last four years, the two packs have butted heads frequently but have grudgingly ended up sharing the territory. They've been too evenly matched for either to dare start a full-fledged war. And then there are the witches, who now step up and enact protections at the full moon each month to make it difficult for the Loups to turn more people." His voice lowered to a mutter as he added, "Too late for me."

Morgen listened, enraptured by the story. In five minutes, Valderas had given her more information about the strife between and history of the packs than anyone, even Amar. She'd almost forgotten about Lucky's problem.

"If the Loups have the mayor and other influential people on their side," she said, curious to learn even more, "it seems like they'd be able to overpower the Lobos."

"You would think so, but the Lobos are strong, scrappy fighters. Only Lucien among the Loups is truly terrifying in battle."

Great, that was the one Amar was supposed to duel. Duel to the death?

"Most aren't as strong as Lucien," Valderas went on. "The Loups rely upon numbers and trickery. Someday, they'll probably succeed in besting the Lobos, but they haven't had the courage to take them on fully yet." Valderas knelt back from Lucky. "All I can tell is that this is the result of magic, not a powder or fungus or skin disease. Unfortunately, that means there's nothing I can do for him. Thus far, it doesn't seem to be bothering him in any way, but I can't promise it won't turn into something more insidious. If I were you, I would consult Phoebe Aetos at the Crystal Parlor."

"Ah." Morgen would have cheerfully done so if Phoebe had been in her store. "Thanks. What do I owe you for the exam?"

"Nothing."

"Are you sure? You had to stick a thermometer up his butt. That seems deserving of a service fee."

He gave her a bland I'm-too-professional-to-find-that-amusing look.

"Well, thanks for your help." Morgen glanced at the bookcase again. "Would you mind if I borrowed your book? Since I find myself surrounded by werewolves, I'm trying to learn more about them." Maybe it would tell her something about their magic that could give her a clue when it came to making a talisman.

Valderas squinted at her. "Such as how to control them? I know whose granddaughter you are and that strong witch blood flows in your veins."

Strong witch blood? Not just witch blood? Interesting.

"That's nice," Morgen said, "but no. I'm trying to help a werewolf friend *resist* magical control."

Valderas studied her, as if trying to tell if she was lying. "If that's true, then you had better keep that project to yourself."

"I'm not driving down Main Street broadcasting it from my speakers." Admittedly, she'd known the vet for less than ten minutes and was blabbing about it to him, but that was only because she wanted to borrow his book.

"The witches have to work hard and use a great deal of their resources to protect the town on the full moon each month. They won't appreciate it if you create something that renders their magic ineffective."

"It would just be for one person."

"Oh? If you succeed in making something like that, your new vet would be interested." His tone was dry, and he smiled for the first time, but his eyes were intense, and she sensed that he was serious.

"Do the witches bother you? You seem like an integral part of the town, not someone who would be a threat to them."

"Oh, I'm not a threat, and I've even treated some of their familiars. But sometimes, being the exotic foreigner intrigues women a little too much." His mouth twisted with bitterness, all hint of the smile gone. "I would give much to ensure nobody ever has control over me. Any werewolf would."

Morgen bit her lip. All of her run-ins with the Loups made them seem awful, so it was probably a good thing that the witches could control them, but what if she succeeded in making the talisman and the word got out? She could end up with Loups at her door—or her throat—demanding that she make more for them.

"I'm just doing research at this point," Morgen said, telling herself she didn't need to worry about it until she found out if it was possible to make a talisman, "but I can let you know if I learn anything useful."

Providing she talked to Amar first and he said the vet was a decent guy.

"I would appreciate that." Valderas took the book from the shelf and handed it to her. "And as I said, I recommend you don't tell anyone else that you're doing this research."

"I won't. Thanks."

The last thing she needed was *another* reason for those three witches—not to mention the vengeful Calista—to come after her. If Phoebe learned that Morgen was working on a talisman for Amar, would she also turn on Morgen?

As she led Lucky to the car, she thought of how she'd originally come to Bellrock thinking it would be like a vacation, an opportunity to recover from her divorce and losing her job. Somehow, her vacation had ended up being much more stressful than her old life.

10

A Treatise on Lycanthropy lay open next to *The Talisman Enchiridion* on one of the workbenches in the root cellar. The single lightbulb dangling between two ceiling beams was on, shedding wan illumination. Lucky, glowing as he snoozed on the dirt floor, didn't brighten the area much more, but Morgen noticed him out of the corner of her eye every time she turned a page. It was hard *not* to notice a lucent dog. At least it didn't seem to bother him.

Morgen wished so many things weren't bothering *her*. In addition to everything else, when she'd returned from the vet, she'd found that the moss she'd stretched out to dry in the kitchen had lost its glow. When she'd touched it, it had disintegrated, no hint of magic lingering. Whatever needed to be done to cure the bioluminescent moss was more than simply letting it dry naturally. The whole bag the sisters had gathered appeared to be ruined. Morgen almost wished she'd let them steal it. At least they would have known what to do to preserve its magic.

She sighed and rubbed the back of her neck. "Grandma should have gotten an ergonomic chair."

For hours, she'd been sitting on a hard stool as she read and took notes, and her muscles were letting her know that they couldn't put up with as much abuse as they once did. She was on the verge of going upstairs to look for a better seat, or at least a cushion she could put on the stool, when a passage in the werewolf book caught her eye.

"'The magic of the wolf relies upon the moon and is most powerful at night. However, wolves must 'ware those who can control the moon's magic for they may manipulate it to their gain and twist its power to control the wolf.'" Morgen scratched her jaw. "Okay, we know about that already. The werewolf-control incantation specifically mentions the moon's magic. But is there anything in here about strengthening their magic so they *can't* be manipulated?"

Lucky, who'd had a big day of hunting around the garden, was too busy snoring to wag his tail or otherwise participate in the conversation.

Morgen flipped back to a page she'd been studying in the talisman book. Thus far, it seemed the closest bet for something that might help. *Talisman of Imperviousness*, the header at the top read.

"It doesn't mention werewolves, but it says it protects a person from magical control. Presumably werewolves count as people, right? Oh, look. There are a few variations listed." She squinted at small print toward the bottom of the page. "Talisman of Flame Imperviousness, Talisman of Sun Imperviousness, Talisman of *Moon* Imperviousness. Hah. Maybe that's what he needs."

A chilly draft wafted down, carrying the sound of raindrops pattering on the dirt steps and the open root-cellar doors. Morgen would have to go up and close them. Usually, she left them open when she was in here, because she found the cellar claustrophobic and a little... eerie. By now, she knew—or at least believed—Grandma hadn't done anything evil with the pentagram on the floor or with any of her witch paraphernalia, but the place still had a Halloween-creepy vibe.

"Other than *spore of blood caps*—presumably, that's a mushroom—the ingredients for making the moon talisman are all things that I've come across since arriving in Bellrock and don't seem like they'd be that hard to scrounge up," she mused, speaking aloud to Lucky, even though he wasn't paying attention. Until she figured out how to get a familiar, she didn't have anyone else to muse witchy things to. "In fact, we might have everything else here. I recognize two of these ingredients from organizing the cellar, and there's mugwort and lavender in the kitchen. Do you think Amar will mind wearing a sachet of lavender around his neck? According to this other book, it's great for warding off evil spirits and protecting against general evil. I'm sure he would put witches into that camp, though I'm equally sure witches don't consider themselves evil, so one wonders if this would work for him."

If Amar was around to consult, she didn't know. She hadn't seen him since returning from the vet. Even if he were around, she doubted he wanted to hear about *witch* things, no matter that she was researching them on his behalf.

She was also keeping an eye out for information on glowing dogs and cultivating glowing moss. She didn't mind having multiple projects. Research was much more up her alley than questioning strangers or snooping in mansions full of slavering guard dogs.

"But where does one get the jewelry that one turns into a talisman, and how does one infuse it with the ingredients? These drawings are all of silver amulets similar to this one, not of people running around with sachets of herbs flapping on thongs." Morgen tapped the silver-chained amulet her Grandma had left behind and that she'd been wearing. "I can't imagine it's like grilling steaks and that you dip the metal in a nice spice rub."

She flipped through the pages of talisman recipes, hoping to find something basic that she'd overlooked.

"Ah, here we go. How to make a *receptacle*. 'A medallion or other bauble should be formed into a cup or hollow that the *magical resin* can be poured into where it will harden. Silver and gold are acceptable materials.' Hm, we're going to have to make friends with a jeweler, Lucky. Or a blacksmith."

Did little Bellrock have either? Phoebe had mentioned that she *wasn't* a crafter but that her sister was. That didn't help. There was no way Morgen would go looking for Calista and ask her to make jewelry for her werewolf friend.

"Oh, this says that the receptacle itself must be made durable with a magical overlay." Morgen grimaced. That meant she would need not only a jeweler but a *witch* jeweler. "'Once you have an appropriate receptacle, you melt the ingredients together in a crucible to make the magical resin. The last ingredient to go in should be the witch's blood.' Er, blood?"

That hadn't been mentioned in any of the recipes. Morgen looked back at the imperviousness-talisman page to double-check. Nope, no ingredient of blood was listed. But the page on receptacles implied that it was a key component in all talismans.

She re-read more closely, thinking maybe it referred to the spores from the blood-cap mushrooms she'd seen listed. Alas, that was not the case.

"'The greater in magic the witch's blood, the more powerful and effective the talisman will be. Also, if the witch cares for the person she will grant the gift of the talisman to, its protective powers will be greater.' That probably means I should use *my* blood and not ask whoever we can find to craft the receptacle to dump theirs in. Unless there's a crafter witch out there who secretly adores Amar." She grimaced. "I wonder how *much* blood is required. Pricking-your-finger-with-a-needle amounts or opening-your-vein amounts? And will Amar appreciate wearing something with my blood around his neck or think it's gross?"

Worse, would he think she wanted to manipulate him through it? She would make sure to show him the recipe and get his okay before going forward.

"He would appreciate that you cared enough to spill your blood for him," Amar said from the steps, his voice a low rumble.

Morgen gripped the bench to keep from pitching off the stool and frowned at Lucky for not warning her that someone was coming. But he was still snoozing. Some guard dog.

"Are you sure?" Morgen feigned casualness as she rotated to face Amar. "Because he's kind of a grump and never seems that appreciative."

"Because he is getting old and jaded and has difficulty admitting when he's wrong." He walked toward her, stopping close enough to peer past her to the books.

She pushed the talisman text to the side so he could more easily see it. "Grandma had most of the ingredients, except these blood-cap mushroom spores, but I'll need to find someone willing to make an appropriate receptacle. A necklace with a cup designed to hold hardened resin, basically."

"Maybe the person who knows how to prepare the moss will also have the ability to make witch jewelry."

"Maybe so. I just need to find them. An ad in the paper probably wouldn't be wise. Someone pointed out that the witches of Bellrock might not approve of a werewolf in town who can resist their control spells." Morgen hoped Phoebe wouldn't find out, but if Morgen's blood went into it, it would probably be obvious to all the witches around who had made the talisman.

"You risk their ire to help me."

"Yeah, cultivating people's ire is my new hobby."

"Unwise."

"I'm sure of it." Morgen turned back to the book and wrote

down the ingredients and how much silver a receptacle required. She hadn't seen any bars of precious metals in the cellar, so she would have to find someone who sold it.

"I came to apologize," Amar said.

She looked curiously over her shoulder at him. "For not being properly appreciative of my enchiladas?"

"For mistrusting you because of your blood. You have stood up for me to other witches, and you have not done anything cruel to me or others."

"I'm glad you noticed." She winced when that came out sounding snarky. That hadn't been her intent. "Seriously. I don't want to fight with you. I'm glad you were around for Grandma and that you've helped me."

Amar nodded, and Morgen thought that would be the end of it, but he spoke again.

"In the garage, when you cast that incantation, I felt its effect on me as it clashed against Calista's spell."

"Did you? I couldn't tell if it was working or if you stopped advancing because of your own willpower. I could tell you were fighting her."

"Yes, and your spell helped."

"That's good, right?" Morgen smiled, though Amar's face was serious, almost puzzled, as if he was trying to work something out.

"In that instance, it was a good thing. But I was concerned."

"That I would try to use it again?" She didn't want him to worry about that and wished she could promise that she would forget the incantation and never use it again, but the words were indelibly imprinted in her mind, and if a werewolf attacked her again, she knew she would blurt them out.

"Yes. I worried that you would like it." Amar held her gaze. "Like controlling me."

His voice was a rumble that sent a shiver through her for some reason. She grew aware of how close he was and thought once again of that kiss, though she was positive he didn't have that in mind now.

"No. I'd like having you not resent me for being an ass. And acting of your own accord. Do you have any silver or know anyone in town who sells it?" Morgen pointed to the recipe to change the subject.

His gaze shifted back to the page, and that relieved her. His eyes got intense sometimes.

"I can get some," he said.

"Good. I'll gather the rest of the ingredients and ask around, hopefully without being obvious about it, and try to find out who in town could make the receptacle. Or maybe teach me how to do it."

She yawned and rubbed the back of her neck again, reminded of how late it had gotten. Her mission would have to wait until the morning. Maybe tomorrow, Phoebe would be back in her shop, and she would have a suggestion. She still hadn't returned Morgen's voice mail about Lucky. Morgen hoped nothing had happened to her. Calista wouldn't have done anything to her sister, would she? Because she'd been willing to help Morgen?

"There is another reason I came," Amar said.

"To rub my neck for me?" Morgen supposed she shouldn't fish for a massage. Besides, with those meaty arms, he probably had the touch of a butcher tenderizing meat. It wasn't as if he was dainty with his art when he wielded his chainsaw.

Amar glanced at the back of her neck. "I do know where those three witches live. Their last name is Braybrooke."

"Oh? Why didn't you say you knew their names and where they live before?"

"I did not want you to go to their home and do something foolish. The older ones, in particular, are powerful, and their property is rumored to be well guarded by wards and magical booby traps."

"Why are you telling me now?"

"After last night, *I* am thinking of going there and doing something foolish."

"What?"

Amar didn't answer right away. Morgen was about to ask again, but he rested his hand on the back of her neck. A sensation between alarm and anticipation shot through her, and she froze. Did she fear him? She wasn't sure. But she wanted to lean closer to him, not away.

"They are all witches and work together," he said, thumb and fingers kneading the muscles in her neck, "but Olivia is the largest threat. As I told you, she is the one who forced me to my knees and branded me. *She* lit the barn on fire. *She* commanded me to kill the real-estate agent."

There was something wrong about getting a neck rub from someone concurrently talking about a man he'd killed. But she'd hinted that she wanted it, and his fingers weren't nearly as blunt and brusque as she'd imagined. Instead, he found the knots in her muscles and gently pressed and manipulated them, sending waves of relief through her.

"The oldest is Olivia?" she asked.

"Yes. They are in the Bellrock coven. Most witches in the area are."

Morgen grimaced, reminded that Phoebe knew the sisters, that she knew them and hadn't ratted them out to Morgen. Why would she? Morgen was a newcomer, not one of the coven.

"I do not know how to remove the brand," Amar continued, "but it would cease to have any power over me if I killed her."

"Uh." Morgen stared bleakly at the books without seeing the words. This discussion had taken an even darker turn. "I agree that she's wronged you—no, that she's a blatant criminal—but she should be arrested and put in jail, not killed."

Not *murdered*. If he did that, and he'd told her about his intent ahead of time, would that make her an accomplice?

"The sheriff will not arrest her. I am the only one who knows she was responsible for the real-estate agent's death, and neither the sheriff nor the deputies will arrest anyone on my behalf. No judge would listen to me in a court. I am a scruffy werewolf who's not from around here. They won't condemn one of their own citizens, or even speak stern words to her, because of anything I say." Anger infused his tone, but he kept it out of his massage. His fingers stroked and kneaded, turning her muscles into pliable goo. Turning *her* into pliable goo.

"I agree that it could be hard to get them to do anything without concrete evidence, but murder isn't the answer. Let's figure out how to put this talisman together, and then she won't be able to control you anymore." Morgen hoped.

"I need your help."

"With the talisman?" She didn't think that was what he was requesting, but she didn't want to acknowledge anything else. "I know, and I'm offering it."

"Getting into their home. Gwen knew how to thwart wards and protections. It must be in some of her books here. Make the talisman, then get me in, and I'll deal with Olivia Braybrooke."

Morgen swallowed. His tone was calm, rational, and determined, not bitter and vengeful, but that didn't make this discussion any less alarming. She would *definitely* be an accomplice if she helped him get into the witches' home to kill one.

"If you have the talisman, you won't need to deal with her," she said reasonably. "You can just let her be, and—"

"She has controlled other werewolves," Amar said, a growl returning to his voice. "If she can't use me, she'll simply use another."

"We can't—"

"*Kissing* is not what she wanted me to do to you." His hand stilled on her neck.

"Uh?" She wished she hadn't uttered even that. She didn't want to know. But didn't she *have* to know?

"She not only wanted you detained but also too afraid to go into the woods alone again."

"Because of you?"

Amar lowered his hand and stepped back. "Because of the monsters who roam the woods—that is what she calls werewolves—and what they might do to you. She'd run far enough away by then that her control wasn't absolute, and I managed to resist her somewhat, to creatively interpret her desire to *detain you*, but if she'd lingered nearby to watch, I wouldn't have been able to do anything but exactly what she wished." He ground his teeth.

Morgen didn't ask for explicit details. Her imagination was bad enough.

"The brand adds to her power and makes her harder to resist than if she cast an incantation," he said, "and she can manipulate me from farther away. I must kill her to be free from her."

"Don't you think a talisman could override the power of the brand? Let's try that first, all right?"

Amar glared mulishly at her. Because he didn't believe a talisman would be enough? Or because he wanted so badly to kill the witch?

"If I'm able to make it, and if it doesn't work…" What, Morgen? Would she agree to help him kill Olivia? No, she couldn't do that. "I'll help you get into her home to *capture* her, and we'll force her—uhm, use *magic,* not torture, to force her—to remove the brand and leave you alone. All right?" Kidnapping and coercion were also crimes, but they weren't as bad as murder, and she wasn't that sympathetic to Olivia after what she'd done. She deserved some magical coercion, damn it.

Amar's expression remained mulish, and she feared he wouldn't agree, but then he gruffly said, "I will help you gather the ingredients for the talisman, you will find someone to craft the receptacle, and if it works, we will storm the Braybrooke home and force Olivia to remove the brand."

Storming the home wasn't exactly what she'd had in mind, but it was better than plotting murder.

"Okay," Morgen agreed, wondering what she would do if she helped him get into the witch sisters' compound, only intending to talk them into removing his brand, and he killed them anyway. Her gut knotted at the idea.

She reminded herself that she had to successfully make the talisman and learn how to thwart protective wards before any compound-storming could happen. Maybe she didn't need to worry about this yet.

Still, she couldn't keep from shaking her head, worried that Amar was on the path to his own destruction. And that he might take her with him.

11

Morgen wrote down her list of ingredients and was ready to call it a night when scrabbling sounds came from the doors to the root cellar. She spun in that direction, wishing Amar hadn't left to hunt or sleep or whatever he planned for the night. Lucky leaped to his feet and barked.

A thump followed the scratches, and Morgen glanced around for a weapon. The antler staff was upstairs in the living room. She grabbed one of the wicked serrated knives from a pegboard full of ceremonial tools. What if it was a werewolf? Someone looking for Amar... or to take revenge on *her*? She'd been right beside Amar in Rainwater Estate, battling Calista and her Loup lover. Admittedly, she'd only taken swings at Calista, not the werewolf, but there hadn't been any witnesses to that battle in the garage, so who knew what story had gotten out?

Lucky ran to the base of the stairs and barked at the doors. Because of the rain earlier, Morgen had closed them. As the thumps and scrabbling noises—those sounded like claws on the wood—continued, she was tempted to *leave* them closed. Unless someone tore them off the hinges, he or she shouldn't be able to get in, not without a magical amulet to unlock the doors.

A screech sounded.

Morgen winced. "That doesn't sound like a werewolf."

Hackles up, Lucky continued to bark.

"Wait, what if it's Phoebe's raven? Here to deliver a message?"

Could a raven make that much noise? Those scratches and thumps were loud.

Morgen crept forward and grabbed Lucky's collar. She still hadn't heard back from Phoebe, so it was possible something was wrong with her. Something Zeke had flown up here to warn her about.

Lucky strained against her grip, wanting to lunge up the steps and outside.

"You can't leap out and eat a witch's familiar," Morgen whispered, shifting to stand in front of him. "Phoebe isn't that delighted with you as it is. I don't think she's a dog person."

At her words, the scrapes and thumps stilled. Something that sounded like wings flapping followed and then silence. Knife in hand, Morgen risked easing one of the doors open.

The night sky was dark and cloudy. The rain had stopped, but water dripped into the cellar.

When Morgen didn't see anything directly in front of the doorway, she eased outside. A faint green glow on the edge of the roof above drew her eye, and she lifted her knife toward it. An owl perched on the gutter, preening under one wing.

The owl was glowing green.

"Uh."

Lucky rushed past Morgen and ran outside. He didn't look up and see the owl, instead charging all around the cellar doors, snuffling at the wet clumps of grass. His green glow was the same shade as the owl's.

"That's unexpected." Though she felt silly, Morgen called up to it. "Are you the same owl that flew into the barn last night?"

Was it possible that her *ritual* had somehow caused the animals around her to glow? That Lucky's green nimbus didn't have anything to do with the ceremony the witches had been performing in the woods?

The owl's head rotated as it looked around. It seemed more like it was searching for tasty mice than paying attention to her.

"The answer to this question is probably *no*, since my dog has the same glow, but are you by chance my new familiar?" Morgen touched the spot on her shoulder that she'd had to wipe clean the night before. If the owl *had* flown out to respond to her spell and have a spiritual connection with her, pooping on her seemed a strange way to start their relationship. "And is it odd to talk to familiars? I assume they don't talk back. Are we supposed to communicate telepathically through our bond, or how does it work?"

Asking the bird was silly, but the ritual hadn't mentioned any details about what happened *after* a witch acquired a familiar. It was as if anyone performing the ritual was simply supposed to know.

The owl rotated its head again until it focused on her. It parted its beak, as if to speak and answer her questions, and she held her breath. A wad of something rolled out of its beak and plopped to the ground a couple of feet from Morgen. An owl pellet.

"Ew."

In a fourth-grade science class, Morgen had dissected an owl pellet to pull out and examine the bones. She had no urge to dissect this one and wondered what it meant that the bird had essentially puked at her feet. Other than that her potential familiar was incredibly irreverent.

"I don't care what Phoebe says, Lucky," Morgen said. "I'd rather have you on the job."

The owl hooted.

Under the green glow, it had pale-brown feathers with darker brown spots, and dark-brown markings also ringed its dark eyes. Those eyes blinked as it gazed down at Morgen, a surprisingly human blink with its upper eyelids descending.

"If you want to clue me in on the best way to communicate with you, that would be great," Morgen said, then glanced around to make sure Amar wasn't in the area. She would feel even sillier if someone caught her chatting up a bird. "Also, let me know if you're male or female. And, uh, what kind of owl you are. I think maybe a Barred Owl, but I don't usually see a lot of owls on my hikes. Up until recently, I never tramped around in the woods at night."

It hooted at her. Morgen pulled out her phone and took a picture before it lifted a wing and went back to preening. She thought about uploading it to one of those sites that identified wildlife, but the green glow might flummox the software.

As she was about to type in a description to search, her phone rang, startling her.

The owl hissed, apparently equally startled. It flew toward the barn and disappeared through a window. Lucky heard the wing-beats overhead and gave chase, but the barn door was closed, so he couldn't run inside and harass it.

"Maybe it's a *Barn* Owl instead of a *Barred* Owl," Morgen said, answering the phone. It was her sister. Maybe she would know about owls. "Hey, Sian. What time is it in Borneo?"

"A bad time to have Dengue Fever," came the flat reply.

"Uh, is that the punchline for a joke over there, or are you sick?" Morgen wouldn't be surprised. Sian didn't call often for purely social reasons.

"I just had the diagnosis confirmed, yes."

"That's not... deadly, is it?" Morgen had never traveled farther south than Arizona, and her knowledge of tropical diseases was limited.

The long pause made her uneasy.

"Most people recover," Sian said. Did she sound wan? Tired? Her voice was never full of energetic enthusiasm, but it did seem wearier than usual, especially given that it was the middle of the day over there. "But this is my second time getting it, and it can be worse the second time around." Her voice grew softer. "A colleague is taking me to the hospital soon."

Morgen swore. The *hospital*? It was *that* bad?

"Is there anything I can do to help?" she asked.

"From seven thousand miles away? Unlikely. I merely called to inform you of the remote possibility that I will be incapacitated for the near future." Sian hesitated again. "I didn't do that well when I got it the first time."

"And you *stayed* in mosquito-infested Borneo?" Morgen assumed there wasn't a vaccine for the fever, else Sian would have gotten it. She remembered her sister getting a whole swath of vaccinations for everything from typhoid to rabies before she'd taken off on her first research trip to the tropics.

"The orangutans I study live here."

"Do *they* get Dengue Fever?"

"Yes. I slather myself in all manner of mosquito repellents and sleep with netting around my bed. I did not expect to get it again."

Morgen stared bleakly at her phone. Her sister's camp was starting to make Bellrock sound like a paradise.

"I also called to check and see if you survived... whatever trouble you were going into when last we spoke," Sian said. "With the supposed werewolves. Your *I'm okay* text the next day was brief and unenlightening."

"It's the witches that have been more problematic than the werewolves."

"Of course." Judging by Sian's dryness, she still thought

Morgen was playing an elaborate hoax on her. Or that she needed a psychiatric evaluation.

"After you get better—" Morgen didn't want to say *if you survive*, "—you should come visit. I'll show you all the witch paraphernalia that was in Grandma's root cellar. Apparently, I have witch blood. I assume that means you do too. Maybe I can look up the recipe for an anti-fever potion in Grandma's grimoires."

"I'm taking Tylenol."

"How's that working?"

"Thousands of studies published in peer-reviewed journals speak to its efficacy as a pain reliever and fever reducer."

"Is that your way of saying you wouldn't take a witch potion?"

"Correct. I have no further news for you. I need to rest."

"Wait," Morgen blurted, not wanting to let her go, not if she was going to the hospital and could potentially get worse. A *lot* worse. But her sister wouldn't stay on the line for idle chitchat. Sian hated that kind of thing. "Can you identify an owl for me?"

"Because my advanced degree in primatology clearly designates me as a qualified ornithologist?"

"I just need to know the difference between a Barn Owl and a Barred Owl, not about flight patterns and migration habits."

"Barn Owls look nothing like Barred Owls."

"I'm afraid the glow will make it hard for a web program to identify."

"The glow?" Sian sounded disbelieving, not curious.

"I'll send a photo."

Maybe *seeing* evidence of magic would help convince Sian that Bellrock and its inhabitants were special. Though a month ago, Morgen also wouldn't have believed any of this if someone had been describing details over the phone. Having Amar leap on her car and change from a wolf into a naked man had been far more convincing than words.

"Given the quality of my cell reception in camp, that should only take three hours to download," Sian said.

A howl drifted out of the woods off in the direction of the Strait. Amar out on the hunt? Another answering howl came from closer to the property, and Morgen shivered. Amar was a lone wolf. She didn't think he would be out there hunting with anyone else. Was she hearing one of the packs passing through? And if so, was it the Loups or the Lobos? Either could be a danger to her. She glanced toward the sky, but it was too cloudy to see the moon.

"It's a Spotted Owl," Sian said, the photo loading faster than her sarcasm had suggested it would. "And it looks like it flew through radioluminescent paint."

"That's magic from a ritual."

"Naturally."

"I was also wondering if it's male or female." Morgen wouldn't try to convince her sister further about the existence of magic. Unless Sian came here and met the witches and werewolves, it was unlikely she would believe any of this.

"The markings are similar on males and females. The females are typically larger. It's hard to tell without a female there for comparison, but I would guess that one is male."

"Thank you. That will help in naming it."

"You're not planning to *trap* it, are you? Even if keeping owls outside of rehabilitation programs was legal, a bird of prey would make a horrible pet."

"No, nothing like that, but it likes Grandma's barn." Morgen didn't mention the possibility that she'd turned the owl into a familiar, especially since that might be wishful thinking. The glow might not have anything to do with her ritual. It could mean that it had been flying by at the same time the three witches had cast their spell—or thrown some powder—at Lucky. "As long as it's loitering in the area, I thought I would give it a name."

"Arianrhod." Sian snorted. "Or maybe Lechuza, given your new preoccupation with witches."

More howls wafted up the hill from the woods. Morgen grimaced and closed the root-cellar doors. It was time to go inside for the night. If only that meant she would be protected. She'd told Deputy Franklin that she could find a way to secure the property; maybe she needed to prioritize that.

"I'm even more preoccupied with wolves," she muttered.

"I hear them," Sian said in surprise. "They truly do sound like wolves. In that area, coyotes wouldn't have surprised me, but wolves..."

"Werewolves. There are two packs of them. I'm not sure which one is out there hunting tonight."

"Two packs of wolves in the same territory?" Sian didn't acknowledge the *were* part of the wolves. "That's unlikely."

"Well, they're werewolves. And they like to squabble with each other and challenge each other to duels."

Sian sighed, sounding tired again. "I don't know how to respond to your fantasies, Morgen. I find them concerning and possibly indicative of drug use. Or a mental disorder that causes delusions and hallucinations. Have you spoken to anyone about your affliction?"

"I'm speaking to you. Let me send you a picture of Grandma's root cellar."

That wouldn't prove that witches existed, but at least it would show Sian to some extent what Morgen had walked into.

Sian sighed again. "Is it also glowing with radioluminescent paint?"

"No. The bioluminescent moss powder is the only thing that glows down there."

"Maybe that's what the owl got into."

"The owl and Lucky. I took him to the vet, and the vet couldn't remove the glow." Morgen didn't mention that the vet was a werewolf or had said the glow was magical in nature. She'd already pushed her sister's willingness to suspend disbelief too far.

"This just looks like a lot of quirky clutter picked up at a garage sale," Sian said when the picture downloaded.

"Including the pentagram on the floor?"

"I don't know. Grandma was eccentric."

"She was a retired librarian."

"An *eccentric* retired librarian who rode a motorcycle and wore her socks outside of her pants."

"I'd forgotten about that. Wasn't she afraid of ticks or something?"

"I don't know, but some of those socks had stripes and went all the way up to her knees."

"Given that you like whimsy, I'm surprised you don't approve."

"I like practical whimsy."

"Like bamboo underwear."

"Yes. I need to go, Morgen. This conversation has been as draining as the fever."

"I always enjoy talking to you too."

Sian hung up.

Morgen shook her head, wishing she'd said something more important. Maybe including that she missed Sian and wished she weren't on the other side of the world. A person who was deathly ill should have family around. But maybe it wasn't that bad. Sian had been able to hold a conversation and be dry and snarky. She couldn't be *that* sick. Besides, she wasn't much older than Morgen and a little overweight but otherwise in decent health. She would pull through... wouldn't she?

"She will," Morgen said firmly. She still wished she'd said something more heartfelt and comforting. Not that Sian ever wanted comfort or a hug or even a pat on the shoulder. "I'll call her tomorrow night and check on her."

With the wolves still howling, Morgen whistled for Lucky and started for the front porch. She'd taken only a few steps when a startling vision formed before her eyes. A mouse skittering across the cement floor of the barn overlaid her view of the lawn and the side of the house. She seemed to be looking down upon it from the rafters until, with a dizzying leap, she swooped down on the mouse, snatched it up, and flew toward a broken window.

Morgen blinked and gripped the side of the house for support. She was seeing what the owl was seeing. Either that, or her sister was right, and she *was* hallucinating.

12

AFTER THE OWL DINED ON ITS CAPTURED MOUSE, SOMEHOW SHARING the vision with Morgen, he flew back outside and perched on the roof of the porch. With the wolves still howling, Morgen had been about to go inside, but this new ability to see the world through the owl's eyes had thrown her off. It didn't help that it was nauseating. She didn't know if that was from the bird's flight or if something about sharing a connection caused queasiness. If Phoebe puked every time Zeke shared his version of the world with her, she should have mentioned it.

Snuffling noises came from the garden. Thanks to his glow, it was easy to spot Lucky hunting for some new critter that must have sauntered through. His hobby was nothing new, but another vision abruptly came over Morgen. For a moment, her eyes seemed to be scant inches from the grass and the mossy side of a raised wooden garden bed. The grass moved as she—as Lucky trotted along, sniffing. He stuck his head in a hole, and Morgen had an up-close look at crumbly dirt sides, lit by the luminescent dog snout thrust in there.

Lucky jerked his head up, and for a dizzying moment, she saw herself, hunched over by the porch and gripping her knees. Then his head went back in the hole.

With queasiness threatening to bring up her dinner, Morgen willed the vision to end. There had to be an *off* switch, didn't there? Too bad she didn't even know how she'd turned the visions *on*. And did this mean that Lucky was *also* her familiar? Because he'd been near the fire pit too? Could a witch have *two* familiars? Or was this something else, something unrelated to the ritual?

She lost the war with her stomach and leaned over and threw up behind the lilac bushes next to the porch. Maybe someone had cursed her. Or maybe she'd done something wrong during the ritual, and that was why Lucky and the owl were both glowing. And why she was seeing through their eyes and puking.

Fortunately, the vision faded, leaving Morgen looking out at the dark lawn as she sucked in the misty night air.

Above her, the owl hooted. Morgen wiped sweat from her brow.

She tugged out her phone again. It was getting late, and she wanted to go inside and wash out her mouth, but she desperately needed Phoebe's advice.

But once again, Phoebe didn't answer, and the call dropped to voice mail. Feeling shaky, Morgen shambled over to the porch and sat on the steps.

The owl flew from the roof down to the railing, his head turning as he regarded her. The dark brown rings of feathers around his eyes reminded her of a mask. It wasn't as prominent as a raccoon's mask, but she decided to call him Zorro. Her sister, with her literary owl-name suggestions, would be aggrieved, but she was already aggrieved at the developments in Morgen's life lately. Besides, Sian had more troubling concerns at the moment.

"Is Zorro okay with you?" Morgen asked.

The owl hooted. It could have been a yes, a no, or a suggestion that Morgen let him into the kitchen to feed on the rats living inside the walls of the house. An appealing notion.

Zorro issued more soft hoots and preened his chest feathers.

"Are you wondering if I can get you to stop glowing?" Morgen asked. "Because I'm not sure how that started in the first place."

The owl ignored her in favor of more preening.

"Do you want to help me out with one of my problems? Familiars are supposed to help witches, right? Not just spit up owl pellets and leave droppings on them."

Zorro ruffled his feathers and switched his attention to a wing.

"That's a vague answer." Morgen drew her phone again and looked up the one ingredient from the talisman recipe, besides the silver for the talisman itself, that she didn't think was anywhere in the house. The blood-cap mushrooms. The internet search returned *Hydnellum peckii* or *bleeding-tooth fungus* as the closest match. She didn't know if that was the same thing but read aloud, "'They grow clustered together on the ground in the Puget Sound area of Washington and are found in association with Douglas fir and hemlock.' Huh, I wonder if there are any here in Wolf Wood."

Zorro hooted. It might have been agreement. It might have been another warning that an owl pellet was on the way. After all, he had recently dined. Thanks to her vision, Morgen had seen the grisly details.

"Do you know the woods well?" Giving up on the idea of feeling silly for conversing with the owl, she held her phone out to show him a picture of the mushroom. "Have you seen any of these?"

He seemed to look at the screen for a moment, though perhaps it was only its glow that caught his eye, then spread his wings and hopped along the railing while clicking and chittering at her.

"I don't know what that means." Morgen wouldn't have associated those sounds with owls. "You're kind of impertinent for a familiar."

He sprang off the railing toward her, and she squawked and ducked, almost slipping off the porch. Wings brushed her hair before the owl flapped off over the garden, startling Lucky.

"*Definitely* impertinent."

Morgen grimaced as Zorro flew up over the trees and headed west before disappearing from view. He was soaring in the direction that she'd heard the wolves howling. What if her new familiar got eaten his first night on the job?

Lucky trotted up to stand beside her on the porch.

"We should probably go in for the night, buddy." Morgen gave him a pat. "I don't know why all those wolves are out there, but I don't want to give them a reason to come up here."

She hoped they wouldn't run into Amar and give him trouble.

Lucky leaned against her shoulder and wagged his tail.

"Are you hungry?"

He licked her cheek.

"I'll take that for a yes." Morgen grabbed a support post and was about to pull herself to her feet when another vision came to her, along with a fresh twinge of vertigo. "Hell."

Once again, she saw the world through the owl's eyes. Zorro was flying over the trees, following railroad tracks down by the water. It was a major north-south line, and Morgen had heard the trains go by at night.

In the vision, a wolf came into view, trotting along the tracks. Amar? No, this wolf was large enough to be one of the werewolves, but it had silvery white fur that stood out even on the dark night. It glanced up at the owl before continuing along its route.

Could the werewolves sense a difference between an owl and an owl familiar? Morgen hoped not. They would be even more likely to attack Zorro if they did.

The owl flew past the silver wolf, then left the tracks, zigzagging his route as he sailed around trees. The uneven aerial flight made Morgen's stomach churn again, and she was tempted to try to break the bond and stop the vision, but if Zorro was flying toward the mushrooms, she wanted to see where he went.

More wolves came into view, large gray wolves. She couldn't tell if they were Loups or Lobos, but she didn't see Amar, who had distinct black markings in his gray fur, among them.

Under the evergreens, the big wolves were rolling on their backs with their legs crooked in the air. Playing?

That was the last thing Morgen would have expected from the surly werewolves. They were rubbing themselves on fir needles and dirt instead of grass, but otherwise, they looked exactly like Lucky when he rolled on his back.

The lumpy ground, with roots and rocks bulging beneath the brown needles, didn't look comfortable. Maybe something had died down there, and they were rolling on the carcass? As gross as that was, she'd caught Lucky rolling in everything from dead fish to duck droppings before. She couldn't assume wolves were any different, though if *werewolves* had that habit, she was going to start hosing Amar down when he returned from hunts.

Zorro landed in a branch overlooking the area and focused not on the wolves but on the base of a large hemlock. With vision far sharper than a human's, he gazed at clumps of mushrooms sprouting from the earth. They had vibrant, solid-red caps that weren't very similar to the ones she'd found online, and she had a feeling this was a different species. But maybe it was the one she wanted. Maybe Zorro could read her thoughts and understand what she wanted, even if she'd shown him something different.

That seemed a stretch, but he was unquestionably focusing on that patch of mushrooms. One of the wolves rolled into his view and brushed one of the red caps. Morgen expected its weight to crush the mushroom, but the stalk only bent, and the cap spat something into the air. A cloud of tiny red particles. Spores? The spores she was supposed to use in the talisman recipe?

Some of them landed on the wolf, and it rolled more vigorously. *He* rolled more vigorously. Thanks to the belly-up view, Morgen could tell that now.

Several other wolves loped over and through the spore cloud before it settled. They ran around, cavorting with each other, then dropped to roll again.

"It's like catnip," Morgen mused. "Magical mushroom catnip for wolves."

Zorro sprang into the air, and she lost sight of the wolves.

Bring me back a mushroom, please, Morgen thought, though she had no idea if the owl could hear her or understand.

He flew away from the area, leading her to believe that he couldn't understand. Or that he did but that he'd done all he was willing to do for her tonight. That meant she would have to go get her own mushrooms. She grimaced, daunted by the idea of strolling into the equivalent of a werewolf opium den.

"We'll wait until tomorrow for that adventure." Morgen gripped her stomach, wondering how to end the vision. "Hopefully, a very sunny day without a hint of cloud cover."

Wind swept through the trees behind the barn, and rain started falling again. Wishing for sun in the morning might be in vain, but she would at least hope it would be too bright for werewolves to take their fur form. She didn't want to run into the pack out there, whether they were high on 'shrooms or not.

Zorro perched in a tree branch and must have closed his eyes, for the vestiges of the vision disappeared, leaving Morgen gazing out toward the garden. Rain pattered against the big squash leaves. Lucky was lying beside her on the steps, his head on her thigh.

She was about to take him inside when he lifted his head, ears cocked, and looked toward the driveway. Was that the rumble of a vehicle?

Morgen checked the time. It was after ten. Nobody had called or texted to say they were coming.

"This can't be anything good." She gripped Lucky's collar so that he couldn't charge off toward the approaching vehicle.

He whined uncertainly. What if the werewolf pack had finished frolicking, turned back into humans, and was coming up here to threaten her? Or, more likely, what if the witch sisters were coming back?

Earlier, she'd set the knife on the porch railing. She eyed it now, though she couldn't imagine using the weapon on another human being unless the person was physically attacking her.

A large white camper van with a pop-up top came into view, rolling into the illumination cast by the exterior barn lights that had survived the fire. The werewolves all drove trucks. Hopefully, this was someone less dangerous.

The camper van wasn't anything that Morgen had seen here in Bellrock. Or anywhere, she decided, as the light played across a mural painted on one side. Maybe on *all* sides. The swamp full of toadstools, grasses, and pools of water sprawled across the hood as well as over the doors, and green vines trailed up to the roof. A giant cartoon frog perched on each mushroom while small frogs hid in the grass. One frog in the water was in the process of catching a fly, its long pink tongue stuck out and wrapped around the insect.

As the van rolled to a stop, Lucky issued another uncertain whine.

Usually, visitors excited him, but he clearly didn't know what to expect from this one. Morgen didn't either.

13

The van door opened, and a young woman stepped out. Wendy.

With her brown hair pulled back in two ponytails, she wore a calico dress and sandals that looked like they'd come off the set of *Little House on the Prairie.* Wendy wasn't armed, as far as Morgen could see, but she wore an amulet, as well as charm bracelets on her wrists. Morgen wagered that all the jewelry had magical attributes.

Wendy also wore a thick fur wrapped around her neck. At least, Morgen *thought* it was a fur... until it chattered.

Lucky barked and sprang off the steps, tearing free from Morgen's grip.

She swore and lunged after him, but he was too fast. He sprinted toward Wendy. No, toward the rodent that was now sitting up on her shoulder. A mink? A ferret?

Though the barking appeared to startle her, Wendy reacted quickly. She shook her sleeve, prompting a wand to slide out and into her grip.

Damn it.

Morgen lunged for the knife she'd left on the porch railing. Afraid she would need it to defend Lucky, she snatched it up and ran after her dog.

Wendy muttered under her breath as she pointed her wand at Lucky.

"Stop!" Morgen yelled.

But Wendy finished the spell quickly, and Lucky halted a few steps away from her. Envisioning the woman turning him into a frog—maybe that was what all the amphibians painted on the van meant she could do—Morgen ran up behind him.

Lucky dropped to his belly and whined, much as he did when he was in the presence of werewolves. Morgen stopped beside him, the knife clenched in her hand, and glowered at Wendy. If anything happened to her dog...

The ferret stood on its hind legs on the woman's shoulder and chattered at Morgen and especially Lucky.

"I'm sorry." Wendy lifted her arms, the wand pointing toward the sky and her eyes wide, as if she were some innocent and misunderstood maiden. As if the other night, she hadn't been in a dark cloak, casting spells and helping her sisters try to steal moss from Wolf Wood. "I know it's late, and you didn't expect me. I didn't know how to contact you or if you would talk to me even if I did call."

"No kidding." Or maybe make that a firm *no*. "You guys burned down the barn."

Wendy looked toward it, though, thanks to Amar's handiwork, all of the burned material had been removed. He was well on his way to having the walls replaced and the roof rebuilt.

"And you *branded* Amar. Like he's a steer you're claiming. And you forced him to *kill* Magnus Christian."

Wendy winced, but she also shook her head in denial. "That wasn't me."

"You were *there*. I saw you pointing your wand at Amar and keeping him on his knees."

Wendy kept shaking her head. "I... helped because he's so dangerous, but I didn't do the other things. I... didn't even want to help. But my sisters— I can't go against them."

"I don't believe you *wanted* to go against them."

Not only that, but Morgen worried the younger sister had been sent here to distract her while the others did... what? Hunted down Amar in the woods? Went back to the spring to finish that ritual and fill another bag with moss? Morgen squinted at Wendy. That had to be it. Dare Morgen run out there and confront them again? While leaving Wendy at her back? If Morgen ran off, Wendy would call her sisters and warn them that Morgen was coming.

"I did. My name is Wendy, and I didn't agree with what they were doing. Really. That's why I'm leaving." Wendy pointed at the frog camper. "I don't know where I'm going yet, but I can't stay here with my sisters. Not when they're doing horrible things just to make money. They don't even *need* any more money. Calista said you weren't selling Wolf Wood, so we don't need to try to buy it."

Morgen had only been half looking at Wendy as she peered into the woods behind the barn, wishing she could see all the way to the spring, but she jerked her gaze back now. "You talked to Calista?"

"Just today."

"In person?" Morgen grimaced, wishing vainly that Calista had called them from another state. Or another country altogether.

"Yes."

The ferret squeaked and chattered while running from Wendy's left shoulder to right and back. Lucky was still on his belly but inching forward, as if he would spring at the creature.

Wendy frowned down at him. "My spell should have frozen

him completely. You've... ensorcelled him somehow. Is he your familiar? A dog is such a weird choice for a witch."

The ferret jumped onto Wendy's head and hissed.

"Yeah, *we're* the weird ones here." Morgen glanced at the van.

Wendy frowned as she removed the ferret from her head. Lucky barked. She hurried to the van, and Morgen thought she might drive off, scared away by the fearsome glowing vizsla, but Wendy merely put the ferret inside and shut the door. She turned and frowned sternly at Lucky. He must have shaken off her spell, for he ignored her and ran around her van, barking at the ferret through the windows. Wendy gave Morgen an exasperated look.

Though this was the last person Morgen wanted to help out, she caught Lucky by the collar and pulled him away. She dug a treat out of her pocket and used it to convince him to sit and be good, though that was a lot to ask of a dog. The ferret kept chattering at him from the dashboard like a squirrel teasing him from high in the branches of a pine tree.

"Like I was trying to say," Wendy said, "I'm leaving home. I don't want to support Olivia and Nora anymore. Or do what they say. They just assume I'll do whatever they tell me to, since they took over teaching me after Aunt Beatrice passed away, but I'm nineteen. They're not my bosses."

"Is that right?" Morgen was torn between the desire to run into the woods and stop the other two and wanting to gather any information Wendy was willing to give her. Not that she could trust anything this woman—this *witch*—said, but Wendy had already revealed that Calista was still in the area. That was valuable information.

"*Yes,*" Wendy said. "Besides, witchcraft isn't supposed to be used to hurt people, even werewolves. And it's not supposed to be about making money either. Especially when they already *have* enough. The sisterhood was just supposed to use what they earned to buy Wolf Wood and other magical lands and keep them from being developed, not sell ingredients at outrageous prices forever."

Uh, sisterhood? Was that something else in addition to the coven?

"Most of the witches in the world can't afford anywhere near what they're charging now," Wendy added. "Even with their special *financing* program."

Morgen blinked a few times at the idea of a bioluminescent-moss-financing program. "Gotta hate price-gougers."

"*Yes*. I knew you'd understand. You wouldn't sell this land, not even for a whole heap of money. That's what Calista said. I thought that would be a relief to everyone, but she was *mad* about it. She still thinks you're a threat to the land, and she *hates* the solo werewolf that chases witches off whenever they come to gather ingredients."

"Amar. He has a name."

"I don't think he'd want me to use it."

"Oh, I'm certain."

Wendy frowned. "Listen, I can understand you not trusting me, but I seriously feel bad about all the things that happened. We didn't even know you. It wasn't right of us to burn your barn and try to scare you out of here." Her words spewed out rapidly, and her eyes were moist, as if she truly was upset by everything that had happened. She lifted her hands imploringly, and the trinkets dangling from her wrists clinked and tinkled like wind chimes.

Morgen remained suspicious. "It *really* wasn't right of you to use Amar to kill someone."

Heinously criminal and *sociopathic* were the words that came to mind.

"That's not what happened." Wendy shook her head. "Yes, Olivia branded him so she could control him—she's terrified of werewolves and was afraid he'd kill her if he could."

Yes, Amar wanted very much to kill her right now.

"And she wanted to get him in trouble for attacking Christian," Wendy said, "so the sheriff would drive him out of Bellrock, but she didn't make him kill anyone. He must have gone into feral predator mode and killed Christian of his own volition. Werewolves are more like animals than humans when they're in wolf form." Wendy lowered her voice. "Even when they're not. I don't know why the coven doesn't just drive them out of the area completely."

"Because they like being able to cast spells and control them? And there's no way Amar killed the agent of his own accord. He's not like that."

"My sister said he did."

"Then she's lying."

"She wouldn't do that, not to me."

"Why not? You said she's terrified of werewolves and wants to get rid of them."

"She has reason to want to get rid of them or at least control them so they can't hurt us, hurt *her*. Like they did before."

"*Amar* didn't do anything to her," Morgen said, sure of it.

"She says they're all the same, that they'll kill us if they get a chance." Wendy glanced toward the dark trees and lowered her voice. "It's not safe for you to stay out here in the woods, all alone. You don't know enough magic, not like Gwen did. Even she shouldn't have lived alone. It was too dangerous."

"A witch did her in, not a werewolf. The witch you were talking to earlier today."

"Not me. Calista didn't talk to me. The elders in the sisterhood all treat me like a child, and like I told you, I don't agree with the way they're trying to control the town and make money off every other witch in the world. Just because so many choice ingredients grow in—" Wendy halted, as if she'd realized she was saying too much.

"Wolf Wood?" Morgen thought of the mushrooms, wondering if they were rare like the moss.

"The Bellrock area. I..." Wendy glanced at her wrist. A charm shaped like a wolf's head started glowing. "I have to go."

"Wait. Did you make those?" Morgen pointed to the bracelets. "Or do you know who did?"

"I made them, and one of my friends enchanted them." Wendy started backing toward her van but almost tripped over Lucky. He'd stopped barking and was engaged in a staring contest with the ferret through a window. He barely noticed her running into him.

"Can you make jewelry of all kinds?" Morgen kept herself from saying magical silver necklaces. *Receptacles.* The last thing she wanted was to clue in these witches about her plans for Amar's talisman, but if one of them could and would make the basic chain... it would be delightful to take their own work and turn it into a tool that could keep them from controlling Amar again. "I'd pay if you could make me something. I have a fondness for silver neckwear."

Wendy was maneuvering around Lucky to open the door and seemed to barely hear her. "Uh, maybe. If you want to talk tomorrow, I'll be at the campground until I figure out where I'm going. Come alone."

Morgen glanced at Lucky, thinking her glowing dog with his desire to nosh on her ferret had offended her, but then a gray-and-black wolf streaked out of the woods behind the barn. Amar.

His growls preceded him. Wendy shrieked and sprang into her van. The engine roared to life as Amar charged across the grass at top speed, looking like he meant to crash through her window and kill her with his deadly fangs.

"Amar!" Morgen lifted a hand, though after all he'd endured at the three witches' hands, she didn't know if she should stop him. But if she didn't, he might murder someone else in her driveway.

She stepped into his path as the van wheeled around, driving across the grass instead of turning on the gravel. The tires spun but quickly regained traction, and the frog-covered vehicle lurched and wobbled down the driveway at top speed, barely slowing for the potholes. Wendy's head had to be hitting the ceiling with each bump.

Without slowing, Amar veered around Morgen and charged after the van. He sprang as it accelerated even faster. Morgen thought he would miss it, that Wendy was driving too perilously fast for even his powerful legs to catch up, but he caught a spare tire mounted on the back under a giant perky green frog cover.

A great wrenching sounded as Amar tore it off. Not only the cover but the tire inside too.

It tumbled free, and Amar landed on the ground beside it as the van continued to roar away, careening down the winding, bumpy driveway far faster than was wise. Morgen wouldn't have been surprised if it hit a pothole and lurched off the road into a tree. Maybe one of the trinkets on Wendy's wrist saved her from such a fate.

Lucky sat on his haunches, his head cocked. He appeared confused by the rapid departure of the ferret. Maybe he'd considered it a new friend, though Morgen was positive the ferret hadn't felt that way about him.

Amar crouched with his hackles up and his tail out straight as he glared after the van disappearing through the trees. He looked like he was thinking about giving chase, but once it reached the paved street, he wouldn't be able to keep up. Already, his chest was heaving as his tongue lolled out, making Morgen wonder how far away he'd been when he'd detected a witch on the property. Maybe he'd sprinted halfway across Wolf Wood to help Morgen. Or to take his revenge.

She walked warily toward him, positive he would be crabby after watching Wendy escape and getting nothing but a mouthful of tire for his efforts. The frog cover lay crumpled on the ground next to the spare, puncture marks from his fangs piercing it and the rubber. Air hissed softly into the night.

"You certainly gave that tire what for." Morgen stopped beside him, stifling the urge to rest a hand on his furry back, though she would have liked to soothe him, if possible.

He shifted into human form to stand nude in the driveway. That made her glad she'd kept her hands to herself. She might have ended up fondling his back—or maybe a lower region.

"Here." She picked up the frog cover and held it in front of him, strategically placing it over his groin. There was just enough lighting coming from the barn and the house that he wasn't entirely in shadow.

Amar glowered grumpily over at her. "My clothes are in the woods."

"Naturally. What would a werewolf need with a closet?"

"I caught that witch's scent and came as quickly as I could. I believed you were in trouble."

"I appreciate that. I think she was the distraction though and that the trouble is happening elsewhere. Will you come to the spring with me?"

"Yes." Amar shifted back into a wolf and loped toward the trail leading into the woods, traveling far faster than she could.

"That's an interesting interpretation of *with*." Morgen dropped the cover, waved for Lucky to come with her, and jogged after Amar.

Thanks to Lucky's glow, she didn't need her flashlight, not until they reached the spring and found Amar standing next to the water, once again in human form. He was turning in a slow circle, gazing up at the branches.

With a feeling of dread settling in her stomach, Morgen shined her phone's flashlight onto the trees around the water. The branches were bare of moss. Not a shred hung from a single twig.

Even the bark of the trunks, which had previously been carpeted with the bioluminescent moss, was bare now.

"They took it *all*?" Morgen shook her head. "Will it grow back? Without any seeds left? Er, spores?"

She had no idea how moss reproduced but worried it wouldn't be able to now. Even if it could, how long would it take? Months? *Years*? Her hopes of selling the valuable moss to pay for remodeling and the taxes that would inevitably be due on the property were dashed.

"I don't know. But the scents of the two older witches linger in the area." Amar's rumbly voice changed to a dark growl. "Including the one who branded me."

"I had a feeling Wendy was a distraction. I shouldn't have listened to anything she said. I bet she's not staying at a campground either."

Amar eyed her. "The Crow's Perch? That's the only campground nearby."

"She didn't say the name. I think she blurted out the first lie that came to mind when I asked how I could hire her."

"*Hire* her?"

"To make jewelry," Morgen said. "She might be able to craft the necklace we need for your talisman. If she could be convinced to."

His eyelids drooped. "I could convince her."

"I'm sure she would enjoy doing favors for you after you ravaged her tire."

"I wasn't going to call it a *favor*."

"Just plant a paw on her chest and force her to work your silver?"

"Something like that. We will check for her in the campground. It would have been unwise for her to tell you where she is staying, but perhaps she is unwise."

"She's young at least. And she claimed to have had a falling out with her sisters, but—" Morgen glanced at the bare branches, "—that could have all been a lie."

"She could have been setting a trap."

"I do love it when my enemies do that."

"I will lead the way while you wait in safety out in the road." Amar looked like he meant to head to the campground immediately.

Morgen held up a hand. "I need to collect all of the ingredients for the talisman before we bother getting a receptacle made. There are some mushrooms that I'm not going anywhere near until broad daylight, and we need silver to give her, in case this *isn't* a trap and we can convince her to make you some lovely neckwear."

"I was able to acquire a small bar of silver from a stash I know about. It's in my pocket."

She glanced at his waist before remembering his nudity, then jerked her gaze back toward the trees. *High* in the trees.

"The pocket in my pants." Amar pointed back into the woods, then looked into the branches where she was looking. "You are offended by my nudity? There is no way for me to carry clothing when I am in wolf form."

"I know," she said, but she thought of the dog backpacks that were available in hiking stores. That's what he needed. But no. A dog—or wolf—wouldn't be able to put one on without a human's help. "And I'm not offended, no. I just assumed you wouldn't want me to gape at your genitals."

Of its own accord, her gaze drifted to a particular tree. The one she'd leaned against—that he'd *pressed* her against—when they'd kissed. She remembered his hungry lips on hers, his hard body molded against her, as if it had just happened, and she had to resist the urge to look at him again.

"Gape if you wish," Amar said. "My genitals are not shy."

"And yet, my *eyeballs* are."

He smiled knowingly over at her, and her cheeks heated several degrees.

"I'll be ready to go to the campground in the morning," she said, eager to change the subject.

"I will get my clothes and the silver. And for the record, my ass is also not shy." He quirked an eyebrow, then headed into the woods, his bare cheeks visible as he strolled nonchalantly away.

Morgen should have kept staring up at that tree branch, but he'd essentially *invited* her to check out his butt. And she did. It was firm and nice and might very well assume a starring role in her dreams that night. Wonderful.

14

MORGEN WAITED UNTIL WELL AFTER DAWN TO LEAVE THE HOUSE with a trowel and bag and trek through the woods toward where Zorro had seen the blood-cap mushrooms. Unfortunately, heavy cloud cover hid the sun, and Amar's promise that werewolves could change during the day if it was dim enough kept coming to mind. What if she ran into that pack, and they were still vigorously enjoying themselves by the mushrooms?

She should have asked Amar about them, but he hadn't shown back up at the house after showing her his butt and heading off to get his clothes. Maybe another hunt had called him—or he'd been in the middle of one when he'd caught Wendy's scent, and he'd wanted to return to it.

A soft owl call of *hoo hoo* emanated from the trees. Her owl? It was hard to imagine a random owl hooting during the day, but she had no idea what was typical in Wolf Wood. Nor did she know if she could truly consider Zorro *her* owl. She wished Phoebe would call her back so she could ask questions about the familiar ritual, familiars, and... everything. It worried Morgen that more than a full day had passed without word from her.

As she made her way down the hill toward the train tracks and the water, she walked into a fog bank.

"Great," she muttered.

Even without the haze, she would have struggled to find the mushrooms. The perspective she'd gotten from the flying owl had given her only a vague sense of where to look.

When she got to the tracks, she would follow them and hope to see a trail or something to indicate the spot where Zorro had flown off. Maybe there would be wolf prints in the ground. Large *werewolf* prints.

The fog thickened as she reached the tracks, making it feel more like night than day, and she wondered if she'd made a mistake by coming here alone. After more than eight hours, the wolves *ought* to be gone, but maybe they weren't. She'd left Lucky in the house, against his wishes, in case she had a run-in with them. She didn't want him to be hurt. Unlike Wendy, werewolves might do a lot worse than pointing a wand and freezing him in his tracks.

Something sparkling on the side of one of the trees made her pause. She veered over and found a pine covered in little dots that glinted, as if catching the sun's light, but there was no sun. She touched one, half expecting it to be glitter that someone had glued onto the trunk, but it grew out of the bark. Warmth emanated from the tree itself, and she pulled her hand back. Was this another magical spell ingredient that grew in the woods?

"No wonder the witches want this place preserved."

Morgen picked at one of the dots with a fingernail, thinking of taking a couple of samples back to the house in case she found a use for them later. A visible charge of energy akin to silver lightning ran up the side of the tree. Her amulet warmed her skin through her T-shirt, and she leaped back. She gripped the star-shaped medallion and shuddered. If she hadn't been wearing Grandma's amulet, the dot might have zapped her. Hard.

"Maybe I'll leave these alone," she murmured, backing up and returning to her mushroom hunt.

As she crept through the trees, the feeling of being watched came over her. The same kind of feeling she remembered having when performing her familiar-finding ritual and spotting eyes observing her from the woods. Though she glanced in all directions, she didn't see anyone around. Nothing but fog.

Fog that had her walking in circles. Morgen grunted in disgust when the train tracks came into view, then veered back into the woods again. She might have to go back to the house and wait for Amar. If all of the werewolves were into the mushrooms, he might know the spot.

A familiar tree came into view, the large hemlock that she'd seen through Zorro's eyes. Morgen picked up her pace, eager to find the mushrooms and get back to the house, but something whitish-silver came into view through the fog, and she halted.

A boulder? An aspen log?

With a start, she remembered the silver wolf that had been traveling by itself. She ducked behind a tree. The fog made it difficult to tell, but the wolf seemed to be lying down. Sleeping? Were a dozen other wolves out there, doing the same? Sleeping off the effects of their mushroom-spore inebriation?

"He's alone," a quiet voice said from behind her.

Even though she recognized Amar's voice right away, she couldn't keep from jumping in surprise. A twig snapped under her foot.

The silver wolf rose to its feet and looked at her. Her nerves jittered, making her want to spring away. She felt as if she'd been caught doing something wrong.

Amar rested a hand on her shoulder. She didn't know if he was clothed or not—his arms were always sleeveless—and didn't look back. The wolf's forest-green eyes seemed to be considering both of them. *Dr. Valderas's* forest-green eyes. She remembered them well.

Between one eye blink and the next, the silver wolf leaped away. It—*he*—loped into the fog, heading toward the tracks and the direction of town.

"I believe I've met that werewolf." Morgen glanced back.

Amar dropped his hand. He was back in his usual brown leather vest and jeans.

"Dr. Valderas is the town vet," he said.

She nodded. "I took Lucky to see him yesterday. He didn't know how to treat his distinctive glow."

"Because that's witch magic. *Your* magic, I thought."

"I'm not sure if it was my accidental doing… or that of our three favorite witches." Morgen waved toward the mushrooms. "Last night, there were a bunch of other wolves here too."

Amar frowned at her. "You were here last night? I've been trying to keep an eye on you, but I haven't wanted to stay in your house. Perhaps that was a mistake."

Morgen resisted the urge to point out that Amar would be welcome to stay in the house; he'd already made it clear that he preferred the barn. "Zorro showed me this place through a vision—I asked for help finding the mushroom spores I need."

"Who is Zorro?"

"An owl that is possibly my familiar now. But possibly not."

"Most witches know if an animal is their familiar or not."

"Yeah, but I'm new."

"Perhaps, as a new witch, you should ask the other witches if naming familiars after movie characters is appropriate. It doesn't seem their usual style." Amar tilted his head. "Or did you mean to call him *el zorro* for fox? That still seems like an odd choice for a bird."

"I'll have you know the book came before the movie, and I hope my Zorro is good at outsmarting the bumbling authorities—

or in this case, Loup werewolves—the same as a fox or the folk hero."

"The witches are more of a threat to you than the Loups."

"Yes, but the *werewolves* are more of a threat to him. I'm sure owls are tasty."

"Not particularly. We prefer small and large ungulates." His eyelids drooped. "They're sumptuous in a mole sauce."

"So are mushrooms. Speaking of that..."

"The mushrooms you're looking for are over here." Amar walked toward where wolf-Valderas had been sleeping. He must have come to enjoy the spores after the other wolves had cleared out.

"It sounds like you're familiar with this place. Do lots of wolves come here? And do you know if those were the Lobos or the Loups that were here last night?"

"The Loups. It's good that you didn't come in person."

She was probably lucky none of them had eaten Zorro.

"I thought you kept people from trespassing in Wolf Wood when you could." Not that Morgen would expect him to stand up to a whole pack. That would be suicidal, and she regretted making what might have sounded like an accusation.

"Not the werewolves. That would be impossible." Amar stopped and pointed at the ground. "We are all drawn to the magic of this place. It's why so many of our kind have congregated in the area."

"Oh, yeah. My sister thought it was weird that two packs were sharing the same territory."

"*Weird*." His flat look said he didn't appreciate the label.

"Well, atypical anyway. She's more of an expert on *wolf* wolves though. She doesn't believe in *were*wolves. I've tried to convince her that you're real, but she's stubborn." Morgen smiled, hoping Sian was stubbornly—and effectively—fighting off that fever.

"Your sister studies wolves?"

"Primates, actually, but she took a lot of biology classes in school and did a report on wolves in fourth grade." Deciding that sounded inane, and hardly counted as *expertise*, Morgen pulled her trowel out of her bag and knelt beside the blood caps. She only needed the spores, but she had no idea how to collect them without taking the whole mushroom. She also didn't want a red fungal cloud to burst into the air while she was kneeling there. Just because inhaling the spores had made the wolves happy didn't mean it wouldn't paralyze her. Or worse.

"What did you do reports on?" Amar asked.

"In fourth grade? Uh, Steve Jobs, Steve Wozniak, and the invention of the Apple I computer."

"Wolves would have been a superior topic."

"I have no doubt, but you can't play games on wolves. Do you think it's okay if I take one of these out of the ground? Or will it shoot spores into my face that prompt me to roll around on my back with my hands and feet in the air?"

"They only emit spore clouds at night. You can likely take a sample."

Wolf Wood was starting to feel like Wonderland. Any minute, a talking rabbit would saunter up.

Careful not to touch the mushrooms with her bare hands, Morgen eased the trowel into the moist earth underneath a lone specimen. Fortunately, Amar was right, and no clouds puffed out. She dug out the mushroom and tucked it into her bag.

"Do you ever come down here to get frisky?" she asked.

"Sometimes. This is one of several places where the magic of Wolf Wood calls us. But I don't come if other wolves are in the area. Like Dr. Valderas, I am without a pack, and it is dangerous to infringe on another pack when they are enjoying themselves." Amar drew a compact silver bar out of his pocket. "This is ten ounces. I trust it will be sufficient for the talisman."

"I think so. By the way, will you be okay wearing silver? I seem to remember folktales saying that silver can kill werewolves."

"Silver *bullets* can. But so can regular bullets."

"Does that mean the folktales aren't true?"

"Silver disrupts magic, so it does have some extra power to harm the magical—including witches—but it's probably also why it's helpful in protective talismans. To disrupt magic cast against the wearer."

"Okay, good." Morgen made a note to avoid silver bullets herself.

"Do you need any other ingredients?" Amar waved toward the woods.

"Yes, but they're in jars in Grandma's cellar and the kitchen." And flowing through her own veins. "The only other thing I need to get is the magical silver receptacle I told you about. Once I have that, I'm hoping I can bring it back to the house and successfully do the ritual and create a talisman of imperviousness."

"That's a mouthful."

"You can call it your lucky charm, if you wish."

Amar gave her another flat look, but all he said was, "We will go to the campground now. Bring your weapons."

"Like the staff with the antlers on top?" Morgen imagined herself running through a campground with that, trying to prong enemies leaping out at her from behind bushes.

"Whatever will protect you if there's a trap. I assume you haven't purchased a crossbow yet."

That had been *his* suggestion for a weapon for her, one that wasn't witchy. Unfortunately, she doubted either would help if Wendy truly was luring her into a trap.

15

MORGEN LET AMAR DRIVE. HE KNEW WHERE THE CAMPGROUND WAS, and nobody would notice if she pronged the upholstery of his beat-up truck. She wasn't even sure the rock-hard bench seat with its split vinyl covering counted as *upholstery*. If he told her there was a wood board under the thin layer of cushioning, she would believe it. It might even have been a bed of nails.

"Leave it to the Pacific Northwest to have thick fog blanketing the area in August," Morgen muttered, eyeing the gray mist wreathing the trees as they drove around town instead of through it. "In some states, it's hot and sunny in the summer."

"Witches, werewolves, and depressed artists like gloomy climates," Amar said.

"Vampires, too, I hear."

"There aren't any in Bellrock."

"But they exist?" Morgen raised her eyebrows, no longer surprised by anything, not when she was on a quest to make a magical talisman for a werewolf.

"Over on the Olympic Peninsula."

"So, the books got it right."

A wooden sign shaped like the state of Washington with a bird crouched on one corner read *The Crow's Perch* and pointed to a paved driveway. After they turned in, following five-mile-an-hour speed-limit signs, tents and RVs came into view through the trees. Morgen looked for the frog-mural van, though she supposed any of the campers wandering around could have told her if it was there. It was hard to miss.

She almost rolled down the window to ask a couple who were walking a dog, but her introvert tendencies teamed up with a sticky crank to thwart that idea. Oh, well. It wouldn't take long to look personally.

Despite the fog and the gloom, the campground was full. With the groupings of camp sites nestled close together between trees, it was hard to imagine witches trying to skulk around to set up a trap. Surely, someone would have noticed people in dark cloaks carrying wands, especially if nude dancing and rituals were involved.

A fluffy Pomeranian on a long lead tied to a picnic table yapped at their truck. Amar, whose powerful, muscled arm hadn't had any trouble rolling down his window, rippled his lips and growled at the dog. It stopped barking and slunk under the table.

"Don't you feel like a bully picking on dogs the size of teacups?" Morgen asked.

"Dogs that aren't properly respectful to werewolves need to be taught manners."

"He could have been respectful of you and barking at me. I'm all kinds of shifty."

Amar eyed her—and the antler staff awkwardly leaning across her lap, the tip brushing the ceiling—and did not refute her statement. She made a note not to fish for compliments from him.

"There is the van." Amar nodded to a group of camp sites in the back next to a sign that pointed to a trail leading to the beach.

Tents occupied three of the sites, making it easy to see Wendy's camper in the fourth. The mural had as many frogs on it as Morgen remembered, though the back looked a little bare with the spare tire missing. The mount that had held it was warped and hanging from the bolts. The pop-up top of the van was up, suggesting it had been used for camping and that the witches hadn't parked it there as a decoy. Probably.

Amar stopped his truck in the road in front of the site and sniffed out the window.

The van doors were shut, with curtains drawn over the windows, and there was no sign of Wendy, other than a stick that might have been used to roast a hot dog leaning against a grate over a fire pit. Did witches roast hot dogs? And make s'mores?

"Can you sense any magical wards around the area?" Amar turned off the truck.

"Uhm, how would I do that?"

"Gwen could tell. I don't know how. She would turn her nose up in the air, much as I do when I check for scents, and close her eyes."

"She didn't leave any instructions on magic sniffing in her letter." Morgen wished she had. No, she wished Grandma were still alive, so she could have taught Morgen some of this stuff herself. And just because. Morgen hadn't realized what an interesting person Grandma had been, and she regretted all those years that she hadn't come up to visit.

Her amulet warmed slightly on her chest, as if it knew what she was thinking about. Strange.

"I can tell that the witch was here," Amar said, "but I don't think she's here right now."

"Where would she have gone without her van? It's a few miles back to town, right?"

"About four."

"A short trot for a wolf. A long round-trip trek for a witch on foot." Morgen eyed the trail sign. "Maybe she went clamming this morning."

"Her sister witches could have given her a ride back to their lair after they set a trap for us."

Amar truly seemed to believe that was the most likely scenario. Maybe it was.

Morgen withdrew the small bar of silver he'd acquired and considered it. They might be able to find another jeweler in town, but would it be a *witch* jeweler? Capable of creating a piece that was a suitable receptacle for a magical resin? She doubted it.

"Stay here." Amar eyed the bar. "I'll check the van."

"I was about to say the same to you. This was my idea."

"If magical wards go off, I can handle the pain."

"This might *protect* me from pain." Morgen gripped Grandma's star-shaped amulet, the medallion still warm. She wore it all the time these days.

"And it might not." Amar opened the door and slid out. "Stay."

Morgen waited almost five seconds before easing her door open. It creaked, as most things on the ancient truck did, and Amar scowled back at her. He'd only gotten as far as the campfire and had been checking out the ashes and roasting stick. Had Lucky been with them, he would have been sniffing around, hoping for fallen hot dogs, but maybe Amar thought it was a likely place for witch wards to be placed.

Morgen strolled toward the side of the van, thinking of taking a more direct approach. It was unlikely that sniffing someone's hot-dog stick would tell her anything.

"You're not an obedient witch," Amar said.

"Observant of you to notice." She leaned her staff against the side of the van and peered through a gap in the curtains, but it was too dark inside to make anything out. She knocked on one of the doors. "Wendy, are you in there? Our chat got cut short last night. And you left your tire in my driveway."

"Are you going to offer to give it back?" Amar asked.

"Sure. You only slightly perforated it."

"It tasted dreadful."

"Hence why there are only a few holes?"

"It crossed my mind to tear it into a thousand pieces, as I wish to do with those witches, but it was like bathing my tongue in a tar pit."

"I doubt those sisters taste good either." Morgen knocked one more time, though Amar had already said Wendy wasn't there. Morgen tried the door and was surprised to find it unlocked.

Before she'd opened it more than an inch, Amar growled deep in his throat.

Morgen paused and glanced around. "Someone coming?"

"No. I'm voicing my disapproval of your flagrant disregard for the likelihood of magical security and traps."

"Nothing bad has happened so far. Maybe it's *not* a trap." Or maybe her amulet was protecting her from whatever wards she'd triggered.

"The witch is not here and therefore cannot craft the receptacle. You do not need to enter her premises."

"It's more of a van than a premises."

And it might be full of clues about the witch sisters, their home, and how one might convince the oldest to remove the brand on Amar's neck.

Morgen opened the door farther. Blue light flashed, and a blast of energy slammed into her chest. A shock of pain rocketed along every nerve in her body as something like a hurricane gale hurled her backward.

She smashed into Amar and would have pitched to the ground, but he caught her, arms wrapping around her to keep her upright. Stars danced before her eyes, and pain stabbed her skull from within.

A long moment passed before her stunned diaphragm recovered enough to allow her to breathe. It took even longer to straighten her crossed eyes and focus on the face looking down at her. Amar's expression contained equal parts concern and exasperation. That had been a dumb move, so Morgen felt lucky to find the concern there.

"Wards," he said blandly, "need not be placed only in a witch's premises."

"I'll keep that in mind," Morgen rasped.

Two kids on bicycles pedaled past, peering in their direction as they headed toward the beach trail.

"Ew," one whispered loudly. "They're going to make out."

"That's *disgusting.*"

The kids pedaled faster to avoid seeing such unpleasantries, but with Amar holding her from behind, Morgen found the likelihood of kisses to be low.

With his help, she put her weight back on her feet and stood straight. The van door remained open, revealing a beige carpet, brown curtains, and a bed and kitchen area. The scents of witch herbs hinted of projects in progress and made Morgen believe that snooping inside might turn up something interesting. The underlying ferret odor wasn't as intriguing, and she wondered how often Wendy and her familiar slept in the van. Maybe she truly was estranged from her sisters.

Morgen grabbed her staff, pointed the antlers at the inside of the van, and braced her shoulders. "I'm going in."

"To assail the upholstery?"

"I'm hoping the magic of the antlers will protect me from further booby traps."

"You know that's a druidic Staff of Earth, right?"

"Uh, no. What's that mean? And why did Grandma have a druid tool?"

"She used to wave it over her garden. It was supposed to keep blight and pests away and make the soil more fertile."

She squinted back at him, suspicious that he hadn't given her that information before. "I think you're messing with me."

"You saw the size of the tomatoes in the garden."

She shook her head and used the antlers to tap the walls, seats, and ceiling of the van before committing herself to entering. For the most part, nothing happened, but when she tapped the mattress, the air buzzed. No zaps of energy smashed into her, but there was definitely more magic inside.

Trusting that Amar would pull her out if she got herself electrocuted, Morgen climbed in for a better look around. She didn't know what exactly she was looking for, but this was the abode of one of their enemies. There ought to be *something* useful she could learn inside.

Unfortunately, most of what she learned was that Wendy ate cereal with marshmallows in it, had posters of boy bands taped to the walls, and had a giant monitor with a black gaming computer that cast purple light onto the walls. It didn't seem like the room—the van—of an arsonist and tormentor of werewolves, but more than once, Morgen had witnessed Wendy helping her sisters with their cruel magic.

She poked in the cupboards and drawers in the tiny kitchenette, found them stuffed with mismatching cups and dinnerware, and was about to give up on her snooping when she pulled open a drawer full of jewelry. Necklaces, charms, rings, and more were stuffed inside, along with crafting tools and collections of beads.

Morgen glanced toward the door to check on Amar and see how much disapproval he was oozing for this trespass. But he was standing guard, his arms folded over his chest as he glowered at more children bicycling past. She smiled. He was a good ally. He might gripe and grump, but he had her back. Phoebe and all of the witches were wrong about him. Morgen couldn't help but wonder how many of the werewolves they were wrong about.

A silver necklace caught her eye, its sole adornment a smooth concave oval without any decoration. She pulled out a couple more that were almost the same, though they had concave circles. They looked like they were *meant* to be decorated. Maybe the pieces were incomplete, and Wendy planned to engrave them later.

Or... Morgen bit her lip. Maybe they were exactly what she was looking for, blank receptacles waiting to receive magical resin created in rituals. She could envision pouring a mixture of spores, herbs, and her blood into the center so that it could harden.

If this was what she needed, there might not be any need to make requests. All she had to do was... steal one?

She grimaced at the idea. Even if those sisters had been making hell for Amar, the idea of committing a crime was unappealing. Snooping was one thing—what harm was she really doing?—but theft?

"Morgen," Amar said quietly. "Someone is driving this way in a campground security vehicle."

"Campground *security?* That's a thing?"

"It's an SUV with a light on the top and the Crow's Perch logo on the side. You may have been reported for your snooping."

"Maybe *you* were the one who was reported."

"I'm not doing anything wrong."

"You're looming intimidatingly and glaring at children."

Morgen held up the two amulets with concave circles, her other hand poised to push the drawer shut, but she paused, wrestling with indecision. She had no idea where Wendy was, so it wasn't as if she could ask to borrow them or propose a trade or a sale. But... she needed one. Ideally two, in case her first attempt didn't work.

"I'm standing next to the table and not doing anything."

"Yes, it's very intimidating." Morgen stuck the two amulets into her pocket, her knuckles brushing the silver bar. "Yeah, let's trade that."

She tugged out the bar and put it in the drawer. It was more silver than had been used in the two amulets. Of course, Wendy had put who knew how much time into making them.... Morgen dug in a different pocket and pulled out forty dollars she had in cash and put that in a drawer too.

"I feel like a horny businessman tipping a prostitute," she grumbled.

She closed the drawer and hopped out of the van as the SUV pulled up behind Amar's truck.

Uh oh.

Amar squinted—intimidatingly—as a woman got out of the driver's seat and walked up to his truck. Morgen closed the door to the van as quietly as possible.

"Do you think she saw anything?" she whispered, hoping the campground was too large for the staff to remember the faces that went with the RVs and tents. And vans.

Amar watched the woman stonily—she was on the other side of his truck from them—and didn't reply. She tucked something under his windshield wiper, then returned to her SUV, backed up, and drove around the truck.

"Not you stealing from one of the campers, apparently," Amar said.

"I left money and your silver bar."

"So, it's not stealing?" He arched a skeptical eyebrow.

"Not at all. It's an equitable exchange of goods." Morgen tapped her pocket and grabbed her staff. "I'm ready to go."

He grunted, walked to his truck, and plucked the slip of paper off his windshield. He glowered at it and showed it to her.

"Is that a parking ticket?" Morgen slid onto the bench beside him.

"Yes."

"You think I should pay it? When I'm here doing this for your protection?"

He crumpled it up and tossed it behind his seat.

"We're just breaking laws left and right now that we're hanging out together." Morgen spoke the words lightly, but she was disturbed by the trend. Just because she'd left money—and silver—for the jewelry didn't make it less of a theft. And this wasn't her first time this month trespassing on someone's property to snoop. Before coming to Bellrock, she'd never even littered or jaywalked. What had happened to her life? "I hope this doesn't end in a high-speed chase with us driving over a cliff."

Amar looked at her.

"Maybe you didn't see *Thelma and Louise*."

Or maybe he didn't appreciate being likened to a woman. Morgen opened her mouth, intending to retract her insinuation, but a queasy feeling came over her, and she found herself looking through someone else's eyes. An *owl's* eyes.

She saw the world from a high branch overlooking a long familiar driveway. A dusty green Subaru was maneuvering past the potholes on its way up to Grandma's house.

"Someone's going to the house," she said.

"You installed security cameras?" Amar put the truck into gear.

"Something like that." After giving her another queasy lurch, the vision faded. "Try to get us back there before they leave. It's not a car I recognize."

"What is it?"

"A green Subaru."

"Those aren't uncommon in town."

"I don't think they're uncommon anywhere."

"One of the witches in the coven has one," he said. "I was passing by once when they were having a meeting at the church."

"They meet at the *church*? I thought witchcraft and witches were kind of pagan." For the first time, it occurred to her that she might be in for an awkward conversation if she ever admitted her new hobby to her pastor back home.

"They meet sometimes in the graveyard behind the church. There are a couple of fancy tombs that seem to mean something to them."

"Huh." Morgen didn't know whether to hope to be invited to one of those meetings or not. Graveyards weren't a passion for her, and thus far, she'd only met one witch who hadn't proclaimed herself an enemy to Morgen. And she was missing.

"I'll attempt to get us to your house before she leaves." Amar bared his teeth—his fangs—at the ticket deliverer on the way past. The woman must have sensed that he wouldn't pay the fine, for she bared her own teeth and shook her pad at him.

"I have questions I'd like to ask the other witches," Morgen said. "Whoever they are."

It could be helpful to talk to members of the coven who hadn't had anything to do with the arson or various murders in Bellrock. Though for all she knew, all of the local witches might be working with Calista and the three sisters.

Another queasy lurch overtook her stomach, and she gripped the dashboard for support as Amar pulled out into traffic. What now?

She braced herself for another vision from Zorro, but the next thing she saw was a close-up of Grandma's living-room window with dog noseprints all over the glass. Ugh, was she seeing through *Lucky's* eyes again?

Through the noseprints, she could barely make out an older woman with curly gray hair walking up the steps to the porch. She knocked on the door.

Lucky ran from window to window, and the vision he shared with Morgen lurched along with his movements. She could barely glimpse the person outside. After putting his paws on no fewer than four windowsills, Lucky ran to the door and reared up on his hind legs as he planted his paws on the wood. That only gave Morgen a view of the door.

"Not helpful, buddy," she mumbled, her stomach protesting the dog-eye view even more than owl vision.

"What?" Amar asked.

Morgen's breakfast threatened to come up. She gripped her stomach and could only shake her head. If she opened her mouth, something more than words might come out.

Lucky returned to the window. *All* of the windows. As he ran from viewpoint to viewpoint, the woman outside only a blur as she rang the doorbell or whatever she was doing, Morgen grew more and more motion sick. How could she end this vision?

She grabbed the crank for the window, but it still wouldn't roll down.

"Pull over," she whispered.

"I thought you wanted to get back before the witch does anything."

"*Pull over!*"

Amar frowned his disapproval at being yelled at, but he obeyed, driving onto the shoulder of the road and stopping. Morgen flung the door open, ran three feet, and threw up in ferns and wild asparagus growing in a ditch. Twice.

It took a minute before she could drag a sleeve over her mouth and sweaty forehead and gather herself to return to the truck. Amar waited behind the wheel.

Morgen slumped onto the seat and waved for him to continue. "In the novels I've read, the hero holds the heroine's hair while she throws up."

"In the novels I've read, the heroine has the stamina of a horse, the agility of a gazelle, and makes her *enemies* throw up when she kicks them in the gut."

"Do those *novels* have a lot of pictures, dialogue consisting of *pow* and *bam*, and women in armor that reveals more skin than the typical Malibu Beach bikini?"

He squinted over at her. "Sometimes, the women wear leotards too."

"I thought so." Morgen wiped her mouth again, wishing she'd brought along water so she could have washed it out. At least the vision had faded. "I'm beginning to see why dogs aren't recommended as familiars."

"What did Lucky's vision show you?" Amar asked, reading between the lines—or the asparagus plants.

"Just what we suspected. Someone who might be a witch is at the house looking for me."

16

MORGEN BRACED HERSELF AS THE TRUCK RUMBLED UP THE DRIVEWAY. It had only taken fifteen minutes to drive back from the campground on the other side of town, but that was an eternity during which a magic-slinging intruder could do something evil. Like setting the barn on fire again or kidnapping Lucky. She hadn't received another vision from him or Zorro and had no idea how to send telepathic requests for updates.

When the barn and the house came into view, neither was on fire, and the Subaru was gone. If Morgen hadn't received visions from Lucky *and* the owl, she might have thought they had been wrong, but she trusted that the person had come and gone.

A breeze whispered through the corn stalks in the garden, and something white flapped on the front door.

"Did she leave a note?" Morgen wondered as the truck stopped. "A nice potion recipe for me to check out? A receipt for a gift subscription to *Witches Monthly*? An invitation to come to a Tupperware party?"

"My experience with witches says it's more likely to be an invoice."

"Uh, what is a strange witch going to bill me for?"

"Setting up shop in their jurisdiction without paying dues to the coven."

"Is that a thing? *Dues*?"

"Yes."

Lucky was barking when Morgen got out and jogged up to the porch. Relieved that he was still in the house and hopefully unharmed, she let him out before removing the envelope taped to the door.

He ran two circles around Amar and the truck, with his nose to the ground, then leaped back up the steps to the porch and sniffed thoroughly at the floorboards.

"I'd know someone had been here even if there wasn't a note," Morgen remarked.

"Someone wearing bergamot, yes." Amar wrinkled his nose and eyed the envelope as if snakes might come out of it.

Morgen wondered how the rest of the witches in town had treated Grandma. She already had a good idea about how they'd treated *Amar*.

After opening the envelope, Morgen withdrew a form printed on computer paper as well as a handwritten note torn out of a spiral notebook. She unfolded the latter and read it aloud.

"Dear Gwen's granddaughter (I'm sorry I didn't catch your name), we're aware that you've been working with Phoebe to modernize her store (good, as it needs it). Nobody has seen her for the last two days, nor is she answering her phone. She never closes her shop, even on the holidays, so this is highly unusual. I was hoping she might be up here, helping you organize your grandmother's belongings or giving you some instruction (she mentioned she might do this), but I see that she isn't. If you hear from her or know where she's gone, please let us know. I've also included a form detailing annual dues required from those who perform witchcraft in the greater Bellrock area."

Amar grunted knowingly.

Morgen ignored the form in favor of frowning at the letter. Phoebe was the only witch she'd met who had been willing to help her and hadn't been plotting against her, at least as far as she knew. What could have happened to her? Her sister, Calista, wouldn't have kidnapped her, not if she was using her to deliver messages. Could one of the other witches have done it? Someone the coven didn't know about? Or maybe one of the werewolves had gotten an urge to put an end to the Crystal Parlor.

That bleak thought made Morgen grimace.

"It's signed Judith Farina, Treasurer of the Sisters of the Trillium Moon. There's a postscript that says she'll accept my dues and also be the one to handle my application if I apply to join the coven." Morgen raised her eyebrows. "I assume this is the same coven that the moss-stealing, pyromaniac sisters are a part of. Why would she suggest that *I* could join?"

"There are even more dues for members," Amar said.

Morgen didn't know if he was serious or not. "How much does it cost to join?"

"I don't know. They've never invited me."

"Odd. You'd make such a fine witch. I bet they'd love it if you suggested all the women should have the stamina of horses and wear bikini armor."

"Don't forget the agility of gazelles."

"Gazelles only live ten years. From what I've seen, most of the witches here are older women." Though Wendy wasn't. And her sisters had only been in their twenties or early thirties too. Maybe they were the young upstarts. "Have you ever met this Judith Farina?"

"No, but I avoid witches whenever possible."

Morgen returned the letter and form to the envelope and stared broodingly at the driveway. She had a lot on her plate, but she wondered if she should go looking for Phoebe. If Phoebe was in trouble, it might be because of her association with Morgen, which could make her disappearance—her kidnapping?—Morgen's fault.

"Just like everything else happening in Bellrock," she muttered.

Amar arched his eyebrows.

"I think... that field trip you want to take to the sisters' house needs to happen soon. I want to talk to someone who's spoken to Calista lately, and Wendy said her sisters have."

Even though it didn't make sense that Calista would have kidnapped Phoebe, Morgen had a feeling the woman knew exactly what was going on in Bellrock. Morgen wished Wendy had been at the campsite when they'd visited so she could have questioned *her*. If Wendy truly was estranged from her sisters, or even just in the middle of a spat with them, she might be more likely to blab than the others.

It was strange that her van had been at the campground and she hadn't. What if Wendy and her ferret had also been kidnapped? What if witches in Bellrock were disappearing left and right?

"Field trips and question-asking are not why I want to go there," Amar reminded her, his voice growing growly.

"I know, but we made a deal, right? You get a talisman, and there'll be no need to murder anyone."

"You can make the protective talisman now that you've acquired the base jewelry?"

Morgen appreciated that he used the word *acquired* instead of *stolen*, but that didn't make her feel better about her theft. "I think so. If it's just a matter of assembling the ingredients and following the book's directions for performing the ritual."

Was it? Thus far, she'd been able to make the incantations she'd been given work, but Phoebe had implied those had been simple for someone with witch blood and an amulet. That didn't mean everything would be simple. Morgen wouldn't be surprised if some things, perhaps such as crafting powerful magical talismans, would take a lot more experience and wouldn't come out right if a newbie tried them. Like a novice chef trying to make a soufflé. Or even getting a risotto right.

"How long will it take?" Amar asked.

"I'm not sure. I can assemble the ingredients and try it tonight." Morgen would have to re-read the entry in Grandma's grimoire, but she remembered night being mentioned. Not a full moon, fortunately, though that was coming the following night. Thoughts of werewolves being able to bite her and turn her into one of their own came to mind.

"My duel is tomorrow night."

"I remember. Are you still planning to go through with it?"

Amar's chin came up, indignation gleaming in his blue eyes. "Of course. An honorable man doesn't back down from a challenge."

"I figured. Do you want me to come with you? The Loups kind of invited me."

Bring your female as a witness, one had said.

"That is not necessary." His eyelids drooped. "Unless you want to see me in battle."

"I'd prefer not to see you torn to pieces in battle, but I can come to support you and cheer for you if you wish."

"I will *not* be torn to pieces. I will be victorious, as long as the Loups don't plan deceit."

That was the part Morgen worried about. They all seemed like such jerks that it was hard to imagine any of them being honorable.

"And if they do?" she asked quietly.

"I will deal with it."

Amar didn't mention that the Lobos had offered to come and

back him up. Even though Morgen didn't like them, she hoped they would follow through on that. For his sake.

"I mention the duel because there is a possibility that I will not survive it." His voice had lost its pomposity, and he gazed steadily at her, serious now. "If I am to force the eldest sister to remove my brand, help you ask the questions you wish answers to, and possibly avenge Gwen's death by finding and slaying Calista… it should be before the duel."

"That's a lot to accomplish before tomorrow night."

Morgen glanced at the time on her phone. It was already after noon.

"Yes," Amar said. "You need to make the talisman, to ensure I can attack the witches without them taking control of me, and study wards to learn how to get past the magic that protects their compound."

"No problem." Morgen had a feeling Phoebe would scoff if she were there. Those sounded like the kinds of things that would take weeks of study, not one day. The memory of being blasted out of Wendy's van came to mind. Her chest still ached, as if she'd been clubbed by a two-by-four. What if the wards protecting the witches' property were much stronger? "Let's hope nobody comes to kidnap *me* tonight."

"I will remain nearby to protect you."

"Thanks."

"Is there anything I can do to help so that you can start immediately?" Amar asked.

"Uh, cook dinner tonight? Feed Lucky. Water the garden. If you're feeling motivated, you could take out the garbage and mop and dust the house."

"Dust?"

"Yes. There's a feather duster in the hall closet." Morgen beamed a smile at him, though she didn't actually expect him to do chores for her.

His expression grew blank. She didn't know if it was because he refused to do such a chore or if he didn't know what a feather duster was. Maybe he used rags? He had to use *something*. Since he was a lone wolf, he presumably had to clean up after himself. She hadn't seen Merry Maids visit the barn at any point.

"When you've been chainsawing in your workshop all day, and there's sawdust all over everything, what do you use to clean up?" she asked.

"A shop vacuum."

"Is a cleaning appliance more appealing to a man if *shop* is in the name?"

"Yes."

"In that case, the shop feather duster is in the hall closet. Also, I'd be okay with you using the shop vacuum on the dog hair on the couch, the shelves, and everywhere else it's appeared. Maybe not on Grandma's decorative pots and vases..."

His eyes narrowed. "These chores will help you make a protective talisman for me?"

"Oh, I'm positive. Especially the garbage. I noticed nobody's come by to collect it since I got here. I guess I have to call to take over the services and get on their route, huh?"

"You need to take the trash bin to the bottom of the driveway on Tuesday nights if you want it picked up."

"The bottom of the mile-long, pothole-filled driveway?"

"Yes." Amar pointed to his truck, the apparent transport mechanism. "That is how it is done in rural areas."

"Wow, the things that don't get mentioned in *Serene Country Living* magazine."

"Should you get parcels, you also need to pick them up at the post office. The mail person won't drive up here."

"Why not? Everyone else does."

"The house is more than a half mile from the mailbox. That is their rule."

"I guess it's a good thing I haven't had time for Etsy shopping lately." Not to mention that she didn't have any money coming in, so she needed to be frugal. This wasn't the time for buying cute vizsla mugs and dragon-shaped soaps.

"I will do the chores. You will craft." Amar strode into the house.

Huh. Not a bad deal. If she could do what she'd promised. She didn't want to disappoint him. Until he had protection from those witches, he would be at their whim to control—and turn against her.

17

In the root cellar, Morgen stood in front of a crucible on a workbench, her ingredients gathered and a sharp knife set aside to cut her finger when she came to that part. *The Talisman Enchiridion* lay open next to the silver necklace, and she'd read the recipe and the ritual several times as she waited for twilight to descend.

She'd also skimmed through numerous books that mentioned defensive wards, magical booby traps, and protective spells. She was still hunting for information on *thwarting* them. It was scant. Maybe witches didn't want to encourage other witches to destroy their defenses.

A scraping at the cellar doors made her jump.

It had been raining all evening, and she'd grown used to the patter of water hitting the wood, but this was something different. Had her owl friend returned? Her owl *familiar*?

Another scrape sounded, and Lucky sat up, his ears cocked. He'd been snoozing since the rain had started. Fortunately, she'd had a chance to walk him through the woods earlier, using the amble to rehearse the ritual in her mind, so he'd gotten plenty of exercise for the day.

As she reached for the door, an animal screech of fear—or pain—came from the other side. What sounded like claws scrabbling at wood followed, and then a thump.

Morgen hesitated, afraid she would open the door to talons slashing for her face. After another softer thump, the unusual sounds stopped, leaving only the patter of rain. She hoped Zorro hadn't dropped a dead rat or some other offering onto her threshold.

When she opened the door and peered warily around, she didn't see anything until she looked up. Zorro perched on an ornamental bracket supporting the eaves, hunkered there to stay out of the rain. If not for his lingering glow—did it seem to be fading?—she wouldn't have been able to pick him out in the dim lighting. Heavy clouds had rolled in, darkening the twilight sky even further.

A tentative squeak came from a tall clump of grass to the side of the door. Maybe there *was* a rat.

As she debated if she should get a lantern and try to find it, the wet grass rustled. A surprisingly long rodent ran out of the clump, down the steps, and between her legs.

Morgen squawked and almost pitched off the stairs. Lucky spotted the long brown creature and rushed after it, his tail thwacking her in the leg as he sped away.

The rodent squeaked as it sprinted across the pentagram and zigzagged between table legs. As Lucky chased it, he almost knocked over the workbench where Morgen had set everything up.

"Lucky!" She lunged after him, afraid he would destroy the place in his quest to catch their invader.

The long furry rodent reached a bookcase in the back and climbed to the top and out of canine reach. Lucky barked uproariously at it, rearing up on two legs and putting his paws on a shelf. Books tottered and threatened to fall out.

Morgen lunged in and grabbed his collar to pull him away. Three books fell from a top shelf. The rodent rose on *its* hind legs, its furry head almost brushing the ceiling as it complained about Lucky.

The lighting wasn't great up there—or anywhere in the root cellar—and it took Morgen a few seconds to realize their invader wasn't a rodent. It was a ferret. *Wendy's* ferret? She hadn't seen any others in town, and it wasn't as if they ran wild in the woods in Washington, but what was it doing here? Besides trying to get itself caught by both Lucky and Zorro?

Could a witch get in trouble if her familiar killed another witch's familiar?

"I'm not a witch yet," Morgen muttered, thinking of the letter. She hadn't applied to the coven or agreed to pay dues.

Even though she succeeded in pulling Lucky away from the bookcase, he kept barking, his tail wagging vigorously, as if he were in a field on the hunt for rabbits.

"That's a familiar." Morgen shifted to stand in front of him, blocking his view of the ferret and forcing him to focus on her. "You're not allowed to eat it. I think *you* may be a familiar now too, so you have to be on good behavior when it comes to witch things."

Normally, she wouldn't have been able to get him to pay attention to her, not when the prey he wanted to capture was in the room with them, and she expected to have to put him outside, but he surprised her by sitting on his haunches and looking up at her. That was his I'm-a-good-boy-and-you're-going-to-give-me-a-treat-right expression. He was usually happy to sit and give it to her, but not when he was distracted by squirrels, rodents, deer, and other enticing critters. This was unprecedented.

"Are you more obedient now that you're a familiar?" Morgen asked, though she still wanted to consult Phoebe about whether that was truly what the glow meant. As with the owl, Lucky's luminescence was fading. What would happen when it wore off? Would the animals still share visions with her? Wendy's ferret wasn't glowing.

Lucky cocked his head, ears perked hopefully.

Morgen dug a treat out of her pocket, gave it to him, and held up a hand. "Stay."

He knew that command, but it was another one she wouldn't have expected to work with such an intriguing distraction in the room.

The ferret chattered, as if to remind Lucky that he was there. Or that *she* was there? Morgen had no idea what sex it was.

Lucky's ears cocked, but he remained sitting.

Outside, the rain picked up, the patter turning into hammering at the doors. Somehow, Morgen sensed Zorro flying from the eaves to the barn and through one of the windows. He didn't send her a vision, so she wasn't sure how she knew, but she was positive Zorro had gone in to escape the storm.

Maybe that was the only reason the ferret had wanted to come inside the cellar. Its fur *was* damp. But that wouldn't explain why it had been in the area to start with. In the area and without its witch.

Before, it had been chattering at Lucky, but now that he was sitting, it dropped to all fours and peered at Morgen.

"Did you come to give me a message?" She thought of the envelope that the other witch—Judith—had taped to the door. That delivery method wouldn't likely work for a ferret. "Or did Wendy send you to spy on me, but you wanted in out of the rain?"

That seemed more likely, though a spy that revealed itself at the first hint of bad weather wouldn't be effective.

The ferret squeaked and sprang to a workbench. Lucky surged to his feet.

"Sit." Morgen pointed for him to plant his butt again, though she expected to have to grab his collar and bring out more treats to get the command to work.

Lucky hesitated, but then sat, though he emitted plaintive whines as the ferret hopped from workbench to counter to bookcase to circle back to the stairs without touching the ground. He went as far as he could, then chattered at the doors from atop an umbrella stand. He looked at Morgen, chattered, looked back at the door with his tail stuck straight out behind him, and chattered some more.

"Like a dog on point," Morgen muttered. "Do you want me to follow you somewhere?"

Barely able to hear her own words over the pounding of the rain, she had no intention of following anyone anywhere that night. The ferret, however, pointed insistently.

"If that's what you want," Morgen said, "I'll follow you out in the morning. Or once the storm passes." Not that she wanted to go anywhere in the middle of the night. "And after I finish the ritu—uhm, the project I'm working on."

She remembered Dr. Valderas's warning not to speak of her talisman plans with the other witches. Though she doubted a familiar could reveal the intricate details of what it overheard, the ferret might be sending a vision back to Wendy. If it had been sitting patiently and staring at her, instead of trying to get her to open the doors and follow it out, Morgen would have been positive her guess about it being a spy was correct.

"A project I'm not sure I should go forward with while there's a strange animal in the room," she said.

The idea of driving the ferret out into the rain seemed cruel, especially when Zorro might risk the weather to swoop down and try to capture it again, but what else could she do? Put it in the house? Would it raid the kitchen and destroy the furniture? It was too small to put in Lucky's crate, unfortunately. She also didn't know if the ferret would let her pick it up.

Lucky whined. He was still sitting, his eyes focused on her treat pocket. Clearly, he knew what a good boy he was being and expected more rewards.

As she slipped her hand into her pocket to retrieve a treat, the door opened. Morgen jumped. She must not have shut it all the way.

Amar strode in, rain dripping from his bare arms and hair. The ferret reeled back, leaped to another high bookcase, and screeched in displeasure.

Amar closed the door and looked blandly at it. "What is that?"

The ferret hissed at him.

"A critic of werewolves," Morgen said.

"Clearly." He growled at it.

The ferret scrunched low and stopped making noise, but it didn't look happy.

"I think it's Wendy's familiar," Morgen said.

"Oh? She must be nearby." Amar frowned at the door, as if he intended to charge back out into the rain to hunt for her.

"I'm not sure that's true. I have the feeling it wants us—or at least me—to follow it. Wendy might be in trouble."

"Those three witch sisters *are* trouble."

"I know, but when Wendy was here, she shared her disgruntlement with her sisters' recent choices. Maybe they weren't pleased by that rebellion."

"Rebellion? I thought her job was to keep you distracted while the others stole all of the moss from Wolf Wood."

Morgen shrugged. "I guess. I'm not sure. She was telling me things she wouldn't have had to if distracting me was her only intent. Maybe she genuinely doesn't approve of what her sisters have been up to."

"I think she was telling you tales to keep you interested but that it was all a trap, including luring you to the campground."

"That's because you're suspicious of all witches."

"Yes."

The ferret peeped in what might have been disapproval. Amar glowered at it.

"Is there any chance you can take it in the house or somewhere while I perform my... project?"

Amar arched his eyebrows.

"In case it's a spy," she whispered, though ferrets probably had excellent hearing.

"I assume he is."

"Which would be a good reason for you to take it—are you sure it's a *him*?—upstairs and put him in a safe place. Maybe the bathroom." How much trouble could a ferret get into in a small, enclosed space?

She'd no sooner had the thought than a memory of one of her sister-in-law's cats unwinding all of the toilet paper from the roll in their house came to mind.

"Maybe the garbage disposal," Amar said.

"That's mean. We're not killing a witch's familiar." She squinted at him. "Or *eating* it."

Never mind that Zorro had already tried to do exactly that.

"I'm already doing your chores," Amar said. "Garbage collection, dinner preparation, *dusting*." He squinted at her, as if that were the most onerous task.

For some reason, an image of him in wolf form swishing his tail back and forth over the end tables came to mind.

"I appreciate that. This small babysitting chore is the last thing I'll ask of you." Morgen shared her warmest smile with him.

Amar glanced at the necklace and ingredients, and she suspected he was only willing to housekeep because he wanted her to make the talisman for him. Mr. Mom, he was not.

"I will remove the ferret," Amar said, "so that he can't spy on you, but I came down here to protest *your* familiar using the barn inappropriately."

"Inappropriately? I think he catches mice in there. Isn't that an appropriate thing to do in a barn? Some people adopt feral cats specifically to keep outbuildings free of vermin."

Amar held up a long brown feather, his posture and his eyes accusatory. Thunder rumbled outside to add dramatic flair.

"Uhm?" Morgen asked.

"The owl is making a nest in a coat rack I'm building for a client and *molting* in the dresser drawers I painted this morning. They're supposed to be drying, not collecting dozens and dozens of owl feathers."

"Well, it's summer. I think owls molt in the summer."

"Not in the furniture I'm building."

"Maybe you can have that discussion with him. Zorro has pooped on me and spit up slimy owl pellets at my feet. We haven't yet reached the stage of our relationship where he respects me."

The ferret hissed at Amar.

"It's possible familiars aren't as obedient and useful as the stories about witches have led us to believe," Morgen said.

Amar growled at the ferret, then reached up and picked him up around his long middle. Morgen hoped the creature wouldn't bite him. Werewolves were likely accustomed to being respected by all the animals they met.

Instead of biting him, the ferret went impressively limp, his eyes closed and both ends dangling from Amar's hand. He looked like one of Lucky's toys after he'd ripped out the squeaker and all of the stuffing.

"Is he... playing dead?" Morgen didn't think Amar had squeezed the ferret.

"Yes. Melodramatically." He headed for the door and added over his shoulder, "Do the stories about witches mention that?"

"I'm actually not that well read on familiars. I'll consult some of Grandma's books and get back to you."

Amar grunted and walked back out into the rain as more thunder rumbled.

Lucky dropped to his belly, his head on his paws, and watched the door. Sad that the evil ferret had escaped before he could pounce on him?

Morgen shook her head and turned back to the workbench. It was dark enough outside now that she could get started.

"Amar is being a good guy by helping out with things," she told Lucky. "I have to make this talisman work. One way or another."

18

Morgen sprinkled in two pinches of dried mugwort and an eighth of a teaspoon of horny goat weed powder, then stirred the concoction slowly over the electric Bunsen burner warming the bottom of the small cauldron. Candles and crackling wood fires seemed more witchy, but Morgen had found the heating element while she'd been inventorying the root cellar. Apparently, Grandma had used some modern tools for her work.

Her index finger stung, a rag pressed to the bleeding cut. She'd already added the six drops of a witch's blood that the recipe called for but was waiting to put on a bandage until she figured out if she needed more—or if she'd screwed up the recipe and would have to start over. Save for the spores she'd laboriously scraped out of the cap of her freshly picked mushroom, the ingredients had all been in vials or jars with plenty inside. It wouldn't be the end of the world if she had to try again. As long as the stuff didn't harden and stick to the jewelry in such a way that she couldn't melt it out again. Even though she hadn't added anything like resin or honey, it had a viscous consistency that reminded her of those things. It would probably harden into a rock.

"Positive thoughts," she urged herself. "This will work."

The concoction in the little cauldron came to a boil, the scent unpleasantly similar to burning hair. Morgen stirred it for another minute, per the recipe's instructions, before removing it from the heat. Feeling like a metallurgist, she tipped the cauldron and dribbled the mixture into the indention in the circular medallion—the *receptacle*—on one of the two silver necklaces.

"A naked metallurgist," she muttered, the damp air of the cellar chill on her bare butt.

She hoped Amar didn't wander in again. Hopefully, he was too busy dusting and discussing with the ferret what he could make for dinner for a vegetarian.

Despite taking care, Morgen spilled several droplets on the workbench. Enough made it into the medallion to fill the shallow receptacle, but she worried that wasting some of the concoction would keep the magic from working. According to the book, the substance was supposed to glow red with *the power of the witch's blood* as it hardened, only losing the glow once the talisman was completely infused with magic.

Morgen set the cauldron down and rested both hands on the workbench as she stared at the medallion, willing it to glow. It didn't.

She glanced at the recipe to confirm that it should have been doing that by now. Maybe she was just making a mess, pretending to be a witch and a crafter. Or maybe this was all hokum. If she hadn't experienced visions and watched a witch take control of Amar and force him to try to kill her, she might have believed that, but by now, she'd seen too much to dismiss magic as nonexistent.

An intense longing for this to work, and for her to be good at *making* it work, rose up in her. Not only did she want to succeed for Amar's sake, but she wanted to be an adequate witch. Maybe even *more* than adequate. It already looked like she had no shot of fitting in with the community—the coven—here, but she hadn't found many places in her life where she did fit in, so that wasn't surprising. She was used to being the one on the outside, being talked about instead of having a tight circle of friends. It wasn't that bad when she was *good* at what she was doing so she knew the taunts had little merit, but the idea of being the bumbling witch who couldn't even get the respect of a familiar chagrined her. She envisioned walking into the Crystal Parlor as the Bellrock residents tittered and pointed at her.

The magical resin still wasn't glowing, and Morgen forced the dumb thoughts from her mind. This was about helping Amar, not her own insecurities. She had to focus on that.

"Wait, maybe I really *do* need to focus on that." She flipped back to the previous page in the book, the part that described the recipe and how the talisman would be stronger if the witch who made it cared about the person who would be the recipient. "But how do I use magic—or blood or spores—to convey to this gunk that I care?"

A peal of thunder sounded above the house, and the ceiling shivered. Lucky had gone back to snoozing beside her workbench, but he bolted upright and whined.

"Just a storm, buddy," Morgen assured him.

He slunk over to the side of the cellar and hid under one of the counters.

An impressive summer storm was raging outside. Morgen was glad the house was built on top of a hill so she wouldn't have to worry about flooding. Other than in the laundry room with the leaky roof. Hopefully, she and Amar could find time to repair that as soon as he finished with the barn.

"Just need to make sure he survives his encounter with the Loups. And the witches." Morgen gazed down at the resin, willing it to glow to indicate that she'd been successful in making a talisman, willing it to turn into a powerful protective amulet that would keep anyone from controlling Amar ever again.

Though she hadn't known him for long, she appreciated how much he'd helped her. He was more of a guide for her than any of the witches in town had been. She'd had to bribe Phoebe to answer her questions, and labor for hours in her store, but Amar was simply helping her because she was Grandma's granddaughter. He'd done *more* than help her at Calista's estate, risking his life to battle a werewolf so she could get away. And he'd fought hard to resist the power of the witches who'd wanted him to hurt her. He'd done a lot for her, even though she didn't think she was that deserving of his loyalty, and she wanted to help him now. She cared about him and hated that others wanted to hurt him and turn him into a mindless minion.

The resin glowed a soft red, like magma in an underground lava tube.

Morgen started to let out a triumphant whoop, but in case her thoughts were influencing it, she kept focusing on Amar and how he would use the talisman to protect himself from those who wanted to use him. And how she *wanted* him to be able to do that, because she cared. She wasn't sure she could voice that to him, but as long as the talisman and the magic knew, maybe that was enough.

The glow continued for several minutes, then gradually faded as the magical resin cooled and hardened. She waited to touch it, not wanting to leave a big fingerprint in the amulet, and pulled out the other necklace. Could she make a talisman for herself? It seemed like a good idea, but she didn't know if the magic would work if she thought about how much she cared about *herself*. She'd never been very good at that.

Something heavier than rain banged at the doors. Lots of somethings. Hail?

Lucky whined from under the workbench.

"For a witch's familiar, you're not very brave." Ready to retreat to the more insulated house, Morgen grabbed her clothes and started dressing. "I bet Zorro isn't worried about thunder."

The owl was probably busy preening himself and molting in Amar's dresser drawers.

Another peal of thunder erupted overhead, rattling jars on shelves, and more bangs sounded at the doors. From the cellar, Morgen couldn't hear the hail hitting the roof, but the pellets sounded large and hard. She hoped they weren't doing damage. With the moss gone, along with her plan of making money from selling it, she didn't know how she would pay for extensive repairs to the house.

As she zipped up her hoodie, more thunder boomed, and one of the doors opened. The light in the cellar went out, plunging Morgen into darkness. Lightning flashed, outlining a large dark figure standing at the top of the stairs.

She gasped and grabbed the knife she'd used to cut her finger.

"It's me," Amar called, his voice barely audible over the hail hammering down outside.

He turned and shut the door, leaving them both in the dark. Morgen suspected the electricity to the house had gone out, not that her lightbulb had burned out. A quick check confirmed that the electric Bunsen burner didn't work either. Well, at least she'd finished her project before the power went out.

"Have you come to romance me?" Morgen patted on the workbench for the talisman, wanting to give it to him to try. They should test it, though she wasn't sure how.

"What?" Amar sounded startled.

"It was a joke. In novels, the squabbling hero and heroine are often forced to find shelter during a storm. They inevitably lose power, have to make a fire and cuddle for warmth, and then somehow end up in each other's pants."

"Are these the same novels where the guy holds the woman's hair while she pukes?"

"Yeah, authors get bonus points if they work in as many popular tropes as possible."

"I came to tell you that the ferret is in a cage and likes the green chips in the bag on the kitchen counter."

"You fed my expensive avocado crisps to some other witch's familiar?"

"He fed them to himself while I was looking for a cage."

"Ugh. Did he make a mess?"

"Yes, but I brought in the shop vacuum. It slurped up the broken chips and shredded pieces of bag that he left everywhere." Amar paused. "Also a small paring knife that I didn't notice until it thunked into the canister."

Morgen rubbed her face. This was not the typical conversation that the hero and heroine in a romance novel had before their storm-induced make-out sessions.

"On second thought," she said, "don't dust. I'll handle that later. In other news, I've finished the talisman. I hope. It glowed, as promised in the recipe, so I found that encouraging, but we should test it." She held it out in the direction of his voice.

With the doors closed, it was pitch dark in the cellar.

"Good." Amar came closer. "I want to show you something first."

"That might be hard right now." She started to reach for her phone, but he spoke again.

"Hold out your hand."

"All right." She did so, then let out a startled squawk when he laid something icy cold and wet in it. "Is this a snowball?"

"A hailstone. They're all over the yard. They're the size of elk balls."

"I, er, *what* balls? No, never mind." She didn't want to hear about the testicles of the animals he hunted.

"Elk *meat*balls," he said dryly. "Stuffed with mozzarella. One of my cousins makes them on the grill."

"Oh."

"They're amazing."

"I'll take your word for it. They don't sound very vegetarian."

He paused. "You could eat the sauce."

"I enjoy meals of only sauce. Very filling."

"It's a red-wine tomato sauce. With basil. You can eat basil, right?"

"If it's a leaf and edible, I can eat it. That doesn't sound like something a grill-master werewolf would make." She'd come across a similar-sounding sauce in one of her fancy vegetarian cookbooks. It was supposed to go with pasta and meatless meatballs, not ground elk.

"José Antonio thinks he's a chef. When he's not laying tile, he spends a lot of time watching cooking shows on PBS. Though the elk balls came from a guy who specializes in game recipes. He has a YouTube channel."

"Nonetheless, for future reference, most people would compare hail to golf balls." She set the chunk of ice on the workbench and wiped her palm as another peal of thunder sounded.

"I don't golf."

"But you eat elk balls."

"Avidly. I brought it in because I think it—the hail—might be magical. You don't see hailstones like that in this part of the country. Or any part of the country where God doesn't hate the inhabitants."

Magical... hailstones? How would she tell?

"The storm is also peculiarly focused on Wolf Wood and this hilltop in particular," Amar said. "It's clear out over the Strait."

"Manipulating weather seems advanced for witches. Or anyone. If I found out there was a spell to conjure up storms, I'd feel compelled to dedicate my witchly life to helping put out wildfires."

"I would guess the storm was brewing, and someone nudged it and refocused it."

"Over Grandma's house? To what end? Scaring me? Damaging the roof?"

"It cracked the windshield on my truck."

Morgen grimaced. That probably meant her little electric car had golf-ball—or elk-ball—sized divots all over it. As Amar had pointed out, it wasn't exactly farm-tough.

She shined her phone's flashlight on the hailstone and touched it again. The temperature had dropped as the storm came in, and it wasn't melting quickly, but it appeared normal. Just large.

Nothing happened when she touched it, and she was about to shrug and return to the talisman when she remembered that some magical items zapped her if she wasn't wearing her grandmother's amulet for protection.

She removed it and pressed a finger to the hailstone. It didn't buzz her with the intensity of the magical lock on the cellar doors, but a faint tingle ran up her arm. She pulled back, abruptly much more uneasy about the storm. What if it could do more than crack windshields? A tornado couldn't pop out of a thunderstorm and swallow an entire house... could it?

"May I try the talisman?" Amar asked.

"Yes, of course. We might be stuck down here all night, so there's time for you to try everything in the cellar."

"Like what? Gwen's motorcycle helmet?"

She'd meant potions and herbs and the like but said, "There's a tie-dye shawl hanging beside it that you might look cute in."

Amar didn't deign to answer that, instead slipping the talisman over his head. The chain was long enough that it didn't need to be clasped and unclasped, and the circular medallion rested between his pecs.

Morgen shined her flashlight over it. The murky, dark-red

resin hardened in the center wasn't the epitome of fashion. Now that it had stopped glowing, a stranger wouldn't suspect it of having any unique qualities, but when she lifted a finger to touch it, a strong buzz of energy rocketed through her. She stumbled backward.

"Maybe you should keep that amulet on," Amar said, dry again.

"I had to test it."

"At risk of personal injury."

"Everyone appreciates a thorough product tester."

Morgen put the amulet back on, her fingers still tingling. It didn't seem right that something she'd made could shock her, but anything with magical energy seemed to do that if she wasn't wearing protection. Maybe that was how young children born into witch families first discovered that they had witch blood. By being electrocuted by random magical objects lying around the house.

"Can you tell if it'll protect me from being controlled?" Amar asked, his eyes intent.

"I don't know how to test for that."

"Chant the werewolf-control incantation, and try to get me to do something."

She grimaced. "I would prefer not to use that on you again."

And she thought *he* would prefer that as well.

"It's the only way to test it," Amar said. "I need to know if it works before confronting those witches."

"I know but..." Morgen looked glumly at her phone lying on the workbench, its harsh flashlight beam shining toward the ceiling. After he'd been so upset about being controlled, and witches in general, she was reluctant to use the incantation on him. Thanks to Calista, Morgen knew what it was like to have someone control her and knew that she felt residual resentment—even loathing—toward the woman for it. True, Calista had wanted her to fly a gyrocopter into a ditch and die, and it wasn't as if Morgen would even ask Amar to do something unpleasant, but he always seemed close to disliking her because of her blood. She would hate to give him more reason to find her unappealing. “I wish there was someone else who could do it. Someone you already hate. Maybe Wendy will come to collect her ferret, and she’ll spell you up.”

“I believe the ferret wants to lead us to where we can collect *her*.” Amar tilted his head.

He hadn’t stepped back after delivering the hailstone, and he was close enough that she could have leaned forward and rested her head on his shoulder. Or maybe run her fingers down the muscles of his bare arms. Or both.

To distract herself from such thoughts, she grabbed her phone to look for an app that would provide less harsh light. She found an *ambient firelight* program and downloaded it. The storm kept railing outside, and the lightbulb wasn’t so much as flickering with the promise of power returning, but at least the cell signal hadn’t died.

“Why do you hesitate, Morgen?” Amar asked.

“I don’t want you to hate me.” She looked up, intending to meet his eyes, but her gaze stopped at his collarbones. Eyes were so intimate. “Like you do every other witch.”

“I’m requesting this, so it wouldn’t make sense for me to feel that way.”

“I know, but Calista cast one of those control spells on me, and I kind of hate her now.”

“She’s vile and killed the boyfriend she was using for his money. You’re supposed to hate her.”

Morgen shrugged. Didn’t Amar think *all* witches were vile? He didn’t like Phoebe any more than the rest of them, and Phoebe had been helping Morgen.

“When did she use that spell on you?” Amar asked, his voice softening.

"Before you came into the garage. She tried to get me to sign away Grandma's property."

"I'm relieved you didn't."

"Me too. It was hard to resist. When I wouldn't sign, she tried to get me to climb into her gyrocopter and fly it into a gorge so I would crash and die. Your entry was fortuitous."

"I didn't know that."

Morgen shrugged. She hadn't told him. It had been enough that she'd managed to resist Calista's compulsion, even if she'd had a few dreams—nightmares—reliving that experience. In them, she hadn't always been able to resist, and Amar hadn't always shown up in time.

"You understand then," he said, "what it is like to have one of them control you, to act as a puppet master making you act out their whims and desires. Forcing you to do horrible things." Amar lifted his hand and touched the back of her head, letting his fingers slide through her hair. "You may have witch blood, but you are more like one of us."

A shiver went through her at the words or at his touch, or maybe both. She held still as he stroked her hair, afraid he would stop if she stirred. She didn't want him to stop.

"You know what it is like to be an outcast," he added, his voice gentle.

Did he consider himself an outcast from his pack? Or were werewolves outsiders in general?

It didn't matter. She did understand.

"Yeah," she whispered, staring at the digital flames flickering on her phone instead of looking at him.

Again, she thought of stepping closer and leaning against him, but that wouldn't be a good idea. Just because he was touching her hair didn't mean he wanted a relationship with her. And she hadn't come to Bellrock looking for a relationship with a werewolf —or anyone. She was here to figure out her life, what she was supposed to do now that the future she'd always envisioned had been shattered. Besides, she was sure Amar still had feelings for Maria. A middle-aged database programmer with witch blood had to be a distant second to the vivacious werewolf woman.

"Say the words for the incantation." Amar's fingers slipped through her hair to massage her scalp.

All right, that felt *amazing*. Her eyes rolled back in her head, and despite her resolution not to get closer, she found herself inching over, lifting a hand to his chest as she leaned against him. Maybe he was trying to control *her*, not with magic but with his touch, trying to convince her to do what he wanted. If so, she could hardly blame him.

And it wasn't as if she minded this, being pressed against his powerful body. He'd mostly dried since coming in from the storm, but his vest was still damp. That didn't keep her from feeling the warmth of his skin or noticing his distinct scent through the leather. He smelled of cedar and pine mingled with… she wasn't quite sure what. Werewolf pheromones. Whatever those were. Maybe someone would make a cologne one day.

"I need to know if this works," Amar said.

"I know. All right." Morgen licked her lips and took a deep breath, though she was tempted to stall so he would keep rubbing her head. But that wouldn't be right. Withholding her magic when he wanted it would be a different kind of control. She gripped her grandmother's amulet and whispered, "Under the moon's magic, turn the snarling hound from angry foe to witch bound."

Amar didn't remove his fingers from her head, but they stopped their massage, stopped sending warm tingles through her.

"Order me to do something," he said.

Kiss me, she thought but didn't voice the words. That would be as bad as Calista ordering her to sign away the property, to do something she dearly didn't want to do. Maybe Amar wouldn't *hate* kissing her, but if it wasn't of his own volition, it wouldn't mean anything. Except that she was an ass.

"Turn off the fire app. This is way too much romantic ambiance, and I'm likely to tear your vest off any second." Morgen made her tone light to make it clear it was a joke, but it wasn't that much of a joke.

The talisman on Amar's chest briefly glowed dark red.

"Tear it off and do what?" he rumbled and resumed stroking her hair. He didn't reach for her phone.

Was he wrestling with the command? Or had he not felt any coercion at all?

Morgen looked up, meeting his eyes for the first time. He was gazing down at her, and a zing of electricity—or was that magic?—ran through her.

"Did it work?" she whispered.

"I felt your power when you said the words and a hint of compulsion to obey, but then there was warmth on my chest where the talisman touches me, and it helped me override the spell."

His eyes seemed to flare with some inner light—inner satisfaction—and his face assumed the most satisfied, contented expression she'd seen from him. Her grumpy werewolf was pleased.

"Deep down," he said, "I doubted that you would do it, give me the power to resist a command from a witch. To resist *your* command."

"I'm not a general." Morgen frowned, not wanting to have this discussion again. "I never wanted to command anyone."

"So you said, but few witches would give up the ability to have a werewolf at their beck and call. They say they only wish to defend themselves, but it is easy for them to justify using one of our kind to further their interests." His eyes narrowed. "Once they get a taste of power, they long for more. They crave it."

Morgen started to step back, not liking where the conversation had gone, but he wrapped his arms around her.

“You are different,” Amar said, his eyes fierce now but not angry. “You have given me a great gift.”

She didn’t know what to say. She didn’t regret making it for him, but what if he used it to take revenge? Not only against Calista and Olivia but against all of the witches who’d ever wronged the werewolves? Or against all of the witches in town?

She opened her mouth, tempted to ask him to promise not to do that, but he leaned down and kissed her.

19

This time, there weren't any other witches around, and Amar's new talisman would have protected him against attempts to control him, regardless. That meant his kiss wasn't out of coercion, wasn't because he was trying to delay Morgen or keep from doing something unpleasant to her. It was because... he wanted to do it.

All of the concerns that had been springing up in her mind tumbled off a cliff as she wrapped her arms around Amar and kissed him back. It had been a long time since she'd kissed a man like this, her body full of passion and desire. Hell, had it ever been like this? She was a rational woman, not someone prone to fits of fervor, and she hadn't thought she was the type of person to inspire such feelings in others.

But Amar was clearly pleased with his gift—with *her*—and pulled her tight, his hand sliding down her back to cup her ass, to keep her pressed against him. Not that she had plans to go anywhere. Morgen slid her hands over his shoulders and locked them behind his neck, thoughts of wrapping her legs around him flirting with her mind. The witches' thunderstorm be damned.

She and Amar were safe down here. Too bad Grandma hadn't put a couch in the cellar...

Morgen's phone rang, startling them both. She broke the kiss to glance over, intending to ignore the call unless it was Phoebe or someone she was worried about.

Her sister's name and number lit up the screen. Her sister who was in the hospital in Borneo with a deadly illness.

"I have to take that," she said, more than a little breathless.

How was she supposed to have a conversation with her sister when Amar's warm hand had slid under her shirt and was sliding up to cup her—

"Go ahead," he rumbled, his lips switching from her mouth to nibble at her earlobe. With a little nip, he sent a blast of pleasure straight to her core.

Oh man, she couldn't speak with her dispassionate sister when all she wanted was to enjoy Amar's touch, to let him continue doing exactly what he was doing... and more. Maybe she could call back in a few minutes. Or a few hours.

No, Sian was sick. Morgen would regret it if she didn't answer and it turned out that her sister had gotten worse. What if this was her only opportunity to talk to Sian again?

Reluctantly, Morgen pulled her hands from Amar's shoulders to reach for the phone. Like a drunk person trying to convince others she was sober, she cleared her throat and answered as normally as she could.

"Hi, Sian. Are you okay?"

"I have Dengue Fever, with symptoms not limited to but including vomiting, stomach pain, bleeding nose and gums, and fatigue. I am not okay." Sian's voice was weak and hard to hear over the rain and hail still pounding at the house.

Morgen thumbed up the volume as high as it would go. "Are you still in the hospital? Can I do anything?"

Amar must have heard Sian's words, for he paused and didn't

make further advances on her earlobe—or up her shirt. Morgen would have gone somewhere private for the call, but she didn't want to walk out into the storm or send *Amar* out into the storm. And if she was honest, she didn't want him to go away. He returned to stroking the back of her head, the gesture supportive, touching.

"You cannot," Sian said. "But I had some thoughts about your werewolves and was moved to call."

"My... werewolves?" Morgen looked at Amar. "I thought you didn't believe in werewolves."

Amar emitted a soft grunt and twitched his eyebrows.

"I am not inclined to do so, having never seen a werewolf nor read about any in respected scientific journals." Sian managed to sound clinical even when she was sick and weary. "As I mentioned, I have considered the possibility that you've developed a mental condition or taken up delusion-inducing drugs to cope with the various crises in your life."

The main crisis in her life currently was that Amar's hand wasn't squeezing her ass anymore.

"I have also considered the remote possibility that you are in your right mind. Hence, I have called to deliver advice."

"On werewolves?"

"On wolves occupying the same territory. You will recall that I said such was unlikely."

"I do recall that, yes." Morgen wondered if this willingness to consider werewolves meant that *Sian* was the one on drugs. Morgen had no idea what the typical treatment for Dengue Fever was, but maybe something was making her sister loopy.

"It's likely that something there draws them," Sian said. "Good hunting grounds or maybe the fudge shop."

Morgen blinked. Her sister *was* loopy. "Is that a joke?"

"Yes. It could be the crystal shop."

"It's not that. A witch owns that, and the werewolves are super not into witches." Morgen brushed her hand through Amar's scruffy hair.

He raised his brows. Asking if he should leave her alone? She let her hand fall to his shoulder and gripped it. There wasn't anywhere for him to go, and if the conversation didn't offend him, she didn't want to shoo him away. What was he supposed to do? Join Lucky under a counter?

The thought made her glance toward the spot where she'd last seen the dog. She felt a twinge of guilt since she'd forgotten he was in the cellar.

Lucky had curled into a tight ball with his thin tail over his closed eyes. He doubtless wanted the storm to be over, but at least he wasn't whining or shaking anymore.

"The witches, right," Sian said in a tone that suggested she was already trying hard to accept werewolves and didn't want to contemplate other magical beings.

"They can control the werewolves with magic," Morgen said. "That's the reason, or one of the reasons, the werewolves don't like them."

Amar nodded firmly.

"Interesting." It didn't sound sarcastic this time. "I assume that's unpleasant."

Amar gave another firm nod.

"Yes," Morgen said. "And I know what draws the werewolves to the area. It's Wolf Wood."

"Wolf what?"

"The woods around Grandma's house. They have some, ah, special attributes. Like magic. The other night, I spotted wolves rolling around next to mushrooms that spit spores into the air when their caps are brushed. They were like out-of-control cats in the 'nip."

That earned a glower instead of a nod from Amar. Maybe he visited that mushroom patch himself.

"There's also a spring that's rumored to have rejuvenating benefits," Morgen continued. "It causes some of the moss and mushrooms around it to glow." Or it had before the witch sisters had stripped away all the moss...

"The witches created those places?" Sian asked.

"I'm not sure. It may all be natural, and that's what originally drew the witches to Bellrock too. Apparently, they were here first. The werewolves came later, and some were dicks to the townspeople, so the witches did some magic to protect the citizens." Judging from Amar's continuing glower, that wasn't the truth, at least not as he believed it. "That's what the vet and one of the witches said anyway," Morgen amended. "I don't know the whole story or who's right, just that the packs don't get along and fight with each other while the witches... I don't know. I guess they're getting what they want. The wolves seem to be more focused on each other than on them or the citizens."

Amar looked like he wanted to protest that, but with his impending duel coming up, maybe he couldn't.

"You know the old saying," Sian said. "Divide and rule."

"I don't think the witches are *ruling* exactly," Morgen said but paused, mulling over the expression, including its origins in Ancient Greece and how often it continued to play out in modern times. "I suppose it *is* possible they're fomenting some of the discord to keep the werewolves focused on squabbling with each other instead of joining forces and turning on *them*."

This time, Morgen raised her own eyebrows, wondering if Amar had ever considered that. All of the werewolves seemed to hate witches even more than they hated each other. It was almost surprising that the two packs hadn't banded together to *ensure* the witches couldn't control them. One way or another.

"They don't get involved in our pack politics," Amar muttered, though his expression was more thoughtful than defiant at the idea. "Or goad us to attack each other. Not that I've ever noticed. We're not fools. We would see through that."

Sian must have heard him, for she asked, "Who is that?"

"A werewolf," Morgen said. "He has opinions."

Amar snorted.

"It need not be blatant manipulation," Sian said. "You're familiar with all the rat studies on shock-induced aggression?"

"Uh, no."

"Your technology-focused education was woefully inadequate."

Morgen rolled her eyes. Leave it to her sister to be pompous even when she was sick. Someday, Morgen would love to challenge her to some academic competition at which she excelled, but Sian was even more of a *mathlete* than she, and asking her to write database queries hardly seemed fair.

"Sum it up for me so I don't have to turn off the flickering fireplace app on my phone." Morgen decided not to mention that she and Amar were enjoying the ambiance. "The power went out."

"In the past, scientists performed numerous studies where they placed a single rat in a cage and administered shocks in such a way that the rat couldn't escape them."

Morgen curled a lip. This was why she was *glad* her degree hadn't included a lot of science classes. She hated reading about animal cruelty.

"The rat would naturally be distressed and have a negative reaction," Sian continued, "but when it was alone in the cage, it eventually stopped doing anything and simply endured the pain. However, when a second rat was introduced and the shocks were given to both, they would react to the pain by attacking each other. Sometimes even killing each other."

"I assume you're implying the shocks need not be literal." Morgen was positive the werewolves would have noticed the witches charging after them with tasers.

"I am simply educating you on the existence of such studies and their results. If you wish to make inferences, you may do so. But I will posit that having two wolf packs in one territory competing for resources may be stressful enough to them to prompt an uncharacteristically aggressive reaction. In the wild, it is natural for wolf packs to avoid each other and not encroach on each other's territories."

Amar's expression had grown thoughtful again.

"I see," Morgen said. "Thank you."

"You are welcome."

"You didn't say if you need anything. Are you getting better?"

Sian hesitated.

"I can send bamboo underwear if that will help. Or fudge. Or a witch talisman that protects against mind manipulation." Morgen smiled. Maybe she *could* make a talisman for her sister, something that might help with illness.

But would Sian wear it? Maybe if Morgen could shape it into an orangutan. Or possibly a unicorn. As a little girl, Sian had watched *The Last Unicorn* even more often than she'd watched *Goonies*, and she'd read the book almost as many times. That had been decades ago, but Morgen was fairly certain some of Sian's bamboo underwear featured unicorns.

"The mail service here is slow," Sian surprised her by saying instead of claiming no interest in gifts.

"That's disappointing."

"Yes." Sian hesitated, then quietly added, "I miss Mom."

"Me too." Morgen blinked as tears came to her eyes, not only because their mother had passed away but because admitting to having feelings was so uncharacteristic for her sister that Morgen worried she truly was dying. The lecture didn't mean anything. If anyone was capable of lecturing on science experiments while on her deathbed, it was Sian.

A female voice spoke in the background in a language Morgen couldn't understand.

"I'm told I need to rest," Sian said. "Never mind that it's the middle of the day here. Apparently, I look wan."

"I hear that happens to sick people."

"Indeed. Enjoy your werewolf."

Morgen didn't know what to say to that—was her sister implying something sexual or just being sarcastic since she didn't believe in werewolves?—but Sian hung up before she had to come up with a reply. Morgen frowned at the phone, wondering if she should leave everything she was doing here, try to get a flight to Borneo, and visit her sister. Could Americans even travel there on a whim? Sian had needed to get a bunch of vaccinations well in advance of flying to the tropics. By the time Morgen was able to get to Borneo, would it be too late?

With her throat tight, Morgen wiped moisture from her eyes. "Damn it, Sian, why didn't you use more mosquito repellent?"

She looked at Amar, no longer in the mood for kissing, but not sure how to tell him. He was gazing toward the doors, as if he was contemplating something else now too. Shock-induced werewolf aggression, perhaps?

A distant howl reached Morgen's ears and sent a shiver down her spine. Why would a wolf—a werewolf?—be hunting on a night like this? The hail had stopped, but rain still pattered at the doors, and the wind railing at the house promised the storm hadn't abated much.

"Is that someone you know?" Morgen asked, though she had no idea if the werewolves could tell each other apart at a distance by their howls.

"Yes," Amar said shortly.

"Are they going to the mushroom patch?"

"No."

"Is it your pack or the Loups?" Morgen assumed it was one or the other, not random wolves coming to check out the house.

That question Amar didn't answer. He merely squinted at the doors and listened to the howling.

"They're not coming here, are they?" She couldn't imagine why either the Lobos or the Loups would. This wasn't the time to come by with a detailed bid for the remodeling work.

More howls floated out from the trees. Lucky lifted his head and whined uncertainly. It sounded like there was more than one wolf out there.

"They are." Amar stepped away from Morgen and walked toward the doors.

"Wait, where are you going? Don't go out there."

"I must." The look Amar slanted back over his shoulder said he didn't feel that he had a choice.

Why? Because the wolves would break down the doors and burst into the cellar to attack them—to attack *her*?—if he didn't?

"No." Morgen ran after him and lifted a hand. "Those doors are ensorcelled, remember? They won't be able to get in, even if that's what they have in mind."

"I must because I'm not a coward." He avoided her hand by striding up the steps. "I won't hide."

20

MORGEN GLIMPSED RAIN SLASHING SIDEWAYS OUTSIDE BEFORE AMAR shut the root-cellar doors firmly behind him. That he refused to hide from the incoming wolves, and that he wanted her to stay there, told her what he hadn't admitted out loud. That wasn't his pack coming. It was the Loups.

But why?

Amar's duel with their pack leader wasn't supposed to be until the night after this.

Morgen charged up the steps and opened a door to peek out. A lone gray-and-black wolf stood between the house and the barn and looked across the lawn toward the woods. Amar's clothing was draped over one of the mirrors on his truck, but the silver talisman hung around his neck. She was surprised he hadn't taken it off before shifting forms but glad the change hadn't broken it.

Though he must have heard her open the door, Amar kept facing the woods. Between the darkness and the rain, it took Morgen a long moment to pick out anyone over there. Then she saw the eyes.

Several sets of amber and yellow eyes glowered out from

between the trees. They seemed to glow with inner light, as if this were some cartoon rendition of *Little Red Riding Hood*. Had the wolves done something to themselves to grant them extra power? If so, that hardly seemed fair. But with so many of the Loups here, they couldn't have shown up for any *fair* reason.

One prowled out of the woods, a big black wolf that was even larger than Amar.

Amar stood his ground, his head low and his hackles raised as it walked across the lawn toward him. Was this Lucien? The leader of the Loup pack? The wolf he was supposed to duel?

"That he's supposed to duel *tomorrow*, damn it." Morgen wanted to demand to know what the Loups were doing here, but they couldn't have answered questions even if she'd asked, not when they were wolves instead of men.

She pulled out her phone as a gust of wind spattered her face with rain. The screen lit up, and the glow must have been noticeable from across the driveway. Several sets of those eerie eyes turned toward her. The wolves didn't have to speak to convey a message to her. Something about the unearthly glow of their eyes made her certain they were warning her to stay out of this—or she'd be next.

Three more Loups slunk out of the trees. They advanced behind their leader as the big black wolf continued toward Amar.

Morgen couldn't stand back and do nothing, especially if they were going to cheat and this wouldn't be a fair fight. But what could she do? Use her werewolf-control incantation? On which one? The leader? She feared it would only work on one wolf, if it worked at all. The others would know right away that she'd used it and charge at her. Could she keep repeating it and try to ensorcel the whole pack?

She doubted it, but if this turned into a bloodbath, she would have to try. She wrapped her fingers around her amulet, the star medallion warm in her palm, tempted to try the incantation on the leader right now.

But Amar would resent that. He would call it witch trickery unless it was clear that the Loups had broken the rules first. Even then, he might be angry and say using magic wasn't honorable. Not that Morgen would care. Not if it saved his life.

The black wolf stopped on the gravel driveway twenty feet away from Amar and growled at him. Amar growled back and crouched, ready to charge into battle. But he glanced at the other wolves. The whole pack hadn't come out of the trees, but the three lieutenants, or whatever the wolves called each other, had. They were close enough to get in the way of the fight. Or close enough to join in and gang up on him.

Morgen wished there was a way to get in touch with the Lobos. Even if Amar was estranged from them, Pedro had said he would come for this battle.

"If he'd been told the right night," she muttered, glaring at the black wolf.

None of the Loups glanced over. They were too focused on Amar. It looked like all four of them would spring at him.

Realizing she *did* have Pedro's number, Morgen ducked back into the cellar. Before throwing away his business card, she'd taken a photo of it and filed it away, just in case. She brought up the picture and dialed his number as the growls grew louder outside.

She had no idea how much posturing the wolves would do before getting physical, but she worried it wouldn't last long enough for the Lobos to arrive. Where in town or the woods did they live? Amar had mentioned the Loups' log lodge but not where his own pack resided.

As she waited for Pedro to pick up, something bumped her leg. Lucky. He'd crawled out from under the counter, but his tail was clenched as he listened to the growls. If Morgen had a tail, she would have clenched it too. The growls were worse than the wind and rain still hammering the house.

"*¿Qué?*" came the terse greeting when Pedro picked up his phone.

"This is Morgen Keller," she whispered. "Amar is in trouble."

"What and where?" Pedro asked, thankfully not dismissing her as an unreliable informant or, worse, saying he didn't care.

"My place. The Loups. They're—"

The growls escalated to snarls, and a thud sounded as the wolves came together. The duel had begun.

"—fighting," she finished.

"I thought that was tomorrow."

"So did I."

"We'll come." Pedro hung up before she could ask when or how far away they lived.

A lupine yelp of pain came from above. Morgen grabbed the antler staff and ran back up the steps. She was afraid to watch the fight, afraid Amar would be hurt, but if the others ganged up on him, and he needed help, she would crack the bastards over their heads.

Before she'd taken more than a step out of the cellar, the black wolf rolled past, as if he'd been blasted out of a cannon. Amar chased after him. The black sprang to his feet before he reached him and managed to turn and lunge at Amar. They came together with another thud, chests colliding as their jaws snapped for each other's throats.

The three lieutenants stalked after them, coming close to Morgen, though they were focused on the fight. They hadn't attacked Amar yet, but they looked like they would. If it was clear their leader was losing?

"Stay back," Morgen warned them, gripping the staff like a spear and turning the antlers toward them. Rain glistened on the tips.

Two of the wolves ignored her. One looked at her, his yellow eyes glowing menacingly, and growled. His head came up to her chest, and he had to weigh two hundred pounds, far more than any dog she'd met.

Those eyes and his powerful build sent a chill through her, making her want to flee back into the cellar and slam the doors shut. She made herself stand her ground.

"Let them fight fairly," she added, hating the quaver in her voice. At least she'd gotten the words out coherently.

She opened her mouth again, intending to try the incantation, but another yelp came from the combatants. Not from Amar but the bigger wolf. Once again, the black skidded across the ground. He splashed through a puddle and leaped up, but he favored one leg. Lightning flashed, revealing a deep gouge in his shoulder.

Amar glanced at the other wolves, then advanced on the black. Two of the lieutenants ran in behind him, jaws opening.

"Look out!" Morgen warned.

They snapped at Amar's hindquarters, but he whirled before their fangs could sink in. His own fangs flashed as he lunged for them.

One scurried back fast enough to avoid his bite, but Amar caught the other by the ear as it tried to dodge. He chomped down hard, tearing cartilage and flesh. The Loup cried out in pain.

The black wolf took advantage of Amar's distraction, the fact that his back was turned. He jumped in and bit him in the rear. Ganging up, just as Morgen had known they would.

She wanted to run in and slam the staff down on his head, but the other wolves were in the way.

"Under the moon's magic, turn the snarling hound from angry foe to witch bound," she blurted instead, trying to focus on all four of the enemy wolves but especially the leader.

She repeated the incantation, hoping that would somehow give her more range, and pointed the staff at the wolves. Maybe it would help her focus the spell. If not, the antlers might at least keep them from springing for her throat.

The three lieutenants turned toward her, even the one who was now missing half of his ear. Two crouched, poised to spring at her. One cocked its head quizzically.

Morgen dashed rain out of her eyes and repeated the incantation. The leader gave her a long look but shook off any effects it might have had. She had a feeling her magic wouldn't work against so many. She was probably diluting whatever modest power she had.

At least the incantation gave Amar time to turn back to face the leader. They snarled at each other and crashed together once more, more like elk butting heads than how she'd imagined wolves should fight.

Growls closer at hand made her focus on the other three Loups. Only one had paused. The other two advanced, cold glowing eyes squinting at her. Their hackles rose on their backs like porcupine quills.

Morgen focused on one wolf and repeated the incantation. He paused, his paw lifted in the air, but the other crouched to spring.

From behind her, Lucky barked. It startled Morgen, but it startled the wolf even more, and he jumped back.

Morgen ran forward and smacked the Loup between the ears with the staff. It flashed blue, unexpectedly discharging energy.

The wolf yelped and wheeled away. She'd had no idea the staff could unleash magical power, but she was glad it did. She pointed it at the other two lieutenants, expecting them to charge next.

But her spell was still affecting them. As Amar and the black wolf kept battling, the two Loups stood still, staring at her. It wasn't a gaze of rapt adoration—or obedience—but all that mattered was that they didn't attack her.

Lucky barked again, his snout pointed across the driveway.

The rest of the wolves were flowing out of the trees, heading not toward Amar and their leader... but toward Morgen.

"Hell."

She'd barely wrangled control of these two. How could she stop all of them? No fewer than ten were running across the wet grass toward her. She would have to retreat into the cellar and slam the doors shut.

But that would leave Amar alone up here. They'd already ganged up on him once. They were bound to do it again.

"Stop those wolves," she told the two who were watching her with glassy eyes. Would they attack their own kind? She had no idea, but when they continued to stare, she repeated the words more loudly and thrust her staff toward the Loups. "Stop those wolves!"

The two lieutenants loped off toward the pack, but their pace and posture made it look more like they intended to join the others for a beer than attack. Morgen checked on the third lieutenant.

He was glowering at her but had backed off and wasn't advancing. Amar and the black continued to fight, both of them rolling on the ground, legs tangling as they pawed and snapped their jaws.

Should she run up and try to crack the black in the head with her staff? Amar probably wanted this fight to be one on one, wanted to prove that he was stronger than the Loup leader, but she didn't know if she could keep the others from joining in against him. Or from surrounding her and tearing her staff out of her hands.

Already, the wolf she'd clobbered was slinking toward her again, murder in his eyes.

She glanced toward the front of the house, trying to think of something else she could do to distract the pack. Jump in her car and drive at them? She didn't have her keys in her pocket.

Lightning flashed, and her gaze snagged on the raised garden beds. Something crouched there, something furry but too small to be a wolf.

A fox?

Someone had mentioned seeing a fox before, hadn't they?

"Amar did," she remembered. "Before the sisters ordered him to kill the real-estate agent. He said it was a witch's familiar."

As the ramifications of the fox being here thundered over her, Morgen almost missed the wolf attacking. It was the one she'd smacked. She whirled back toward it, trying to blurt the incantation one more time.

But the wolf was too fast, and she had to break off to jump back and swing her staff at it. Oh, how she wished she had more tools to use against enemies.

The wolf ducked under the antlers and kept coming, snapping for her legs. Morgen scurried farther back, hoping to escape its reach, but her heel caught on a tuft of grass. She tripped and barely kept from falling down the stairs.

Lucky jumped at the wolf, but his seventy-pound frame was small in comparison to these creatures. The wolf knocked him away and snapped for his throat.

"No!" Morgen cried, terrified for her dog.

She found her balance and lunged at the wolf with the staff. The Loup had interrupted her incantation, and she had no hold over him, but she managed to clip him with the antlers.

No blue energy came out of the staff this time, but her blow drew the wolf's ire. Before she could retract her weapon, his jaws came together around it like a vise.

Cursing, she pulled, attempting to yank it away from him. But those powerful jaws wouldn't be dislodged. He jerked his head and tore the staff free from her grip. It flew twenty feet and landed in a puddle.

The wind blew the cellar doors shut as Morgen retreated

toward them. She started to turn, but the wolf lunged after her with the speed of the flashing lightning. With no weapon left, all she could do was fling up her arms and try to utter the incantation in time.

As the wolf's jaws came in close, hot breath washing over her wet face, she knew she couldn't. But a gray-and-black bullet shot in from the side before the deadly jaws closed around her arm. Amar.

He slammed into the lieutenant, and they rolled away from her.

The rain picked up, drenching Morgen's hair and clothes as she put her back to the house and looked for the Loup leader. She was afraid that he would take advantage again and attack the distracted Amar. But the black wolf was more wounded than before, one leg dangling limply as he slumped against the side of the barn.

With the fury of a tornado, Amar laid into the lieutenant. Morgen wanted to retrieve her staff, but the battling wolves were between her and it, leaping and rolling about, mud and fur flying. She feared she wouldn't be able to circle around them without being knocked down.

Growls came from across the driveway. The two wolves she'd ensorcelled faced the rest of the pack. Somehow, they'd succeeded in getting the others to stop, not with their fangs but by planting themselves in their route. Those growls were from the others—an attempt to break her spell ensorcelling their comrades? Whether they did or not, the pack would soon continue past to attack her and Amar.

Morgen dashed water out of her eyes and glanced toward that fox, wondering if getting rid of it might stop this. What if whoever controlled it—Olivia?—was somehow influencing the wolves through it? Morgen still didn't know why the pack's eyes were glowing.

She looked around for a rock, something she could throw at the fox. But Lucky spotted the animal first. Spotted it and sprinted toward it.

He either knew what she wanted, or he took off after it because of his natural prey drive. Morgen hesitated, worried that he would be hurt if the witch was nearby and could attack him, but it was too late to stop him.

Even as Lucky barked loudly and closed on the fox, a winged form flew out of a high window in the barn. Zorro. Both of her glowing familiars arrowed toward the fox.

It whirled, leaping over the garden beds, and sprinting toward the woods.

"One problem taken care of," she whispered.

Unfortunately, the wolf pack was now facing her again. That included the two that she'd controlled. She sensed from their cold stares that she'd lost that control.

The entire pack loped toward her and Amar and the lieutenant. Near the barn, the injured leader seemed to have gotten his pain under control, for he also approached. He limped, but that didn't keep him from striding forward with deadly intent.

21

As the pack drew closer, Amar leaped away from his fight to stand in front of Morgen. The Loup lieutenant he'd been battling was down, blood matting his fur, but more than a dozen wolves loped toward them, fangs bared.

Amar put his back to Morgen, his hackles up as he growled at their approaching enemies. She gripped her amulet, wishing she had the staff back in hand, but it still lay in a puddle, and she couldn't reach it in time. It wouldn't have mattered anyway, not against so many.

She opened her mouth to try the incantation again—if she could turn one or two wolves to her side, maybe it would make a difference. But before she finished it, the entire pack paused. Their ears rotated toward the driveway, and Morgen soon heard the thumps of a truck coming up it, hitting the potholes at top speed.

"I called your pack," Morgen whispered. "I hope they're the ones coming."

Amar looked back at her. When he was in wolf form, she couldn't read his expressions and had no idea if he was pleased or annoyed. Given their current situation, she didn't care if he was irked. They needed help. She just hoped it was the Lobos and not more Loups.

The headlights came into view, beaming through the trees and across the dark hilltop, highlighting the house and the barn and the dozen wolves in between. Soon, a black truck appeared. It was the Lobos' construction vehicle, and Morgen let out a sigh of relief.

It sped onto the property, tires kicking up mud and gravel, and didn't slow down. It rolled straight toward the wolf pack, causing them to scatter.

Two people were visible inside the cab, Pedro and Maria. Gray wolves sprang out of the open truck bed and charged for their furred counterparts on the lawn.

Morgen thought the Loups would flee—they were poised like children who'd been caught with their hands in the cookie jar—but another noise rose over the rain and the rumble of the truck engine. It sounded like a helicopter's blades.

What the hell?

Yips and snarls erupted as the two wolf packs engaged in battle. Ignoring the rain and the wind, they sprang for each other's throats.

Amar crouched, as if he meant to join his old pack, but he paused and looked back at Morgen again. Afraid to leave her unprotected?

"You can go help them," she called over a gust of wind that blew damp hair into her eyes. "I'll be fine."

She hoped. For the moment, the wolves were too busy with each other to pay attention to them. Even the injured leader had joined the fray.

Still, Amar hesitated.

With the way finally clear, Morgen ran around him and picked up her staff. "Really." She waved it. "I'll be okay. You know what a badass I am with a weapon. I should buy some of that bikini armor and pose for comic books."

Since he was in wolf form, he couldn't make sarcastic comments—or point out that she'd thus far done a lot more damage to her car's upholstery than any enemies.

One of his pack mates yelped, and after another pause, Amar charged off to fight alongside the Lobos.

Morgen wiped her face again and glanced toward the garden. Neither Lucky nor Zorro—nor the fox—had reappeared. She hoped her dog was all right, but she dared not run off to look for him with all this going on.

More lights appeared, not from the driveway but above the trees to the west of the house. Confused, Morgen gripped her staff with both hands and peered into the rain. The *whomp whomp* of helicopter blades grew more pronounced, and a flying contraption bobbed into view over the evergreens.

Morgen gaped. It was Calista's gyrocopter. It had tipped over back in the garage when Calista had thrown an explosive, and Morgen had assumed it destroyed, but perhaps not.

At first, she assumed Calista was the one piloting it, but one of the three sisters occupied the single seat. The blonde. Nora. Did that mean Olivia and Wendy were in the area too? Goading on the Loups?

Morgen clenched her jaw as the witch fought the wind to fly the gyrocopter over the yard, circling and watching the wolf fight. Or trying to control it. Nora's mouth moved as she peered down.

What if the brand on Amar's neck allowed her to take control of him and the talisman wasn't strong enough to stop her? What if she forced Amar to turn from the battle and attack Morgen?

Most of the wolves were too busy fighting to glance up, but a few did. One moved away from the fray and sat on its haunches and howled, as if warning all of its pack mates about the witch up there. A couple of the wolves looked up, but they could do little from the ground. Thus far, Nora hadn't attacked them, at least not physically, but her lips kept moving. She was doing something.

As Morgen hunted around for a rock or something she could throw to keep Nora from casting spells, the gyrocopter turned toward her. Morgen glanced toward the closed doors to the root cellar. She would feel cowardly hiding inside, but if Nora had a gun or a wand capable of ranged attacks, she might have to. And quickly.

As the gyrocopter flew closer, Nora raised her hand. She gripped something. A grenade? Did witches throw grenades?

Morgen ran to the root-cellar doors only to find them locked. She pulled the amulet off her neck, pressing the medallion into the indention, but she still couldn't open the doors, couldn't escape. It was as if something had enlarged them and made them fit too tightly to open.

Nora threw what she was holding, not at Morgen but at the side of the house. Confused, Morgen rose to her feet again. That had either been bad aim… or Nora had been targeting the house.

When the item struck, it shattered and broke open like a glass jar. A pitchy black substance smeared the siding, and flames burst forth.

Morgen cursed. The witch was trying to burn down her grandmother's house.

In the rain, it shouldn't have worked, but that pitch had to be something magical. Magical and flammable. The fire spread quickly and burned heartily.

"The *barn* wasn't enough?" Morgen yelled, her fury making her shake. Why wouldn't these horrible witches leave her alone?

She sprinted for the hose and wrenched on the spigot. The gyrocopter bobbed, the wind battering it, and flew around the house. Nora lifted another glass jar.

Morgen turned the hose on the patch that was on fire, glad for the spray gun on the end that gave the water more strength but fearing it wouldn't be enough. She glanced at the fighting wolves, wanting to call for Amar to help, but he was wrestling on the ground with the big black leader and another wolf. It wasn't as if he could have done anything anyway.

As she sprayed water onto the fire, glass shattered, announcing another attack, this time on the roof of the porch. Morgen had no idea how she would reach that with the hose. She had to stop the witch, or the entire house would burn to the ground.

The gyrocopter flew close again, bobbing along twenty feet above the ground. Either because of the wind and rain or inexperience, Nora didn't seem to have a good grasp on controlling it. Maybe Morgen could force her down.

As the first patch of pitch flamed and smoldered, the fire threatening to spread, Morgen risked turning the hose away from it and onto the low-flying witch.

She had the pleasure of seeing water blast Nora in the face, startling her into releasing the controls. The gyrocopter tilted wildly, its blades whizzing close to the roof of the house. They blew off shingles that flew into the lawn, one almost striking Morgen.

She ducked, hoping the gyrocopter would crash, but Nora got it back under control. She snarled something as she produced a wand and pointed it at Morgen.

"Damn it." Morgen flung herself into the tall grass beside the root-cellar doors.

It didn't matter. What felt like a blast of electricity wrapped around her entire body. Her legs twitched, and her hands spasmed. The staff and the hose dropped from her hands, and she clunked her head against the side of the house.

Morgen groaned and rolled away in case a second attack was coming. The feeling of being electrocuted faded, but for a few seconds, all she could do was pant and try to still the quakes coursing through her body.

In the driveway, truck doors slammed.

"Now what?" Morgen lifted her head, damp hair plastering her face, and patted in the wet grass until she found her staff.

Pedro and Maria leaped out of the cab of their truck with shotguns in their hands. Morgen worried that Nora had control of them and that they would aim the weapons at her, but they fired at the gyrocopter.

Pellets pinged off the contraption's hull, though a few seemed to pierce it. Nora shouted at them, the words familiar. It was the werewolf-control incantation.

Morgen found the hose and turned it on the woman again, hoping to interrupt her. But Nora had time to finish the incantation. Even though they were in human form, Pedro and Maria were affected. They lowered their guns and stood slack-jawed, like robots powered down for the day.

One of the Loups noticed and broke away from the battle and charged toward them.

"Amar!" Morgen shouted, not knowing if he could escape to help but certain he would be crushed if he lost his brother.

Amar didn't seem to hear. Two enemy wolves lay bloody at his feet, and his eyes were crazed with battle lust as he fought two more.

Morgen strode away from the house and shouted the incantation as she focused on Pedro and Maria, hoping she could override Nora's hold on them. Not only did they need to defend themselves, but Morgen wanted them to go back to shooting at the gyrocopter. They were the only ones with range weapons.

But they didn't hear her over the wind. The gray wolf reached Pedro and bowled into him. Pedro's instincts kicked in, and he got his arm up to protect his throat, but that didn't keep the wolf from snapping down on his shoulder, puncturing skin and crushing bone. Pedro screamed.

Amar might not have heard Morgen's earlier cry, but he heard that. He left his battle and sprang for his brother's attacker as Maria stirred, breaking the spell's hold. She pointed her shotgun at the wolf.

The gyrocopter flew back into view, wobbling as Nora prepared to throw another jar. Already, flames leaped from four spots on the house and its roof. And they were spreading.

Morgen snarled in wordless rage. This time, instead of turning the hose on the woman, she used her staff. Though she worried she would lose the useful weapon, she hurled it antlers-first into the air. Her target was Nora, but she'd never had any athletic prowess or marksmanship abilities. The weapon sailed too high. Instead of hitting the witch, it caught in the blades of the gyrocopter, clattering uproariously.

The blades would have destroyed a normal piece of wood, but the magical staff flared blue as they collided with it. Somehow, it caught up there, and the gyrocopter lurched violently sideways as the blades hiccupped and threatened to stop. Nora shouted in alarm, cursing Morgen's name as she struggled to keep control of the craft.

Arcs of lightning streaked from the staff, as if it were shorting out, and wrapped all around the gyrocopter. The blades stopped moving, and gravity took over. With Nora screaming, the gyrocopter crashed into the side of the barn. Wood snapped as it plunged halfway through and stuck briefly before toppling to the ground with a thunderous crunch.

22

Out on the lawn, all sounds of battle disappeared. Numerous wolves were down, but the remaining combatants looked at each other in confusion. Maybe Nora had been using magic to rile them up and *force* them to fight.

Pedro knelt in the driveway, his shotgun in one hand as he gripped his bloody shoulder with the other. Maria stood protectively next to him. Amar had knocked down the wolf who'd attacked Pedro, tearing a huge chunk from his flank, and now they stared at each other and exchanged soft snarls.

The other Lobos drifted closer to each other, creating a united front as they faced the Loups. Challenging them?

But the Loups must have had enough. Led by the injured black wolf, they slunk off toward the woods. Two of them were too injured to rise, or maybe they were dead. Morgen swallowed, dreading the idea of calling the sheriff's department about more bodies in her driveway.

Her staff was on the ground, and she headed over to grab it. Several of the antler tips had been sheared off. She was surprised it hadn't fared worse.

A clunk sounded as a gyrocopter blade fell off the wreck. Morgen couldn't see Nora, but nothing over there was stirring. What if the woman hadn't survived? Or what if she had, and she was incredibly pissed?

Morgen was tempted to let the werewolves handle Nora, but she feared the woman had come because of Morgen and that this was her problem. Why those sisters had it out for her—and the buildings on her property—she didn't know. They'd stolen all of the moss. What more did they want?

The fires burning on the house gave Morgen a reason to avoid going over to check on the wreck. She grabbed the hose and turned the water on the burning areas. It was still raining, and that did as much as her spray gun to dampen the flames. Fortunately, the wind had died down. Maybe Nora had been responsible for revving up that storm and centering it over Wolf Wood, and now that she was... incapacitated, it would stop.

Morgen had managed to put out one of the fires and was trying to figure out how to direct water at one burning on the porch roof, when Amar came up to her side. He'd turned back into a man and gathered his clothes, but they were sodden from being abandoned in the rain, so he carried them instead of wearing them.

Numerous deep gashes on his arms, chest, and back wept blood, and someone had torn a chunk out of his hip.

"You don't look good," Morgen said inanely. She didn't know what else to say. She didn't even know what had prompted this mess, though she had a feeling they would find out that Nora had goaded the Loups into attacking tonight.

"Better than those I battled." Amar's chin lifted as he glanced toward the two wolves that hadn't stirred.

Morgen doubted they ever would again. Even as she looked, one transformed back into a man. At first, she thought that meant he was alive and that he would stand up and follow the other Loups into the woods, but he appeared even deader as a human.

Maybe when werewolves died as wolves, the magic disappeared and they returned to their human form.

Morgen swallowed and turned her focus back toward the fire, though she noticed Maria standing by the crashed gyrocopter and Pedro pulling aside wreckage with one hand. A tangle of wet blonde hair was visible, along with a single arm, but Nora wasn't moving. If she was dead, Morgen had been responsible.

Her stomach flip-flopped with anxiety and dread. It was hard to feel that she'd been anything but justified in her actions, especially when she was in the middle of putting out the fires Nora had started, but knowing she might have caused someone's death stunned her. Once again, she wondered when and why her life had gotten so crazy. So... criminal.

"What did she want?" Morgen whispered.

"If we can find the younger sister, maybe she can tell us." Amar touched the brand on the back of his neck, then met Morgen's gaze. "The witch attempted to command me, but I resisted it."

Though naked, he still wore the talisman. It dangled next to his thong necklace with the tooth.

Morgen resisted the urge to comment that he was on his way to looking like Mr. T and only said, "Good."

"Yes. That is *very* good. But your firefighting method is ineffective." Amar took the hose from her and pulled himself up a porch post and onto the roof so that he could hit the flames with the spray gun.

"Silly me, not climbing onto the roof myself."

He nodded down at her.

Pedro left the wreck and walked over to Morgen. He'd spent half the battle trying to run over enemy Loups and the other half shooting at the gyrocopter, so he had never shifted into wolf form.

"The witch is dead." Pedro sounded more triumphant than disturbed at the thought of having to explain a dead witch—or dead werewolves—to the authorities.

Why not? The bodies weren't on *his* lawn.

"Her contraption crushed her when it crashed," he added.

Morgen's stomach did that unsettled flip-flop again. "Do you think the sheriff will… try to figure out what happened?"

Pedro twitched the shoulder that wasn't injured, though the pain that flashed in his eyes suggested he shouldn't have twitched anything at all. He, Amar, and several other Lobos needed medical attention. She thought about recommending the vet, but Pedro had to already know about Dr. Valderas.

"She crashed while flying a dangerous contraption in a storm," Pedro replied while giving Morgen a significant look. "That is what their report will say. If they ask, that is what I will tell them."

Morgen doubted the sheriff or any of the deputies would consider the werewolves reliable witnesses, but it *was* what had happened. And Pedro seemed to be saying that he wouldn't rat her out.

"And they care little what happens to our kind." Pedro waved at the dead Loups. "We will remove the bodies."

"Thank you."

"We do not usually kill each other, but the witch's frenzy spell drove the pack to madness. It is good that she died. Life will be better for the pack."

Morgen nodded, even if she didn't necessarily agree. This meant one of the sisters wouldn't be able to keep coming after her, but what about Calista and Olivia? Where were they?

"It is also good that you called us." Pedro nodded to her.

"I'm glad you came. We were in a bind."

"No lone wolf can face an entire pack. But my brother fought better than I remembered he could."

Morgen thought of Amar's claim that he'd let Pedro win when they'd battled over Maria, or for the right to rule the pack. She didn't know if she'd gotten the exact story.

Maria stood off to the side, gazing up at the roof—at Amar firefighting on the roof. Her lips parted and curved into an appreciative smile.

Morgen tried not to frown but couldn't help but wonder what would happen if Maria had seen him fight, been impressed, and decided she wanted him back.

"What is that on his neck?" Pedro didn't seem to notice Maria's interest. He was watching Amar. "Not just his usual tooth."

"I made him a talisman. It's supposed to protect him from people trying to control him."

"People? Witches?" He squinted at her.

"That's the hope. I think it worked."

Pedro nodded slowly. "Yes. I wondered. The witch's enchantment didn't seem to bother him while it made me..." He pulled back his lips and growled like a wolf.

Even though his ire wasn't focused on her, standing next to a growling man made Morgen uncomfortable. If there had been another hose, she would have made an excuse and gone off to help put out fires.

"You made that talisman for him?" Pedro focused on her with intent eyes. "You can make others?"

Uh. If she did that, all the witches in Bellrock would resent her. And she already had more enemies than she wanted.

Still, the witches were wrong to use magic to control the werewolves. Unless it was true that they needed to do so to protect the townsfolk from the packs. Did they? Morgen wished she knew the whole truth.

Maybe she needed to have another chat with Dr. Valderas. He had no reason to love the werewolves or the witches, so he might be a reliable third party.

Amar sprang from the porch roof to the main roof to address another burning spot. Fortunately, the fires hadn't spread too far, and the hose water worked to put out the flames. They had done damage though. The house would need even *more* remodeling.

"Witch." Pedro poked her in the shoulder. "Can you make more talismans? For me? For my pack?"

"It's Morgen, and I'm not sure. That was my first one, and the recipe... Uhm, it was more involved than simply pouring ingredients into a cauldron." Morgen touched the cut on her finger that she'd never gotten around to bandaging. "I have to care for the person who's going to get the talisman. I don't know how the recipe—or the magic—can tell that, but it did."

"Care for?" Pedro glanced at Amar.

"Yeah."

"Like lovers?"

"No, no," she said, though the earlier kiss she'd shared with Amar sprang to mind. "Just as friends."

"Friends? His scent is all over you."

Hell, the rain should have washed away any lingering scents. Maybe werewolf pheromones were sticky.

"Don't friends share scents with friends?" she asked. "The recipe didn't say anything about lovers. Just that the talisman works better if the person making it cares about the person receiving it." If that glow was any indication, it hadn't worked at all until she'd started thinking about how she felt about Amar.

"Well, then." Pedro grinned and clapped her on the shoulder, almost knocking her sideways. "You can learn to care about the Lobos. We can all be your *amigos*."

He waved to the side, where the rest of the pack, all back in human form and most naked, had joined Maria. They must have caught the gist of the conversation, and liked the possibility that they might be able to get protective talismans, for they lifted their arms and shouted, "*Sí, amigos!*"

"Uh," was all Morgen could manage.

"We'll remodel your home for you. No charge. We'll even scrounge up the materials." Pedro glanced at one of the smoldering walls. "And add fire retardant. You'll *have* to care about us."

"That could start to prompt feelings of warmth."

"Good, good." Pedro thumped her again, then wandered over to sling an arm around Maria.

She saw him coming and turned her attention and a warm smile on him, but Morgen caught her glancing at Amar again as he strode around naked—naked and magnificent—on the roof.

Chattering noises wafted out the open kitchen window. The ferret.

Hearing him reminded Morgen of Lucky, and she turned worried eyes toward the trees again. Even if the fox had led him on a chase, he should have returned by now. It was possible he'd treed the fox and refused to leave the spot, but it was also possible the animal—the witch's *familiar*—had tricked him and led him into trouble. That was what foxes did, wasn't it? Out*foxing* their adversaries.

Amar jumped down from the roof to land beside her. "The fires are out."

"Thank you." She hugged him, careful not to grab any of his wounds. "I need to go look for Lucky. He chased off a fox while you were fighting."

"I've seen that fox before. I believe it's a familiar."

"I know. So do I. But Lucky just chased it because it's a fox, I think." Morgen rubbed the back of her neck. "I might have ordered him to. I'm not sure, but Zorro took off after it too."

Amar arched his eyebrows. "You are able to command two familiars?"

"I really don't know."

"We will help you find him."

"We?"

"I will speak to the pack. You helped defeat the witch. They should agree that they owe you assistance."

Oh, she had little doubt they would help. Now that they

wanted her to make them all talismans, getting them to *stop* helping would be the problem.

The ferret chattered again from whatever cage Amar had found for him. He'd been about to go talk to Pedro, but he paused and gazed thoughtfully at the window.

"We believe that is the familiar of the youngest witch sister, right?" he asked.

"Wendy, and I think so. I saw it riding on her shoulders."

"And the fox is likely the familiar of one of the other two witches. Perhaps hers." He pointed to the wreck.

Morgen avoided looking. "Maybe."

"I can follow your dog's trail." This time, Amar pointed to his own nose. "But since the ferret wanted to lead us somewhere, we might want to follow it."

"I need to find Lucky first," Morgen said. They could feed the ferret more chips and let it give them a tour in the morning. "If you're not too injured to help me?"

"I am fine," he said, as if oblivious to all of his wounds, "but I have a hunch the ferret may take us to the same place the fox would logically run. To its home. The witches' lair."

"Wendy was staying in the campground, not with her sisters."

"Her *van* was staying in the campground. She was missing."

Morgen was skeptical that someone would have kidnapped Wendy, only to take her back home, but finding Lucky was her first priority. Especially since she'd sent him off into danger.

"We can let the ferret go," Morgen said, "but it's your furry nose I want to follow."

"It is a fine one."

She thought he would change back into his wolf form and head immediately into the woods, but he trotted into the house first. The chattering escalated, punctuated by an alarmed squeak, then halted abruptly. Morgen frowned in concern and almost ran inside, but Amar wouldn't have harmed the ferret after talking about following it.

He soon returned with the ferret in hand. Once again, its long body hung limply.

"Is he playing dead?" she asked.

"Again, yes." Amar handed the ferret to her, the warm furry body feeling like it had no bones. "As soon as I walked into the kitchen, he flopped over melodramatically in his cage."

"Maybe your nudity scared him into fainting."

"My nudity is as fine as my nose." Amar changed back into a wolf, dropping to all fours as fur sprouted and his hands and feet changed into paws.

The ferret shrieked and wriggled free from Morgen's grip. She lunged after him as he hit the ground but then remembered that she hadn't wanted a ferret in the first place. He chattered as he ran between the garden beds and toward the woods. She thought the ferret was fleeing from the large and ferocious Amar, but he paused at the tree line and rose up on hind legs to look back at her.

"I'm coming," Morgen said.

Amar loped after the ferret, and she followed, hoping the familiar would indeed lead her to Lucky.

23

SEVERAL OF THE LOBOS LOPED ALONG BESIDE AMAR AS HE navigated through Wolf Wood, pausing only when the ferret did and occasionally lifting his snout to test the air. Morgen, ungainly and awkward on her two human feet, especially in the dark with only her phone's flashlight guiding her, grew more self-conscious every time the wolves stopped to wait for her. It didn't help that the antlers of the staff kept catching in the brush.

It wasn't her fault that she was slow—they weren't even following a trail—but that didn't keep her from feeling frustration. Why had so many people—werewolves—come along on this journey anyway?

She almost snapped that question when two of them looked expectantly back at her, but if the ferret led her to a houseful of angry witches, she would be grateful for the help.

Amar's nose and their ferret guide took them all the way down the hill, over the train tracks, and to a pebbly beach. The calm waters of Rosario Strait lapped at the shoreline. Not pausing, the ferret turned north and led them in the direction of Bellrock. If they ended up on Main Street, or somewhere else she could have easily driven to, Morgen would be grumpy. Thus far, there had been no sign of Lucky.

They passed houses perched above the beach, then turned up a creek and into a wooded area choked with undergrowth. It had stopped raining, but all the foliage they passed through was wet, so there was no chance of drying out. Morgen's sodden clothes chafed with each step.

Amar paused and shifted back into his human form. The presence of nearby cottages and cabins made Morgen wish she'd thought to grab his clothes for him.

"I know where we are," he said.

"A romantic beach getaway?" Morgen leaned on her staff and looked at the other wolves, who had also stopped, though they remained in their fur forms. "For six?"

"You have fantasies of romance with half the Lobo pack?"

"I do not." She remembered the pit-stained tank tops of the construction workers and shuddered. "It was a joke."

Up ahead, the ferret chattered at them from atop a log.

"I think he wants us to keep going." Her feet ached, making her wish she'd grabbed her hiking boots.

"He does. But we've almost reached the boundary."

"Boundary?"

"This is the sisters' property." Amar waved toward a densely treed area, no lights providing illumination. "We'll reach the warded perimeter soon."

"All I see are trees."

If there was a road or driveway, it wasn't apparent. They must have approached from the back side of the property.

"Their home is *in* a tree," Amar said. "A tree house. Protected by magic."

"Lucky doesn't know about wards. He would have barged right onto the grounds."

"He may be injured then."

Morgen winced and stepped forward, but Amar halted her with a hand.

"Did you study how to defeat them so we can gain access?" he asked.

"No. I was busy learning how to make wolf talismans."

"I'm glad for that, but—"

The ferret squeaked and spun circles on his log. He hopped off, ran through some tall grass, then darted back to the log and reared up on his hind legs.

Amar growled at him. The ferret flopped over on his side, playing dead again.

"Maybe he can lead us past the magical security system," Morgen suggested.

"Without fainting?"

"If you don't growl at him, maybe." She tried to ease past Amar, but he kept his arm up, blocking the way. "I may be able to sense the wards," she said, more to get him to let her through than because she believed it was true. "I'll step exactly where the ferret steps. Maybe there's a safe path through."

"Or maybe he doesn't trigger them because he's one of the witches' familiars. You didn't sense the protective spells on the van."

"True." Not until the magic had knocked her across the campground, fortunately into Amar's arms.

As she considered how they might find a safe route, barking came from an elevated position ahead of them.

"That's Lucky." Morgen knew his bark. But how would a dog have climbed up into a tree house?

Their guide looked back at them and chattered again.

"I'm going in." Morgen headed after the ferret. "I have to."

This time, Amar didn't try to stop her, but he didn't look happy. He said something in Spanish to the wolves lurking nearby. Hopefully asking them to rescue them if they landed themselves in trouble.

The ferret led Morgen and Amar along a zigzag route through overgrown grass, chest-high thistle, and towering trees. There wasn't a path, but the deliberate zigging and zagging made Morgen hope the ferret was indeed avoiding booby traps.

"There's a wolf up ahead," Amar murmured.

"A Loup?" Morgen stepped onto a log in precisely the same spot the ferret had, wobbled, and caught her balance when Amar put a hand on her back to steady her.

"No."

"A Lobo?" She frowned at the idea of Amar having to fight one of his own people.

"No."

"Not a werewolf?"

"It is one." Amar sniffed, as if he were trying to place a familiar scent.

They stepped around a copse of trees, and the massive trunk of an ancient cedar came into view. It was as tall and wide as the California redwoods, and one could have driven a car through it. Or put a *door* in it. A large silver wolf stood in front of a round wooden door reminiscent of the entrance to a Hobbit house.

Morgen had seen that wolf before. Recently.

"It's the vet." Amar rested a hand on Morgen's shoulder to stop her.

The ferret had also stopped. With a questioning chitter, he peered at the wolf. He seemed confused to find it standing in front of the door.

"He shouldn't be a threat to us, right?" Morgen asked.

The wolf—Dr. Valderas—growled.

The ferret wilted like a flower and flopped down to play dead again.

Lucky had stopped barking, and Morgen peered warily up the

cedar. There were few branches growing out of the first twenty feet, so even in the dim lighting, she could make out the bottom of a large wooden platform extending from the trunk. From below, she couldn't tell if there were structures built atop it, but she assumed there were.

Valderas's growls drew her attention back to the door. He crouched, his silver hackles up, his focus on them. What looked like a red ruby on a chain hung around his neck, the gem glowing slightly. He hadn't been wearing that at his house, nor at the mushroom patch. Maybe it was something like Amar's brand that allowed the witches to control him. He hadn't seemed like someone who would voluntarily work for them.

"How do we get past him?" Morgen glanced up again, hoping to spot Lucky's nose sticking over the edge of the platform.

"I may have to fight him." Amar sighed wearily. Enough time had passed for his body to stiffen after his battle and for those gashes and bites to start throbbing with pain. He should be seeing the vet as a patient, not for a fight.

Morgen wished she'd thought to grab him some ibuprofen out of the house before they'd started this trek. She hadn't expected to have to walk miles and battle another wolf before finding Lucky. Where was the fox?

Amar pointed to something lying in the grass to the side of the tree. Morgen shined her light in that direction and slumped, recognizing the brown feathers of her owl familiar. What had *been* her owl familiar. Zorro still glowed faintly, but from the way he lay crumpled on his side, she suspected he was dead. The fox's doing? Or the wolf's?

Bleakness filled her at the realization that something else had died because of her. She hadn't even intended to send Zorro after the fox.

What if the same thing had happened to Lucky? That bark could be a recording or some audio illusion.

Morgen clenched a fist. She had to get into that tree to check.

The growls intensified, and Valderas left the door to prowl toward them, his hackles still up.

"Under the moon's magic, turn the snarling hound from angry foe to witch bound," Morgen said, gripping her grandmother's amulet.

The ruby on Valderas's chest glowed brighter, as if it were some antimissile device deflecting an incoming attack. He kept advancing.

Amar growled, stepped in front of Morgen, and shifted into his wolf form. That didn't make Valderas pause.

"Try not to hurt him," she whispered, though as Valderas drew closer, she realized he was as large as Amar. As large and as powerful? And not injured from a previous battle.

Amar glanced back, giving her the wolf version of an are-you-kidding look?

"At least try not to *kill* him," she amended. "I doubt he's working for them voluntarily."

Based on her short meeting with the vet, she couldn't truly know that, but she wanted to believe it.

Valderas turned his prowl into a charge and sprang for them. Morgen skittered to the side as Amar leaped forward to meet the silver wolf.

Pain blasted Morgen's heel, and she couldn't keep from crying out. It felt like something had bitten her, and the pain lingered after she jerked her foot away.

As the wolves came together, snarling and biting, Morgen shined her light on the ground, expecting to find a viper coiled there. But there was nothing. She must have stepped off the ferret's path and come down on one of the magical defenses.

The wolves rolled to the side, almost clipping her, but she made herself hold her ground instead of jumping back. She didn't want to land on another booby trap.

She hefted her staff, thinking to help Amar by clubbing his foe, but they were thrashing and rolling around too quickly. She couldn't target the right wolf. Besides, whether he wanted to fight or not, he might not thank her for interfering with his battle with her witchy ways. The ideal tactic would be if she could slip that ruby off Valderas's neck, but with fur and saliva flying, she couldn't even see it.

A lupine yip of pain came from several yards back, the spot where they'd left the rest of the wolf pack. One of them had tried to come onto the property to help Amar. She had a feeling the wolf had found a similar booby trap.

Several of the Lobos started howling their distress from the perimeter. The noise made Morgen wince but did nothing to affect the fight as Amar and Valderas snapped their jaws, trying to reach each other's throats.

Beyond the battle, the ferret jumped to his feet and ran for the Hobbit door. It opened for him.

Morgen hesitated, torn between wanting to help Amar and wanting to use this opportunity to run inside and find Lucky. If the witch who'd given Valderas the ruby was inside, maybe Morgen could also find a way to break its control. By cracking *her* over the head with the staff.

The wolves rolled past again, and something spattered Morgen's cheek. She touched the moisture, assuming it was water from a puddle, but her fingers came away with blood on them.

She swallowed. Whatever she was going to do, she had to do it now.

Staff in hand, she ran for the door. The ferret had disappeared into a dark chamber, though chattering from within suggested he was waiting for her.

Before she reached it, the door started to close. Morgen shifted her run into a sprint. She turned sideways and leaped through before it closed fully, the thick wood muffling the snarls from the wolf fight. It was pitch black inside the tree. The ferret chattered uncertainly.

"You're the leader here." Morgen pushed on the closed door, but it didn't budge. "Or maybe the bait," she grumbled, afraid she'd walked into a trap.

The floor lurched, and she swore, envisioning a trapdoor opening and pitching her into a dungeon. Or straight into the abyss. But the floor went up instead of down.

"An elevator?"

It rose with several jolts, as if it were catching on knots inside the hollow tree, then stopped. A door opened behind Morgen. She spun, holding her staff up defensively.

The ferret ran onto the platform she'd seen from below and toward the left, into what looked like an ordinary living room with sofas and end tables and even a hearth. Windows in wood walls peered out toward the dark trees, the view too elevated to see down to the wolf battle. The ceiling was made from woven branches that appeared to still be alive.

Morgen inched out, surprised she hadn't yet been attacked.

Barks almost made her drop her staff. She spotted Lucky chained to a post with barely enough room to rear up on his hind legs when he saw her. He barked again, his tail whacking against the post, then snatched up something from the floor. A piece of fabric. The floral pattern and material made Morgen think of a woman's blouse.

"Are you alone, boy?" Morgen whispered, her gaze snagging on something to his side.

A marble pedestal that was out of place in a room made almost entirely of wood held another glowing ruby, this one several times larger than the gem dangling around Valderas's neck. It not only glowed, but it projected a hazy red cloud around it.

The ferret's chatters and a concerned squeak pulled Morgen's attention to the living room. She crept farther from the elevator and peered over a couch. Two women sat on the floor with their backs against a wall, their shoulders slumped against each other. Phoebe and Wendy.

"What are you—" Morgen stopped, noticing handcuffs capturing their wrists and a glazed aspect to their eyes. They also wore ruby necklaces.

The ferret ran back and forth in front of Wendy, then hopped into her lap and head-butted her. She didn't react.

Morgen started toward them, but Lucky whined.

"You're right," she said. "You release your familiar before the other witches. That's the rule."

After looking around the room again to make sure nobody lurked, preparing to jump out at her, Morgen hurried to the dog and hugged and patted him. He nearly knocked her over with his enthusiasm, and she dropped her staff as she tried to unclasp his collar from the chain. Lucky licked her face, further impeding her progress.

A lupine cry of pain came from below, reminding her of the wolf fight.

"Sit, sit. Let me..." Morgen finally got him undone.

Lucky ran in circles around the room. Though he was only demonstrating that he was happy to be free and wasn't a threat to anyone, the ferret spotted him and flopped down, playing dead in Wendy's lap.

Neither Phoebe nor Wendy reacted to any of that. Their glazed eyes remained unfocused.

"I bet this thing is responsible." Morgen eyed the ruby on the pedestal and picked up her staff again.

Electricity, or maybe that was magic, buzzed in the cloud floating around it. She was tempted to knock the ruby to the floor and hope that broke its spell, but her heel still ached from where she'd stepped on a booby trap. If this had some magical protection, who knew what it would do to her if she touched it?

"I might not have any choice," she muttered, after peering all around the pedestal and the ruby. There wasn't anything as handy as an on/off switch. Maybe a spell could have stopped the flow of magic, but neither of the incantations she knew would accomplish that.

The howls of the Lobos started up again. It sounded like they were still at the perimeter of the property and still agitated. Or were they *more* agitated?

"Amar might be losing the fight." Morgen glanced at Lucky, who'd stopped running around and sat beside her, the fabric in his mouth again. "I wish you could talk, buddy."

He wagged his tail, and an image popped into Morgen's mind. A *vision*.

She saw the room through Lucky's eyes as he leaped up and down, trying to escape. This had to be a vision from the past, when he'd been chained.

To his side, a woman leaned forward, her hands on the ruby as she faced the pedestal. It was Olivia, the oldest sister. She glanced over her shoulder, barking orders to a man standing by the elevator, his eyes glazed and a smaller ruby around his neck. Dr. Valderas.

"The bitch killed my sister," Olivia growled. "She's more dangerous than Calista said. And I can't count on my *other* sister." She glowered toward the wall. Phoebe and Wendy were in the same spot, handcuffed and vacant-eyed, already under the ruby's effect. "I'm getting out of here while I still can. Hold them off. Don't let them track me."

Valderas shifted into wolf form and stepped into the elevator.

Olivia faced the ruby again, chanting under her breath, and stepped back and raised her hands. It started glowing, the red haze forming. She moved away from it but got too close to Lucky, and he lunged, catching the hem of her blouse. He growled and tore it off her.

She shrieked, kicked him, and ran shirtless for a door that led to the deck outside. She grabbed a rope and swung over a railing, disappearing from Lucky's view.

The vision faded, leaving Morgen focusing on the ruby through her own eyes. Unfortunately, the glimpse into the past hadn't given her any advice on how to turn it off.

More agitated howls wafted up, followed by another yelp of pain. Amar? Valderas? Or had one of the Lobos tried again to find a way through the ward?

"I have to stop this," Morgen said. "One way or another."

She raised the staff like a baseball bat. Her meager plan might not work, but the weapon had been strong enough to survive being thrown into helicopter blades. She hoped it would survive this—and that she would as well.

She swung hard, clobbering the ruby. It flew from the pedestal, red lightning bursting from it and running up the staff. A blast of power struck Morgen and knocked her backward. She hit the floor headfirst, and the world went dark.

24

"SHE'S WAKING UP," A MALE VOICE PENETRATED MORGEN'S consciousness.

She grew aware of the hard floor underneath her, her shoulder mashed against it, and the pounding in her head.

"That's your professional assessment? She's not moving."

"I professionally assess animals, not humans, but I am fairly certain. You can hold a mirror in front of her nose if you wish."

"The advanced veterinary techniques you employ must create a frenzy of repeat customers."

"Hilarious. You use a lot of big words for an uneducated orphan from another country."

"I read books."

"He reads comic books," Morgen slurred, her muzzy brain catching up with the discussion and identifying the speakers. "Starring gazelle women in bra armor."

"What did she say?" Dr. Valderas asked.

"Nothing coherent."

Morgen scowled, certain Amar had understood her. She pried

her eyelids open, and two pairs of bare muddy men's feet came into view. Also a copper-colored snout. Lucky leaned in and licked her face.

"What happened?" she asked, simultaneously petting him and pushing his tongue away from her eyeballs.

"We weren't here," Amar said. "You'll have to tell us."

"Though we surmised that you bashed a hypnosis control gem with your large stick. Hard." Valderas had something cradled in his bare arms, but Morgen couldn't tell what from below.

"Very hard," Amar agreed.

Both men looked toward a wooden wall where the ruby was now embedded. The heavy pedestal it had rested on was toppled on its side near Morgen's feet. She was lucky the magic had thrown her back so that it hadn't landed on her. Alas, the ruby didn't appear to be cracked or damaged in any way, though it was no longer glowing. Maybe that and the fact that Amar and Valderas were up here in human form and talking to each other were good signs.

"Did I break its hold on everyone?" Morgen squinted up at them but looked away before she got more than a glimpse of gashes and bite wounds. They were both naked, and she didn't want to be perceived as assessing anything more than their freedom from spells.

She looked toward the wall where Wendy and Phoebe had been handcuffed, but the couch kept her from seeing the spot.

"You broke its hold on *me*." Valderas bowed to her. "I thank you for that, and I will attend to what I believe is your owl familiar."

"I had no hold that had to be broken." Amar lifted his chin, either because he was proud of himself or to show off the talisman hanging from his neck. Perhaps both.

"My owl?" Morgen started to say that Zorro was dead, but a few brown feathers were visible over the side of Valderas's arm. *That* was what he was holding. "He's alive?"

"Barely, and his wing is broken, but I've nursed such wounded birds back to health before."

"I would appreciate that," she said.

"We're free of the spell too," came Phoebe's voice from beyond the couch. "It would be nice if someone freed us the rest of the way." Handcuffs clanked.

"The werewolves weren't willing to," Wendy added, then lowered her voice. "I was afraid they were going to eat us."

"*I* was afraid they and their naked penises were going to ravage us," Phoebe said.

Valderas scowled in their direction. "I assure you that you were never in danger of that."

"I'd be more likely to ravage the ferret," Amar muttered, lowering a hand to Morgen.

"The ferret that plays dead when you come near it?" Valderas asked, apparently having already seen a demonstration. "That seems an inauspicious trait in a lover."

Morgen, feeling dizzy and with her head still throbbing, accepted the hand up. No sooner were her feet under her than blackness encroached on her vision, and her legs threatened to give out.

Amar gripped her to steady her. "I think I originally objected to the idea of you learning how to become a witch and suggested you learn to use mundane weapons instead."

"You did. I remember." Morgen blinked, hoping to drive away the sensation that she might pass out again.

"Now that I've seen you get into trouble by clubbing things a few times, I'm changing my belief. You should learn more spells so you have more than one tool to use against magical devices, magical people, and witch-piloted aircraft."

"Seems like a reasonable suggestion."

"Morgen?" Phoebe lifted her handcuffs. "There's a key in the table drawer over there."

"We should leave them locked up." Amar frowned at them.

Phoebe and Wendy were still sitting with their backs to the wall, though their glazed expressions were gone. Now, they appeared more peeved than anything else. Wendy's ferret was peering at Lucky from behind her back and alternating between squeaking and hissing at him.

"They could be a threat to us—to you—if they're freed," Amar added.

"Our unwillingness to be a threat to Morgen is *why* we're locked up," Phoebe said.

"All *I* said was that maybe we shouldn't steal your moss and keep lighting your buildings on fire," Wendy said. "My sisters were positive they had to scare you out of Bellrock, that you would end up being a huge threat to them and everything the coven has set up if you were allowed to stay."

When Morgen was steady enough to walk without support, she headed to the table and opened the drawer. There didn't appear to be anything magical about the handcuffs or the key inside, but she picked it up gingerly.

"I'm not a threat," Morgen said.

"That's not what Calista was assuring us of," Wendy said.

"Amar is the one who chewed up her werewolf," Morgen said.

If she was a threat to any of the witches here, it was only because they'd made her so. They'd started all of this. All she'd done was inherit a property and drive up here to fix it up.

"On your behalf?" Phoebe eyed Amar.

He and Valderas stood shoulder to shoulder, eyeing her back just as warily.

"I didn't command him to, if that's what you mean. I appreciated that he did it since the werewolf was trying to tear my leg off at the time." Morgen brought the key over to release them. She didn't want to argue further. Phoebe was the closest person in town she had to an ally. And Wendy... Morgen didn't know what Wendy was, or how she would react when she learned of her sister's death. Morgen didn't want to make an enemy of her, but it might be inevitable now.

"Thank you." Phoebe rubbed her wrists as soon as she was free.

"You're welcome." Morgen moved on to Wendy. "Have you been here the whole time, Phoebe? I've been looking for you for two days. The treasurer of your coven left me a note. They were looking for you too."

"Of course they were. My shop provides a valuable service, and I'm a valuable part of the community. People notice when I'm gone."

"She said you hadn't paid your monthly dues," Amar said.

Phoebe snorted. "Figures. She harasses you in person if you're a day late. The gods forbid if they don't get enough dues to repaint the parking lot lines at our meeting place."

"He was joking." Morgen shot Amar a quelling look.

He appeared unrepentant.

"My sisters brought us here and locked us up so we couldn't warn you about the Loups," Wendy said, "and that they were going to drive you back to wherever you came from."

"Seattle," Morgen said.

"Yeah."

Once free, the women stood and shook out their arms. Lucky thought that meant they wanted to pet him and came over and leaned against Phoebe's thigh. The ferret hissed at him.

"This is an inappropriate familiar," Phoebe said, though she deigned to pat Lucky's head.

"*Is* he one?" Morgen raised her eyebrows. "I wanted to ask you about that, about his glow. That was why I was looking for you."

"A glow after the familiar ritual shows you that you've successfully bonded with an animal. I told you that a dog isn't proper for a witch. Why did you claim him?"

"I wasn't trying to. He was rolling around in the grass near the fire when I did the ritual. And an owl came to me, so I thought I'd gotten *him* as a familiar." Morgen pointed to Zorro over in Valderas's hands. "They've both been giving me visions."

"Yes, that's typical," Phoebe said. "It's how familiars communicate with those they are bonded with."

Howls started up again outside.

"I had better let them know that I'm okay," Amar said. "I hadn't realized they still worried about me."

"They could be distressed because they don't know what happened to *me*," Morgen said.

Amar started to scoff but stopped himself. "That's true. They *do* want you to live long enough to make them... gifts." He glanced at Phoebe and Wendy and didn't expound, but they'd probably seen the talisman he wore. His lack of clothing made it rather noticeable.

"Not surprising." Valderas gazed wistfully at Amar's talisman.

Maybe Morgen would use the second piece of jewelry to make one for him. As another lone wolf, he probably needed protection more than the pack members. Although... she remembered that she'd taken the base pieces from Wendy's van and looked warily at her, wondering if she'd recognized Amar's neckwear yet.

Wendy *was* eyeing Amar's chest, as if she'd just noticed the piece.

As the two werewolves walked to the elevator together, Morgen cleared her throat, looking for a polite way to admit that she'd taken the jewelry.

"Earlier today," she said, "we went to see you at the campground. I wanted to try to pay you for jewelry that I could make into protective talismans. You weren't there, so I, uh, borrowed a couple from your drawer. I left some silver and money as payment, but if there's something else you would prefer, let me know."

Morgen hoped Wendy wouldn't say that she would prefer to have them back. There was no way she would be able to convince Amar to give up his talisman now that he knew it worked.

"Oh, it's okay. I can make those pretty easily." Wendy cocked her head. "How did you get into my van? It's protected with magical defenses."

"Yeah, I triggered one. With my body. Amar was kind enough to catch me before I hit the picnic table."

"Such experiences would deter *some* people from entering a witch's premises," Phoebe said.

"I'm kind of stubborn."

"That's why Calista and Olivia are afraid of you," Wendy said.

"I think it's more that they were angry that Morgen got Wolf Wood and that she's making talismans for the werewolves," Phoebe said. "The werewolves we all feel a lot more comfortable around when we know we can control them if necessary."

Morgen suspected most of the witches wouldn't add those last two words to that sentence, but she kept the thought to herself. "How did they find out about that?"

Phoebe and Wendy shrugged, but Morgen realized that Valderas's presence here might answer that question. Olivia must have chosen him to defend their premises tonight because he was a reliable werewolf, one she'd controlled before. Morgen would like to think Valderas hadn't shared the news of her talisman plans as soon as she'd left his office, but it was possible he had. Or that Olivia had called him that night, and when he'd been under her sway, he'd admitted it.

Morgen shook her head. She never should have opened her mouth about that.

But maybe it didn't matter. The witches would have figured it out as soon as they saw Amar and realized they couldn't control him anymore. Whether Morgen wanted enemies or not, she kept putting herself into positions to gain them.

She sighed deeply, well aware that Calista and Olivia were still out there and still hated her.

EPILOGUE

Morgen sat on the front porch steps with a glass of iced tea and a cookbook and tried to enjoy the late afternoon sun filtering through the trees. With no fewer than ten Lobos banging, sawing, and pounding inside and outside of her house, serenity was elusive. Since the werewolves were fixing up the place, including replacing the leaking laundry-room roof and all of the siding that had burned, she couldn't complain, but she was already looking forward to the process being complete. They had only started the day before though, so it would be a while.

Two burly men in tank tops walked past carrying armfuls of wood as their jeans sagged around their hips. Her cousin Zoe would have appreciated the view. Morgen merely fantasized about them going home for the day and quiet returning to the property. Had her sister been here, she was positive Sian would have locked herself in the root cellar with a book or perhaps run off to find a quiet cave in the woods.

Emotion tightened Morgen's throat as she wondered if Sian would ever make it up here. She'd called twice since her sister's possibly drug-induced hypothesis on the witches dividing and ruling the werewolves, but both times, it had dropped to voice mail. She'd also called her brothers to see if any of them had updates, but they hadn't even known Sian was sick. If Morgen didn't hear from her in another day, she would call the university that funded Sian's research and find out her status through them. She tried to tell herself that if things had turned truly bad, they would have already called. Since Mom had passed away, Morgen was her sister's emergency contact.

A gruff shout in Spanish came from Amar. He was by the barn, repairing the wall where the gyrocopter had crashed. The wrecked aircraft, Nora's body, and the bodies of the two Loups had all been gone when he and Morgen had returned to Wolf Wood the night before last. She'd assumed the Loups had retrieved their own dead, but she had no idea if they'd been responsible for removing the wreck. What would werewolves want with a broken gyrocopter?

But she hadn't asked around. She'd been relieved that all signs of the chaos, save for the damage to the house and barn, had been gone.

One of the Lobos banging away on the roof paused long enough to yell a reply to Amar. In the exchange that followed, Morgen picked out enough to know they were teasing each other about who had the bigger biceps. At least, that's what she thought *músculos del brazo* meant. It was possible they were comparing penis size.

Since the clash between the Lobos and the Loups, the pack had been friendlier toward Amar. Oh, they were razzing each other and throwing insults left and right, but the barbs seemed more affectionate than biting. Part of it might have been that Pedro hadn't been around. During the fight, he'd been wounded badly enough that he'd ended up visiting Dr. Valderas, and now, he was resting at home for a few days.

Maria hadn't been around for the renovations either. Morgen

was glad about that. She and Amar hadn't spoken about their kiss, nor had he been sleeping in the house where she might have easily knocked on his door and asked if he was interested in making out on the couch, but she liked to think there was hope for... something.

What, she didn't know. They had nothing in common, he loathed witches, and they couldn't even go out on a dinner date without one being disgusted by the other's food. It wasn't as if they were a logical match.

"Not like me and Jun, huh?" Morgen snorted, regretting that she'd spent so many years with a man who found her cold and aloof.

Though it wasn't as if she knew what she would have done if she hadn't been married to him all that time. Probably the same as she'd done while with him: focused on her work and only later wondered if maybe it had been a mistake never to have kids.

Morgen shook her head, pushing her ex-husband from her thoughts. She highly doubted he was spending time dwelling on her. Besides, she had more important things to worry about. Like what she would do when the tax bill came due, especially since all of her valuable bioluminescent moss had disappeared, and whether Calista and Olivia were out there plotting further assaults on her and her property.

A text message popped up on her phone with an image. Zorro with a bandaged wing and leg. Morgen's throat tightened again in sympathy for the poor owl, but at least his eyes were open and alert and Dr. Valderas's message was encouraging.

Your familiar is recovering and screeching at any unsavory clients that come in the door. This includes but is not limited to people, cats, dogs, rabbits, snakes, and parrots. The only visitors he didn't complain about were the gerbils that little Bradley Braun brought in a shoebox, but it's likely he was plotting how to hobble over and eat them.

Morgen smiled and thanked him for the update, though she

mentally added *vet bill* to the list of things she would soon have to pay.

At least Lucky had stopped glowing, so she wouldn't have to take him to see any specialists. He was lounging in the sun by the truck full of lumber that the Lobos had brought to the house. Every time one of the men had to grab a few boards or a forgotten tool, he wagged his tail and positioned himself just so, to ensure they stopped to pet him.

Amar left the barn and headed in her direction. He grunted at his pack mates as he passed them, and there was a swagger to his step. Given how bruised and cut up he was, and that he'd been favoring his left leg since the battle, Morgen suspected the swagger was more to hide a limp than because he felt exceedingly hale and invincible.

He eyed the cookbook as he sat beside her. *The Art of Authentic, Traditional Mexicano Desserts.* She'd found it in Grandma's cupboard along with numerous other recipe books and had been contemplating making something special for Amar. He kept getting beat up on her behalf, and since she'd started cooking more, she'd found it a nice way to say she cared for someone without actually speaking the words. That was something that was always difficult for her. She wondered if most bakers were introverts. Why say things aloud when one could instead present pastries to express one's feelings?

"You're not going to try to make churros, are you?" Amar asked.

"I thought I might make you something from your homeland. Do you like churros?"

"Not the way that book tells you how to make them."

"The recipe isn't right?" Morgen flipped to the churros page.

"When Gwen used that book to make them for me, they were always raw on the inside."

"Oh. I'm sure that's not the recipe's fault. She probably heated the oil too much, and the outsides got done before the insides."

"*Well* before the insides." His eyebrow twitched. "You don't have to make anything for me, but I like American desserts just fine."

She felt a little disappointed that he didn't want her to ply him with authentic Mexican desserts, but if there was something else he would prefer, she would happily select from another cookbook. "What's your favorite?"

He gazed thoughtfully at the lawn. "Girl Scout cookies."

"*Girl Scout cookies* are your favorite desserts?"

How was she supposed to show him that she cared through something that came out of a box?

"They're good. I like the shortbread ones. And the peanut-butter patties."

"Most people like homemade desserts or fancy cakes from restaurants best. Cheesecake, chocolate tortes, tiramisu..."

"Do I look like a fancy-cakes kind of guy?" Amar waved at his ripped jeans and leather vest.

One of his pack mates sauntered past with an armful of lumber and threw insults at Amar in Spanish. They spoke of muscles again, and how women liked bigger ones, and Morgen was positive from the hand gestures that penises were *definitely* implied somewhere in the exchange.

"Maybe I can find one of those recipes that deconstruct Girl Scout cookies and bake some homemade peanut-butter patties," she offered, deciding to pretend she couldn't understand anything the werewolves were saying.

"You don't have to make things for me."

"I want to. Because..." Morgen waved at him, having a hard time admitting that she'd developed feelings for him. Maybe being an introvert wasn't the problem. Maybe it was having been hurt recently. Or the fact that he hadn't exactly amended his statement that he wasn't interested in her and didn't like witches. Just because they'd made out in the cellar during a storm didn't mean he wanted to have a relationship with her. "Reasons," she finished lamely.

"Because I dusted your house and you want to show your gratitude?" He arched his eyebrows.

"You didn't dust. You used the shop vacuum on my kitchen and slurped up a paring knife, a dish towel, and the meat thermometer."

"I didn't mention anything but the knife."

"The other things were implied by the fact that they aren't in the kitchen anymore."

"The rats may have carted them away along with your pea snacks. For their lair."

"Oh, I'm sure. Nothing brightens up a lair like a meat thermometer from Ikea hanging on the wall."

Amar rose and walked across the driveway to his truck. Morgen frowned after him, afraid she'd offended him somehow.

He clambered halfway into the truck, bending to hunt for something under the bench seat and giving her a view of his butt while he did so. She thought about looking away, but the way he wiggled around, then held the pose for several long seconds made her wonder if he was deliberately giving her a show.

Only when one of the pack called, "*Buen culo!*" to him, which she was fairly certain meant something like *nice ass*, did he hop down and close the truck door.

He ambled back over with a plastic-wrapped row of shortbread cookies. "This is the *last* of my Girl Scout cookies. They're out of season now."

"Yes, you'll have to wait for another box to ripen." She lifted a hand, wanting to tell him that he didn't have to open them on her account, but he broke the seal and handed her a small stack. "Thank you. You don't need to share your favorite treats with me though."

"I want to."

"Because you like me even though I have all that tainted witch blood?"

"Because *reasons*." He took a chomp out of a cookie and smiled at her.

THE END

Thanks for reading! The adventure continues in Book 3: *Any Witch Way*.

Printed in Great Britain
by Amazon